Tracking
The Carpaccio

To Renee
with all good wishes,
alice Heard williams
march 2010

Tracking
The Carpaccio

❖

A suspense novel set in Venice
featuring American Emma Darling

Alice Heard Williams

To order additional copies of this book, contact:
Xlibris Corporation
1-888-795-4274
www.Xlibris.com
Orders@Xlibris.com
67168

Contents

To the Memory of My Parents, Daisy Huffman Heard and

Joseph Richard Heard

~~ Venice 1975 ~~

1

You've Paid the Rent, Now I have Nowhere to Go!

The excitement she felt leaving the train station at Santa Lucia was short lived as Emma began walking briskly toward the water taxi stop. She felt a lightness of the suitcase in her left hand and glanced down as the handle gave way and the bag plummeted to the pavement, landing on her left shoe.

Good grief! An omen? Surely not. She had assumed everything would go smoothly for her first look at Venice in a decade. She had been hired to research a private collection of paintings, with free time to explore the city its citizens called *La Serenessima,* and she would pocket a generous stipend. What could be better?

Picking up the case by the broken strap she continued on, willing herself to keep moving. She could see the water taxis moored about fifty feet away. She threaded through streams of early morning commuters from the mainland bound for work.

The boatman she approached gave every appearance of honesty in the clear-eyed, open face. Clean, neatly mended white shirt, black trousers, thinning grey hair. Had he sensed she was hopeless at haggling over price and would agree to pay what he asked? No, the fare he quoted her was reasonable, perhaps a little less than she remembered.

She sank back on worn leather cushions of the water taxi and surveyed her fellow passengers. Too early for tourists, these were affluent commuters, those who hadn't finished breakfast soon enough to take the slower *vaporetto*, with its frequent stops. Glancing at her watch, she noted it was almost ten o'clock, when most offices opened. Venetians conducted their affairs efficiently, centuries of merchant blood coursing through their veins. However, business eased into life slowly, even the crowds of tourists stirred themselves later: in Venice, living would not be rushed.

Emma's life had been had been greatly enriched by travel after leaving Virginia to study art history in England. In Italy, life moved to yet a different beat. Relishing every moment held highest priority, even the pleasure of arguing was a part of it she mused, watching a dispute over the fare erupt at steps leading down to the boat. Both the young man, nattily dressed and carrying a brief case, and the boatman were enjoying themselves immensely.

Agreement on a price reached, the two leapt gracefully aboard, the craft shuddered into action accompanied by the din of a spluttering motor. A gentle rocking motion set them underway, making for the Grand Canal, signaling a shiver of delight through Emma. As she strained to take in weathered facades which had withstood centuries of eroding wind and water she was aware some of the *palazzi* lining the canal dated back to the Byzantine age. At that moment golden sunlight struck the stones bringing to life shimmering colors, set dancing by the wake of boats plying translucent waves.

She thought of the great art critic John Ruskin and the *Stones of Venice*, his book of tribute. Ruskin had been right. The reflected light of water on old stone walls defined Venice. Emma believed passionately that art changed people, their outlook. It could and did enrich lives.

Emma admired loggias and open spaces on the facades. At roof level, greenery fluffed from gardens atop sumptuous palaces. Others were faced in precious marble of exquisite shades ranging from pale pink to light amber. Windows, heavily mullioned in the Florentine style, others light and airy, capped by the pointed arch typical of Gothic, reflected enhanced light bouncing off the water. Overhead a dome of sky blended into the cerulean blue of Tiepolo's ceilings. Emma sighed, content as she sailed on, broken strap and a throbbing left toe forgotten.

The taxi chugged by fabled *palazzi Ca' Pesaro* on the right, *Ca' d'Oro* on the left. Sailing under the noisy Rialto Bridge markets, she saw cordons of shoppers of every possible description smelling the fish held up by vendors, listening to musical entreaties to buy as green grocers hawked their wares, inspecting baskets brimming with pears from Tuscany, oranges from Morocco. Ages and sexes looked and mingled, haggling, as they touched, prodded and sniffed the offerings for Venice's dinner pots.

She knew the route would reveal the basilica of *San Marco,* the five glorious domes shimmering in majesty, the bronze horses dating from antiquity straining toward the heavens on the terrace above the entrance. The Doges Palace and the Bridge of Sighs would be visible from the water. Hidden behind San Marco stood the church of *San Zaccaria* where her favorite altarpiece in Venice by Giovanni Bellini hung in a small side chapel. These unseen delights to be sampled arose in her thought as Emma glided along.

The water taxi also would carry on to pass the Gritti Palace Hotel where the *traghetto,* a public gondola ferry docked, waiting to transport a single row of standing passengers across one of the widest spans of the Grand Canal. She sighed, content, absorbing the color, the beauty of it all in her thoughts.

The taxi shuddered to a stop drawing up alongside the arching Accademia Bridge, Emma's departure point nearest her lodging. They were now in the Dorsoduro *sestiere,* home for many musicians, writers, artists. She stepped out, thanked the boatman as he placed her two bags on the *molo,* dock, in front of the vast museum of art, the Accademia.

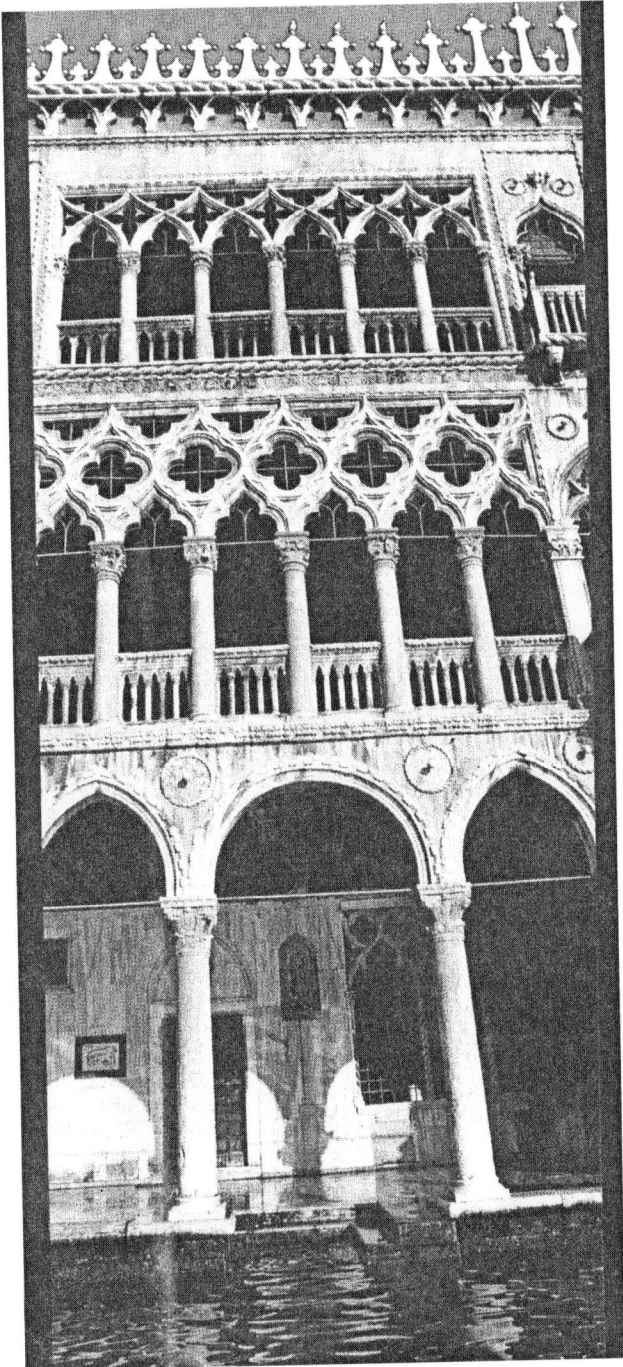

Palazzo Ca' d' Oro, Grand Canal

Consulting a small map before lifting her burdens, she found the street she wanted, Calle del Pistor, near the bridge. It should be only a short walk to the flat she had rented, sight unseen, belonging to one Rosamund Belfrage, a typist at the British consulate and a distant cousin to Emma's friend in London, Jane St.Cyr.

Emma longed for a shower and a lie-down to ease her throbbing toe. Struggling on as fast as possible, she found the small three-story building from directions outlined in Rosamund's letter. Strange so few houses in Venice bore numbers. How people ever found their way around was a tribute not only to instinct and intelligence but tenacity. Everything seemed to hinge on designating the nearest church, museum, or *campo*, the small squares, as a guide point.

Inserting the larger of two keys into the heavy door she stepped into a foyer with an open stairway of curving, delicate wrought iron. Slowly she climbed, admiring the airy space. The building was not old by Venetian standards. Emma guessed it dated from around the 1930s, but it had been skillfully blended with the existing houses on either side. Probably a courtyard garden had been sacrificed to make way for a few money-producing flats.

Rosamund's reply had been concise; she included the keys and a receipt for Emma's check for the first month's rent. It should be a satisfactory arrangement for both of them with Rosamund off on holiday to England. The flat was affordable in expensive Venice and she could put by a nice little nest egg. Emma would have a safe, convenient place to stay.

She reflected on her assignment as she struggled upward with the cases. She would research for Lord Elmley paintings collected by his late father, the Seventh Earl, who had lived in Venice some forty years before his death in the 1950s. She knew little about the collection, only that it comprised Venetian paintings by second tier artists, works of the twentieth and nineteenth centuries plus a few earlier pieces.

After teaching art history at the Celia Drummond School several years, Emma had resigned her post to prepare for an autumn wedding to a young surgeon from Scotland, Dr. Sam McGregor, working at Guy's Hospital in London. The tempting offer from Lord Elmley, an acquaintance of Jane's husband Charles St. Cyr, came unexpectedly and was too good to turn down. Sam agreed wholeheartedly. The wedding arrangements were complete, thanks to their early planning.

What art historian wouldn't be delirious with such a plum dropped in her lap? Venice! For two whole months! Being paid handsomely for doing work she loved. Emma could hardly believe such a prize was hers, like a purse full of emeralds from Aladdin's cave. And when she mentioned to young Lord Elmley that her wedding was set for early autumn, he immediately urged her to invite Sam to come for her final week in Venice.

The Accademia Bridge

"He can bunk in one of the empty rooms at *Ca' Sospira*," he had offered. "He'll be out seeing the sights with you most of the time and the half-closed aspect of the place won't trouble him.

"It would be entirely too gloomy for you, living there around the clock, Emma," he added gallantly, "working all day, remaining at night. And Riccardo Montgano, the resident curator of the furniture collection, can be rather moody when he puts his mind to it.

"To be fair, I've added an ample cost of living stipend to your salary. You should easily be able to sublet something suitable for two months. Many young people from the consulate go on holiday at that time of year, I believe." And with Jane's help, Emma had made arrangements.

Emma wondered what the earl had meant by that remark about Riccardo and she also wondered about working at the Elmley *palazzo, Ca' Sospira,* on San Marco. She had heard it was beautiful. She reached the top and inserted the smaller key into the lock into the door of Rosamund's flat. She took a deep breath and entered.

Was that the sound of someone weeping? Surely she was mistaken. Rosamund had left for England by this time. She stopped. Beyond the folding screen separating a tiny foyer from a reception area she could see a girl about her own age slumped on the sofa, handkerchief in hand, the other clawing at a sofa arm. She looked at Emma with alarm through red-rimmed eyes of a startling, blue. Emma took a step back.

"Oh dear, I am so sorry to disturb you. My name is Emma Darling. I have rented the flat for the next two months. I thought Rosamund had left for England. I can't think what has happened."

The girl quickly jumped up, began smoothing a rumpled skirt and blouse and making nervous jabs at the wild mane of hair like liquid red silk tumbling over her shoulders.

"Emma? *I'm* Rosamund. Aren't you early? What day is it?" She glanced at the small clock on the sofa table. "Mercy! Surely this isn't the second? What a complete simpleton I am."

She approached, putting out her hand.

"Something horrible, well, unsettling has happened, and I've lost track of the last few days. I've been so muddled I didn't even send you a wire or anything. Whatever must you think?" The distress in her eyes sent Emma's feelings of euphoria plunging, a punctured balloon.

Oh no, so this is Rosamund. Poor thing. Will I be chucked out on the sidewalk with my broken case, or will I have to creep along to *Ca' Sospira* and settle in among the dustsheets and shuttered rooms with the dour Riccardo? Clearly something major had upset Rosamund's plans. For once at a loss for words, Emma took a step back and waited.

"I've had a shock," Rosamund continued, downcast eyes fixed on the frayed but beautiful Oriental carpet underfoot.

Composure dissolving, she looked directly at Emma and blurted everything out.

"Oh, bother! Why cover it up? The story is all over Venice. Cyril Meadowes, the man I was planning to marry, received a surprise posting to Prague only a fortnight ago, a big promotion for him, but he had to leave immediately. He worked at the British Consulate, as I do; he was one of the diplomats in training.

"We had planned to leave on holiday together for England and celebrate our wedding there. When Cyril left for Prague, our plans were still in place. Then rumors started buzzing around the consulate like wildfire. Cyril had taken more than his brief case when he left for Prague. He took along one of the Italian junior clerks in the records room, a very pretty brunette with a sultry smile. He married her! Everyone knew who she was. I didn't even know her name. And he didn't bother to say a word to me. I've never been so humiliated in my life!"

Emma inhaled a large gulp of air.

"How absolutely rotten for you. I am so sorry." She paused. "But Rosamund, surely in a horrible sort of way, it seems lucky you found out about Cyril and his failings before a wedding took place."

Thoughtful, the blue eyes raked over Emma like searchlights as though a possible solution might be taking shape in Rosamund's mind.

"Yes, there is that, I suppose. I certainly haven't any feelings of tenderness left for him, if that is what you mean. But the disgrace! Everyone at the consulate is looking at me and chuckling behind my back. I can feel it." Delphinium eyes locked with Emma's welled up again. Emma quickly took her hand.

"Oh no, surely that isn't true! People admire courage, they do. He is the one to be pitied."

She waited for Rosamund's reply and ran fingers through her hair. Glimpsing herself in the mirror behind the sofa she blinked. Was hers the unkempt face with shiny nose and palest lips? Rosamund wasn't the only one who needed freshening up. But where? That was the point. Discreetly Emma's eyes swiveled around the pleasant, colorful flat which would have been hers for the next two months. It seemed spacious and desirable.

She watched as over Rosamund's face a glimmer of hope was born. Could she possibly brazen it out as though nothing had happened? Emma saw she had planted a seed in her mind. With her support, Rosamund might be strong enough to cope, show a little grit and determination. Rosamund's face revealed she had arrived at a decision, gathering up her thoughts like rolling up a ball of yarn.

"Emma, you have paid the rent, but now *I* haven't anyplace to go. What if I said to you, stay here with me? I'll move into the little room. We'll share the bath, but you'll pay only half of the agreed price. Would you be interested in an arrangement like that?"

Emma hesitated. "I'll accept your very generous proposal, but only on this condition: you let *me* have the smaller room; you keep your bedroom. I only have a few clothes to unpack, I'm here for such a short time. It will be easier for both of us if I take the second room."

Rosamund brightened but insisted she should first show Emma what her quarters would be like. She led her to what probably started life as a servant's room opposite the flat's one bathroom at the end of the hallway. Emma stepped into the small space. It held a daybed along one wall, a comfortable, worn armchair, a small dressing table and bench. One window, a roundel of thick glass covered with several layers of dust, overlooked the rooftops of Venice. Emma drew closer and saw the outline of the Accademia gallery and a portion of the arching Accademia bridge over the Grand Canal on the horizon, a stunning view.

Her spirit soared. She could gaze out on one of the greatest art museums in the world's most beautiful city. She knew a good omen when she saw it. Her smile told Rosamund a deal had been struck. Rosamund's face brightened.

"Oh Emma, we'll be flat mates!" She smiled, hardly able to grasp her good fortune after the dreadful week which had just passed. Emma nodded.

"It will be a turning point! I can actually go back to my job and put that horrible creep Cyril out of my mind."

"Of course, and you'll begin to see this for what it really is, a lucky escape, Cyril bolting, I mean."

"Right Emma. Now, come along and I'll show you the kitchen. Then we can have a cup of tea. I've got some Earl Grey and a packet of chocolate digestive biscuits."

After tea, Emma showered and unpacked, nursing her bruised toe with a band-aid and resting on the narrow bed. Later, Rosamund took her on a walk about Dorsoduro.

La Fenice Opera House

2

Mental Gymnastics with Riccardo at Ca' Sospira

The following Monday at nine-thirty, Emma boarded the crowded *vaporetto* number one at the Accademia Bridge and arrived at the San Marco stop only a few minutes away. Stepping along narrow pavements beside the network of small *rios*, she kept map in hand as she wove her way toward *Ca' Sospira*, the Venetian home of the Earls of Elmley. Specifically, Lord Elmley, her employer, for whom she must begin researching the collection of paintings and write a new catalogue.

La Fenice, Venice's fabled opera house was her goal; she knew the Elmley property was near it, just past it, in fact, on Calle della Fenice. When I know my way around better, she thought, I can reach the house another way, by walking over the Accademia Bridge from the Rialto district on to San Marco. It was actually closer that way. She folded the map and put it in the handbag slung over her shoulder, already feeling at home in her surroundings.

Emma was unprepared for her first glimpse of *Ca' Sospira*. So this was the House of Sighs. Lord Elmley had described it to her as, "Rather small and unappealing in its present state with the furniture smothered in dust sheets and the shutters closed tight." But he had given no hint about the outside to prepare her for the dazzling small *palazzo* in front of her. The exquisite, rose colored façade, faced with marble in a reinvented Gothic style, had been built late in the nineteenth century, Emma guessed, sometime after Ruskin had awakened the world of art to the beauties of the Gothic in *The Stones of Venice*.

The house shone in the reflected sunlight of morning, enhanced by its mottled, pinkish tones, leaded casements sparkling with diamond shaped panes of a pointed Gothic design. The roof line included two small minarets balanced on either end of the building, confirming Emma's guess as to its dating, for she knew it was typical of Victorian architects to incorporate divergent styles into a single design. A singular building Emma thought, watching as the warm light of the sun bathed the facade in movement reflected and enhanced by the water.

It was the young earl's habit to understate, she recalled, thinking of her earlier meeting with him in England. He had worn the relaxed country gentleman's uniform of tweed jacket, given birth in Jermyn Street or Savile Row, legendary London haberdasheries; blue jeans and a white shirt open at the throat. Supple leather loafers finished her impression of him. His only jewelry consisted of a small onyx signet ring bearing the Elmley crest, its gold band worn almost into oblivion, for it had embellished the finger of three previous earls. Emma recalled his forthright gaze, open face, red hairs and freckles sprinkled generously on the backs of his hands. Was he a copy of the man who had lived here, his father, the seventh earl? She had set herself the goal of understanding the man who assembled the collection she would be researching.

She gazed up at a railing around the flat roof beyond which she could see sprouting green branches of a roof garden, the *altana,* a place to catch the sun and the breezes, enjoy the boxwood and oleander planted in tubs. Downspouts ornamented with open-mouthed fish and scowling gargoyles managed to look benign rather than menacing. Emma, admiring the total effect, was guessing who might have designed the house, when the heavy front door opened and an impatient voice called out to her in accented English.

"Do come in, *per favore.* You are *Signorina* Darling?"

Emma hurried toward the voice and stepped over the threshold. The man standing before her pressed her hand and spoke in a rich baritone; he had presence. The face with its finely modeled features, large *espresso* eyes was pleasing. His thinness bordered on shocking.

"I have been expecting you. Young Lord Elmley said you were an American art historian?" The words, delivered in a puzzled tone, sounded to Emma as though he doubted such creatures actually walked the earth, certainly unknown within the rarified air of *Ca' Sospira*.

This must be Riccardo. She heard pride and uncertainty meet in combat in his tone. His words told her he could hardly find her more provincial had she been an Indian dressed in buckskin and feathers standing before him.

"And you must be Riccardo Montgano?" She turned her reply into a question as she studied the face. "Lord Elmley told me of your expertise in furniture and sculpture."

She looked straight into his eyes and was rewarded by his pleasure at her words. He had not been expecting a compliment. His dark suit of superior fabric but aging style fit loosely. Eyes under fine brows took her measure. Black hair reached just above the shoulders, turned under in a pageboy style, popular in Venice in the spring of 1975, just as it was in London. Movements fluid, full of grace, and his courtesy, although lacking warmth, was faultless. He really is quite good looking, in a Byronic sort of way, she decided, moving inside.

"I am Riccardo Montgano," he answered in clipped tone, his gaze seeming filled with disapproval. "I believe you have come to research *Ca' Sospira's* small collection of paintings."

Why did his words demean the paintings, make them sound like worthless rubbish collected by some dotty earl with more money than sense? Emma felt her face turn red, temper rising. She felt a familiar prickle at the back of her neck as she reined in her anger. Was she imagining his disdain?

"Yes," she answered. "Lord Elmley asked me to revise an outdated catalogue and research the collection." Recalling her meeting with the young earl, she remembered his final words.

"Riccardo Montgano is indeed an expert on Venetian sculpture and furniture of the eighteenth and nineteenth centuries, but do not let him bluff you into thinking he knows a bean about painting. That is precisely why we are engaging you. So you can tell us exactly what we have in the way of paintings at *Ca' Sospira*."

"I am in charge here," Riccardo declared, looking put upon. "I was the late earl's advisor on artistic matters. The *furniture* collection at *Ca' Sospira* was the pride of the late earl." He squared his shoulders and glared, daring her to contradict.

"Of course," she murmured politely, countenance serene. He must be worried about his job and me upsetting his little kingdom. Well. I'll do what I can to win him over, but I won't be a flunkey. He is not my employer. Is that why he's so touchy?

Riccardo guided her through an airless *portego,* a central hallway. The principal reception room containing sheet-shrouded tables, sofas and chairs was visible through an open door, the glimmer of daylight coming through shuttered louvers at the windows. Approaching a closed door on the opposite side of the hall, Riccardo turned to usher her inside.

Here dustsheets had been removed, heavy draperies thrown back onto open windows admitting a fresh breeze. She stood in a library furnished with an imposing desk and chair, a Chesterfield sofa tufted in well-worn brown leather and book-lined walls. A comfortable wing chair with frayed arms covered in faded brocade stood conveniently near the books. Fortuny damask, Emma noted with approval, running her fingers over the chair back, a holdover from the art deco age.

The faint smell of leather bindings and furniture polish enriched the air, transporting Emma at once back to England. But of course, she reflected, this had been the library of a wealthy English nobleman who had spent his later life in Venice. There was even a slight depression in one of the cushions of the Chesterfield, as though it had served as a napping spot. The room had the look of worn comfort and solitude. She loved it at once.

"I've set you up in here to work. I hope you find it adequate," Riccardo murmured stiffly.

"Adequate?" she echoed, drinking in her surroundings, approval shining in her eyes. "It's heaven! Thank you, Riccardo. I'll try hard to be worthy of it." He gave a pleased smile and turned to fuss with a cushion of the Chesterfield.

Emma wondered how best to go about discovering just what sort of a man the former earl had been. Obviously he loved books and shared her passion for art. She felt certain he had been a collector who bought paintings he loved, unmoved by greed to possess something that would make money for him. She longed to know everything about him and his collection. But she knew she must make Riccardo her ally. This might take time.

Riccardo left to let her settle in, still nursing suspicions she feared, at any rate where her work was concerned. She must prove her worth to him. He must understand she was in no way a threat.

She opened the slim catalogue lying on the desk, PAINTINGS AND DRAWINGS OF CA' SOSPIRA. She studied titles and names of the artists, disappointed as they meant virtually nothing to her. Naturally there would be many she had never heard of, but she had allowed herself to hope for a few sketches by the likes of Tiepolo, Tintoretto, Titian, Giorgione.

Leafing through, she came upon a small pressed flower, a rose, it's color faded almost to ivory, its substance in a tissue paper state. It had been stuck to a piece of paper, where penned in faded script she read,

> "In visions of the dark night
> I have dreamed of joy departed,
> But a waking dream of life and light
> Hath left me broken-hearted."

She recognized the words of the American poet, Edgar Allan Poe. The late earl was perhaps a romantic? The faded rose spoke volumes to Emma about the man's melancholy, contemplative nature. Continuing to peruse the catalogue, she came upon another insert, a scrap of paper stuck between the final two pages. She reached for the magnifying glass at her elbow, for the writing was faint and blurred, almost illegible.

"Whatever happens, do not ever give up the Carpaccio!" she read.

Emma raised puzzled eyes. What could that mean? She knew who Carpaccio was, of course. A preeminent Venetian painter working during the Renaissance, who produced wonderful scenes of life, dress, buildings, customs of Venice in the 1500s. But he wasn't listed in this catalogue of the Elmley Collection. Most of his work was in Venice, in the Accademia or the Correr Museum, and there were examples in the *Scuola di San Giorgio degli Schiavoni, in situ* since the fifteen hundreds. Carpaccio was indeed a big name in Venetian painting. Had there once been a Carpaccio in this collection?

Pushing doubt aside, she began a thoughtful rereading the catalogue, badly in need of updating since its publication in the nineteen fifties. She knew of course in her field of art history, patient research by art historians often unearthed new information about masters of the past. She marveled at their ability to ferret out hidden facts, obscured by the passage of time. Many of these diligent art history sleuths would be useful on detective squads, gathering secrets for the CIA or MI-Five. For a few moments Emma's thoughts rambled on this path.

What if there had been a Carpaccio in the collection? It would provide a focus, star quality if you like. A centerpiece for the new catalogue she must prepare. Emma quickly turned the pages of the outdated work again. There was no entry of a Carpaccio. If there had been one in the collection, where was it now?

3

A Ghost Perhaps, or Possibly George Washington?

Later that morning after working quietly for several hours at her desk, Emma was interrupted by a discreet tap at the library door. She straightened up, rubbed the crick in her neck.

"*Avanti!* Come in!"

Not Riccardo, but a ghost from the past grandeur of Venice stood before her. The *palazzo* was quickly revealing itself as a step back into another era, another time. Wizened, slender, tottering on thin legs encased in white stockings, knee britches of a pale blue damask with matching coat, a dignified man of advancing years fingered the lace cascading down the front of his shirt and bowed in her direction.

"*Buongiorno Signorina,*" he smiled. "I am Filiberto, I was Lord Elmley's man."

Valet, he means, Emma noted, taking in the snowy white hair which in her mind gave him the appearance of a bewigged George Washington. The waistcoat fell to his knees and was richly frogged, encrusted with braid and gold buttons in a perfect adaptation of eighteenth century Venetian dress. He would surely win first prize at a costume party.

"I have been in Elmley service almost my entire working life. In Venice more than thirty years. Twice I accompanied the late earl back to England and the horrors of the English winters came back so vividly I never wanted to return. So when he died, I stayed on. I should be put out to pasture for all practical purposes, but here I am, assisting Riccardo in keeping everything in good order." The warmth of his smile wrapped around her.

Emma nodded, amazed. "You are English? But Filiberto, I would have sworn you were Venetian born and bred. Your Italian is impeccable."

"Haw!" he roared, hugely pleased. "I don't mind telling you *Signorina* Emma, England is too hustle and bustle for my taste nowadays. In Clapham, the East End of London where I was born, they're all rushing about in motors, going nowhere in my opinion. No, give me Venice, a paradise in summer. Well, winters can be a bit cold and damp. Nothing like as bad as Worcestershire, mind! But in the kitchen there's always a warming cup of tea, and before you know it, spring is bouncing the sunlight around on palace walls and canal waters." Here was a friendly spirit Emma realized, approving the combination of wrinkled cheeks and merry eyes.

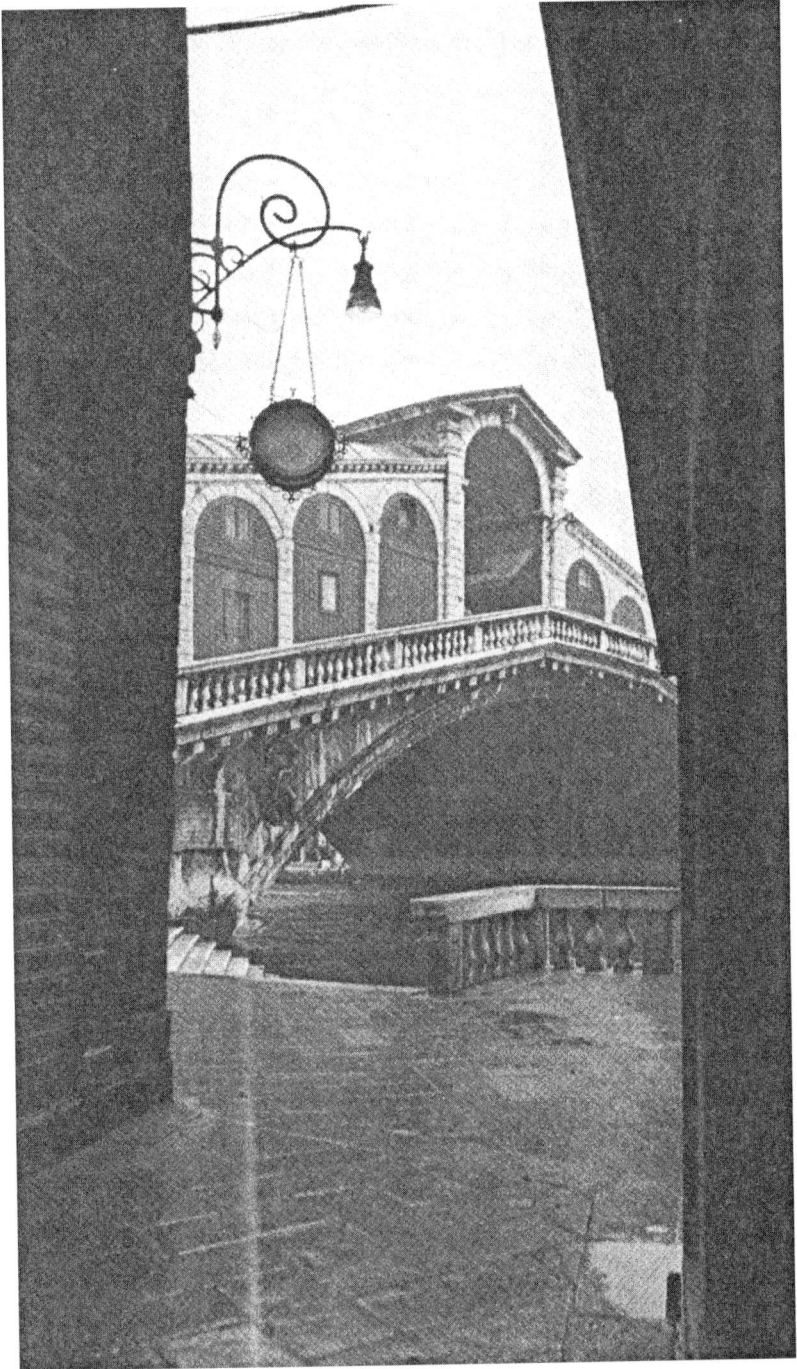

Rialto Bridge

"I came to tell you luncheon is being served in fifteen minutes. Cesara the cook doesn't look kindly on latecomers. Wash room just across the hall," he motioned, giving a jaunty wave as he hurried out, summoned by a distant bell.

Emma made the motions of tidying her desk and hurried to wash her hands. Soon after she returned to her desk, Riccardo breezed in, seemingly in a more genial mood.

"Riccardo, look what I've found!" She handed him the piece of paper from the catalogue.

"Ah, yes, I failed to mention that to you. It is of no importance. A joke perhaps, of one of the late earl's children when they were here on visits, years ago. Come along, now!" he urged in a nanny voice. "We must not be late for luncheon."

Disappointed, Emma replaced the slip of paper and meekly followed him toward the dining room. She had recognized the handwriting of the late earl. Earlier as she rummaged through drawers of the desk, she had stumbled upon a small notebook bearing the Elmley seal on its leather cover. The notations inside were about dinner guests rather than paintings, but they matched the writing on the slip of paper.

"You do realize the collection was never supervised by an expert who would have advised the earl properly of what he should buy? He was a mild-tempered man, but at times he could be immoveable," Riccardo intoned over his shoulder as they made their way toward the dining room.

"He preferred to purchase only works which awakened a response in him. It is that sort of a collection, very personal," Riccardo droned on in a superior air.

Implying, Emma thought, that collecting in a haphazard manner was a practice studded with pitfalls and produced inferior results. But Emma disagreed. Such a collection was an effort of the very best type: highly original, dictated by the personality of the owner, a hands on *collezione*, in some ways a work of art in its own right, provided of course, the collector had discernment and taste as well as money. And judging from the beauty of *Ca Sospira*, the late earl had not only taste and style, but plenty of The Ready, as Filiberto might have expressed it in Cockney parlance.

"Just don't go looking for Titians or a Georgione," Riccardo concluded. "You won't find any." Emma swallowed a pert reply and they entered the dining room.

The beautifully proportioned space had been freshly cleaned, stripped of the gloomy dustsheets and polished to its former grandeur. Instead of the long mahogany banquet table in the center of the room, which could easily seat twenty or more, a small pedestal table had been laid for three beside a generous, leaded bay window crowned with pointed Gothic arches overlooking the *rio*, the small canal.

Emma's hopes lifted as she saw the third place setting. Talking with Riccardo imposed a strain, littered with verbal minefields as it seemed to be. She welcomed the presence of a third person.

Filiberto tottered in, trailing a plump, pleasant-faced young man with rosy cheeks and a shock of fair, unruly hair reminding Emma of stocky Dutch students she had known in her Uni classes. Riccardo introduced Nigel Sleight of London, working at Gallery Vianello near the Rialto Bridge. They took seats at the round table and were immediately served soup by Filiberto from a massive silver tureen on a nearby sideboard.

Emma, glancing up at the Murano glass chandelier hanging above, dreamed of grand balls, *carnivale* parties which might have taken place beneath it. She studied the clear glass branches ending in blossoms of red, cerise and pale rose thinking until the eye became accustomed, Venetian glass blowers seemed ruled by a passion for the gaudy. But set in the ornate ceiling covered in beautiful *stucchi*, plaster decoration, the chandelier looked magical floating in the soaring space.

"Emma, Nigel's expertise is in English painting," Riccardo looked at her severely, demanding her attention. "I knew you would enjoy learning about his gallery's collection."

"Not very impressive to someone who's an expert on London's offerings, I imagine," Nigel said smoothly, giving Emma a nod as Riccardo began spooning his clear soup in which the tiniest of shrimp, a Venetian specialty, floated in a flavorful broth along with bits of red pepper, sweet corn kernels and miniscule green peas.

"It is true I took my students to visit galleries each week when I taught art at the Celia Drummond School," Emma reflected.

"My students, a few of them, enjoyed tea and scones in the gallery restaurant at the conclusion of our visits as much as the paintings. Not all my girls, of course; some were positively brilliant. Is your gallery's collection made up principally of watercolors?"

"Not as many as you might think, knowing Venetians live surrounded by water. Traditionally, Venetians have never put a lot of money into works on paper. The dampness here has something to do with it, I imagine. Paper, as you realize, is at risk here."

She nodded. Foxing, the small brown specks or dots which could blossom on a paper's surface, cost the earth to remove and were caused by damp. England had that difficulty, but not the punishing summer heat of Venice, which could, and did, compound the problem. In *Ca' Sospira*, thank goodness, the hum of the dehumidifier was never at rest. She had heard it in every room. She turned her thoughts back toward Nigel who was describing some of the paintings at his gallery.

"No, Gallery Vianello has a few notable watercolors by Peter de Wint, William Turner of Oxford, John Varley. Venetians, strange to say, have a liking for the English countryside. None of the slick little Sickert interiors or the gypsies of Augustus John, no indeed! Give them acres of meadow dotted with chewing cows and perhaps a pretty milkmaid in the foreground, and they are blissful.

"I say, we've got some jolly good Bloomsbury oils, Duncan Grant, Vanessa Bell and all the others. Acquired very cheaply from a house designed by Palladio on the Brenta Canal near Vicenza, an estate sale, as I recall. They're gathering dust and have been for years. The collectors I've met in Venice haven't a clue about Bloomsbury artists; in that they lack the fervor of the Americans. Come by and I'll give you the tour. It will explain a lot about Venetian taste, what sells and what does not."

"That would be most helpful. I'm trying to discover the philosophy which guided the late earl to buy what he did. Riccardo's been telling me he had nobody advising him, that he amassed the collection himself."

"That is interesting to hear. I'd like to see the *collezione* when you untangle everything," Nigel replied. "It's one of the mysteries of the art establishment in Venice. Nobody's ever laid eyes on it, as far as I've heard."

Riccardo was listening intently. Emma was sure he picked up on the references to the unsophisticated taste of some of Nigel's clients and was probably wondering if his words were meant as an affront to all Venetians. Or did Riccardo resent the implied lack of taste, the uninspired spending of their millions by the newly rich of Venice? My, he was touchy! As to the Elmley art collection, Riccardo made no comment at all, she noted with surprise.

Fascinated, she watched as Riccardo accepted a third roll from Filiberto's proffered basket and slathered it with butter. How could he be so thin, eating all that food? And what a sensitive nature. She felt she was treading on eggshells whenever she spoke to him.

Unlike Riccardo, Nigel had an open personality. Emma felt drawn to him immediately. It was impossible not to like him, he was so engaging. She looked at him and saw a rotund skater skimming the ice, a figure in a Pieter Bruegel painting, red cheeks, long wool scarf flying in the wind, a winter scene in Holland, a canal dotted with skaters.

"The first thing she plans to do is photograph the paintings," Riccardo was speaking, answering Nigel's question about her duties. "Then she can study each one without constantly having to dart everywhere over *Ca' Sospira.*"

"I will consider the works individually later; this first step will help me get acquainted with them, you see." Emma explained, looking at Nigel, gauging his reaction.

"Wise, wise indeed, Emma. You have the right approach." Nigel moved his untouched roll slightly on the bread plate. He ate sparingly, in contrast to Riccardo who had finished a second bowl of soup and was obviously ready for the next course. Emma wondered how great a portion was allocated to room and board in Riccardo's salary,then shushed her thoughts. She must not descend to pettiness. Riccardo began telling them of the late earl's style of collecting.

"The seventh earl bought only works that awakened a response; he took little advice from anyone else. It was his mantra and everyone understood it. He certainly did not lack discernment. Look around you at *Ca' Sospira.* Filled with life and color and beautiful objects. He favored drawings over oils, but watercolors over drawings," he continued. "In that he was much like his countrymen. Nobody in the world has equaled England in the genre."

Emma gave a polite sigh behind her napkin. She supposed he thought that in America, populated by Red Indians, they favored cave drawings. His preconceived ideas about English and American taste knew no bounds. Perhaps she could provide more correct information in subtle ways.

"And the *collezione?* Have any of Lord Elmley's so called unknowns risen to prominence or staggering prices in the sale rooms?" Nigel asked, looking at Emma. But it was Riccardo who answered.

"There have been modest increases, certainly. But no spectacular surprises unfortunately. I fear the Elmley *collezione* remains what it has always been: interesting, but undistinguished." Riccardo's eyes swiveled from Nigel toward Emma, whose protest died on her lips. She had meant to tell Nigel about the slip of paper she had found which mentioned a Carpaccio, now unaccounted for, but she was halted by an exclamation of satisfaction from Riccardo as the main course arrived.

How she would love to prove Riccardo wrong about the worth of the late earl's collection of paintings! Well, she would take up the challenge. She began anticipating her first move:

photographing each painting would place each of the works at her fingertips. It would prove invaluable. She longed to begin.

Cesara the cook sailed into the room bearing a large platter of *fegato*, calves liver, a dish typical of Venice. Cooked in a little butter, olive oil and rosemary, it was presented thinly sliced, garnished with crisp *pancetta*, the uncured bacon of Italy, caramelized onions, and surrounded by a ring of yellow *polenta*, molded like a pudding, a savory corn meal accompaniment for meats. Similar to Virginia grits, Emma mused, made with yellow, not white corn meal.

Behind Cesara Filiberto carried in an even larger tray of roasted vegetables including squash, peppers and eggplant from a specialty grower on the mainland, Filiberto proudly informed them, their shape and color being so perfect they proclaimed hothouse origins.

While the men studied the platters hungrily, Emma, served first, had a moment to observe the cook. Cesara, younger than Filiberto, had the sturdy build of cooks everywhere who enjoyed sampling their own culinary efforts, a silent advertisement really. Ample brown hair fluffed around her face escaped the bun at the back of her neck. Head high, shoulders back, she looked assured, competently handling serving duties. A ruddy complexion suggested good health, or, at the very least, long hours bent over the roasting spit. She deftly served the table with an unwavering smile outlined on a serious face. Here was someone else she might befriend, a good thing, since Riccardo seemed so withdrawn.

He quickly began tucking into a plate piled with meat and vegetables while Emma and Nigel exchanged information about London gallery openings and exhibitions. In typical Venetian fashion, there seemed little hurry to bring the meal to an end. When luncheon plates had been removed, small cups of steaming black coffee appeared with a froth of whipped milk on top.

Emma earlier had heard the hiss of an *espresso* machine coming from the kitchen. *Ca' Sospira* obviously provided lavishly for its employees and guests, yet the meal had not been fussy or pretentious.

Emma listened to the men as she nibbled tiny, sugar-sprinkled wafers. They discussed a coming auction of fine furniture which was expected to fetch high prices. After leisurely talk they rose from the table and Nigel prepared to leave. He again urged her to visit the gallery Vianello, a stone's throw from the Rialto Bridge. She assured him she would be delighted. They shook hands and Riccardo escorted him outside.

Later during the afternoon Riccardo came to the library and offered to give her a quick tour of the collection so she might locate paintings on her own whenever she wished. Rapidly he took her through the principal rooms of the house. Emma hastily jotted down names of the artists and locations as they hurried from room to room. She would have to photograph them later.

Riccardo, it seemed, had pressing duties demanding his attention. Silently Emma wondered, what could they could possibly be? There was no longer any acquisition of furniture now that the old earl had died. Lord Elmley had mentioned that during her interview. With the family seldom in residence in Venice, there was little need. Emma, on second thought, realized Riccardo's duties would include keeping *Ca'Sospira* secure from theft or natural disaster, as well as halting the onset of decay, an onerous job, however much Riccardo might prefer to haunt the sale rooms ferreting out additional furnishings.

The pair made their way through shaded rooms where graceful tables by Sheraton or Hepplewhite stood beside continental pieces. Glass and porcelain-filled cupboards held more Murano glass. With dustsheets removed and shutters opened, Emma could drink in the exquisite beauty of the Elmley property.

"Such a bother to remove the sheets, but the young earl insisted. He said it wasn't fair, forcing you to work in such a gloomy, cave-like setting." Riccardo scrutinized the room in which they were standing. "I must admit, it does make the effect much more pleasant."

Many of the paintings were scenes of Venice. Emma recognized the Basilica of *San Marco* of course, the *Church of the Redentore, Santa Maria della Salute.* There were views of gondola strewn canals, facades of various *palazzi*, a charming scene of the interior of *La Fenice*, the opera house, where a sprited scene from Puccini's Turandot was being enacted, Emma guessed, recognizing the Chinese mandarin costumes. There were a few early twentieth century watercolors of tourists peering into a bookstall on an unrecognized *piazza*, feeding the pigeons on *San Marco* in front of Florian or Quadri she was not certain which. Silently she marveled that tourists still were taking coffee under those awnings and paying the earth for the privilege. Some things never changed.

The tour finished and Emma had seen nothing remotely similar to the artist Carpaccio. It seemed as though Riccardo must be correct. If there was no picture on the walls, nor anything noted in the catalogue, it must be a myth.

Yet the remembered scrap of paper tucked into the final page of the catalogue nagged at her, an irritant like a small grain of sand working inside an oyster shell.

"Whatever happens, do not give up the Carpaccio!"

It seemed to be such an emotional admonition. She couldn't believe it was a joke, or a prank of children, as Riccardo suggested. No, there was too much passion in those faded words written by the late earl.

Was there a pearl of great price to be found in *Ca' Sospira?*

4

A Surprising Discovery at the Museo Correr

A week into her duties at *Ca' Sospira*, Emma began to feel she was making progress. The paintings were now familiar to her. They had been photographed and each day as she toured the rooms, she felt more comfortable with the *collezione*. A stack of photographs on her desk meant the image of each one was nearby as she read, gleaning new information about the artists. Library shelves yielded precious biographical data on these little known artists, and Emma's respect for the late earl grew.

The artists were lesser names it was true; however most of them held solid reputations in the Venetian art milieu. The thought crossed her mind that Lord Elmley's collection of art books, some embellished with gold leaf, all beautifully bound in soft leather and titled in gold, might equal his painting collection in value one day in the future.

Riccardo had become more friendly and less resentful of her presence. On several occasions she'd had the chance to let him know a little of her plans: her wedding in the autumn, the fact that her future husband was a surgeon whose career would determine where she lived and it would most likely be England, certainly not Italy. She confided in Riccardo how much she missed her family in Virginia, yet she was marrying someone who would probably remain in London and open a practice there. It became obvious she had no wish for a permanent job in Venice and he slowly lost some of his suspicions. They became more at ease with one another.

Although Emma had obtained few facts as yet, she guessed Riccardo's slightly eccentric behavior might be the result of having been an only child, growing up without the noisy companionship of brothers and sisters. His introverted personality reminded her of certain former classmates in Virginia as she was growing up. But she had learned little else either about Riccardo, or his relatives. She knew he was single, Venetian born, an only child. Period.

Filiberto became Emma's confidante. On the other hand, Cesara, a widow of many years, proved difficult to befriend. She seemed distant and unapproachable. She learned from Filiberto that Cesara had a married daughter living in Dorsoduro, not far from Emma's flat. Emma hoped to invite mother and daughter along with Filiberto for tea when she and the cook were on friendlier terms.

Filiberto amazed her with his depth of knowledge about Venice. He knew the city's turbulent history backward and forward and was helping Emma gain her bearings as she explored *campos,* as Venetians referred to their smaller squares, and *rios,* the canals connecting them, during occasional strolls after luncheon.

Emma learned that Venice was a city of neighborhoods each with its own bars, cafes, restaurants. Many held open-air markets in the *campos,* or a floating green grocer's boat tied up on the *rio* on a specified day each week.

Filiberto looked like a Venetian and spoke the language so expertly Emma had to remind herself daily that he was an Englishman. The exception of course, remained his passionate interest in the English peerage. He read and studied everything about it he could find in society periodicals. *Burke's Peerage* was never far from him, its worn pages hastening toward total decomposition.

When Emma reached saturation point in her work, she climbed the outside stairs at the rear of *Ca' Sospira* to the *altana,* Venetian rooftop gardens. There among oleanders and boxwood growing in ornamental tubs she listened to Filiberto as he told her about the Elmleys in interesting detail.

"The late earl was extremely genial and well-liked by his peers in England before giving it all up and moving to Venice with Lady Sybil, his wife. He was active in the House of Lords and held many honorary posts and positions. The children had been sent to boarding school when they were small. That is customary in England you know, and they were absent the greater part of the year. The earl had come under the spell of Venice by this period in his life, and the thought of living elsewhere became increasingly intolerable. It was one of the amazing things about him, certainly to those who knew him only slightly. But I understood: His seduction by Venice, *La Serenissima*, was absolute and complete. However there remained many unknown facets to the man. He was extremely complex."

Emma waited for more details, but Filiberto became silent. He revealed no more about his employer. It was as though a conduit of rushing waters had quickly been shut off. She continued to speculate on the Carpaccio notation tucked into the catalogue. Perhaps after all, the painting had been sent to England when the late earl died. But Filiberto offered no answers.

Filiberto returned to his duties and Emma took out the folded envelope from her pocket and began to reread the letter from Sam. She sighed. Life was never simple. She knew every line of the letter by heart. Sam, she had thought, had been comfortably settling in at Guy's Hospital in London where he was assistant to the hand specialist on the surgeon's roster. She had assumed this would be an assignment of a semi-permanent nature, at least for five years, so they could establish themselves as a married couple. And of course, London offered Emma unlimited opportunities for her pursuit of a career in art history.

Now Sam was writing about an offer he had received from a hospital in Oxfordshire to head up a surgical team. The hospital had lost a large number of doctors through death and retirement, so the surgeons would be younger than usual. The practice would serve Oxford and environs, and would provide Sam with experience in a smaller, less heavily populated area as opposed to metropolitan London. Those surgeons offered positions would be expected to report in the autumn of the following year.

A year was short in terms of a move like that, Emma thought as she sat idly on the rooftop porch, watching the busy scene below. The power of the sun's rays had been unleashed, dancing on the waters, creating reflections on walls, on sparkling glass of a thousand palazzo windows turned into prisms of reflected light.

At that moment she watched a woman's voluminous red scarf flapping over her shoulders as she sat in a stiff wind in the forward seat of a moving *vaporetto*. The scarf echoed the terra cotta tiles of a projecting facade in a crumbling palazzo on the far bank. The reflected reds morphed into liquid fire in the waters of the Grand Canal.

Venetian seduction, sorcery, Emma thought, and a longing enveloped her, to see and experience the world of architecture and art in this amazing city longer than just the few remaining weeks of summer, before settling down into a partnership with the man she loved most in all the world, Sam.

Was her love for Sam strong enough to give up the aims and ambitions in her heart? That was the point. Sam wished to broaden his horizons. Emma too had dreams of her own. She saw them in Oxfordshire, Sam, duly installed on the surgical team, returning home each evening bursting with enthusiasm for his new duties at the hospital. She saw a picturesque cottage with thatched roof, boiling in summer, cold like the Russian steppes in winter. Suppers eaten at a table for two near a roaring fire, tea in the dappled shade of the garden's riotous color on long Sunday summer afternoons. Women's Institute meetings, the flower rota at the parish church presided over by controlling old biddies giving orders in flutey tones for the flower arrangements in a sixteenth century gem of a village church.

'But we've always had hydrangeas massed in front of the altar, dear, the roses in vases belong behind, on either side, don't you see?' Was this the life she wanted?

What would be her chance of cataloging an art collection such as Lord Elmley's in such a village? What project could she find to care passionately about before a succession of darling little McGregors began arriving? Glancing about her, Venice seemed so precious, and Oxfordshire so, well, so provincial.

"Nor fair!" The invisible imp perched on her shoulder, Emma's nemesis, bellowed in her ear. "You tried this before, when Sam worked in Aberdeen. You stayed in London, and you both agreed, no separations again. Now here you are, off to Venice, with Sam's blessing, and you're racked with dissatisfaction. Wanting more. Greedy Emma! Fairness or greed? Which is it going to be? A little objectivity, if you please!"

The imp had seized her attention.

"You might be surprised at what could turn up in an English village. Samuel Palmer painted those glorious Shoreham landscapes in rural Sussex. Turner's paintings from Petworth House stand unsurpassed, the experts say. Henry Moore's sculptures in his sheep field at Much Haddam, barely a pinpoint on the map, made his reputation. You might be amazed. And I do not believe I have ever heard Oxford University described as provincial." He folded arms and subsided.

Emma squirmed in the garden seat. I haven't decided anything. She sniffed self-righteously. I simply want to think while there is still time. She folded the letter and replaced it in her pocket.

~~~

Back on Dorsoduro, Emma and Rosamund were getting on nicely in the flat. Rosamund had a flair for cooking and most evenings offered to prepare something inviting while Emma assisted as salad chef. An excellent *panetteria* provided a variety of interesting breads and cakes for dessert, or pudding, as Rosamund called it. And frequently they visited some of the charming little *ristoranti* nearby which had the added cachet of being favorites of artists and writers in the neighborhood. Of course when will power failed them, they hurried over the Accademia Bridge through the campo *San Vidal* to Paolin for a table at Venice's fabled *gelataria* on campo *Santo Stefano*.

A Small Canal near San Marco

"Why did I not know earlier we were so close to Venice's world famous ice cream parlor?" Emma teased, trying to control rivulets of pistachio running down her spoon as they sat at an outside table on the campo, watching strolling couples and children on cycles and scooters dipping in and out around pedestrians. The neighborhood reclaimed its outdoor space in the cool of evenings as the heat loosened its grip.

"Ah, that was a secret, until I was sure you were stopping," Rosamund grinned as she tucked into a coffee and banana *gelato*. The two girls complimented each other. Emma learned a lot about Venice on their evening walks after supper. Rosamund drew assurance from Emma after the shattering experience with Cyril. She had resumed her job at the British consulate.

On that evening they were joined by a friend Rosamund had met at a party earlier. Samantha Satchell, an American, was an intern at the Correr Museum on San Marco, the museum of Venetian History and Painting. She was taking a semester off from graduate school to serve six months at the museum. She hoped to secure a post as an art historian at some university back home, specializing in Italian Renaissance art. Emma, after five minutes in her company, had no doubts she would reach her goal.

Clear brown eyes, hair worn in a sedate knot at the nape of the neck, her facial features were unremarkable, but the musical quality of her voice quickly emerged as her most compelling attribute. Emma could easily imagine Samantha lecturing to students. Her voice alone would charm them, and Samantha's knowledge, which eased out in unassuming spurts and bursts, was impressive in its depth and range.

Emma's questioned her about her work at the Correr. Samantha replied that most days were routine, answering letters of specific requests, guiding special visitors around the collections. She was working on several research projects. Samantha told Emma the privilege of studying great art at such close range made her feel humble and reinforced her wish to become a professor of art history.

"To show you what I mean, let me tell you about the most amazing thing which happened today. A once in a lifetime event, really." The soft brown eyes took on a faraway look.

"Vincenzo Dalle Deste was a Venetian painter, born in Treviso. But he worked in Venice at some period, around the 1530s-1540s. I know you've never heard of him." She grinned at Emma.

"I'd think you were a walking freak if you had! I certainly had not. Anyway, there is a painting by him is in *Santa Maria dei Miracoli*, not far from the Rialto Bridge. Many Venetians believe the *Miracoli* is the city's most beautiful church, by the way. You think you are in a jewel box standing inside, everything is so precious. Go see it. Now, we have one of Dalle Deste's paintings in the Correr also, a Deposition, nothing special, competently executed you understand, but not wildly exciting."

"Venice is so full of painters and their work, it makes my head swim," Rosamund sighed, a tiny frown wrinkling brows above the spectacular blue eyes.

"Don't take it so seriously, Pet," Samantha answered, smiling, "Just remember, art historians need work and Venice does her part in supplying our salaries. Now let me tell you what happened today." They leaned closer.

"I was in the restoration workshop downstairs watching while Alvise and Fabrizio moved Dalle Deste's Deposition. They were planning to give the old frame a polish; the painting was okay. Just as they lifted the frame, which was front side down on the worktable, the backing cloth came away. Attached to the underside was another painting, this one smaller, on vellum, a secular subject, fresh and bright as the day it was painted, in 1542!"

"Was it Dalle Deste also?" Rosamund asked, rolling the musical sound of the name around on her tongue. Samantha nodded.

"How can you be sure of the date?" Emma wondered.

"Because in the corner of the reverse side Dalle Deste had penned both his name and the date. The prettiest Madonna and Child you ever saw in the guise of a young Venetian mother of the period! Her dress alone would make it priceless for all the costume details. The clothing experts were called in to verify the date and they immediately began slavering over it. It is that good. Such a remarkable face. The nose is the straight Roman nose you still see occasionally, with rosy cheeks and the sweetest smile. It has to be a portrait.

"And the baby! Adorable. Plump and rosy, holding a little coral ring, like so many children in pictures of the period. Even Fabrizio and Alvise were rendered speechless. I'm telling you, it's a stunner. One of the loveliest things I've seen in Venice. I am quite bucked up by such a discovery."

Emma's thoughts flew immediately to the lost Carpaccio. She musn't give up hope. Discoveries similar to Samantha's happened in the art world. The missing Carpaccio painting had to be somewhere in *Ca' Sospira*. But why was it not listed in the catalogue? Had it already disappeared when the catalogue was published? Was its omission intentional? Was it hidden because of its value? She realized the answer could lie in the date it was acquired by the late lord Elmley. She must find out more.

"Hey, Emma. You're in a trance. What's going on?" Samantha looked at Emma. Impulsively, Emma let her concerns tumble out.

"After hearing of your discovery, I am more convinced than ever something fishy is going on at *Ca' Sospira*," she began. Warning them to treat what she was about to say in absolute confidence, she told them about the scrap of paper found in the earl's notebook about the missing Carpaccio and Riccardo's dismissive reply. Samantha whistled in amazement while Rosamund looked wide-eyed.

The three sat, mulling over what Emma had said. A missing painting by Carpaccio, one of the best-loved of Venetian painters. But how to find it? That was the problem. Perhaps the most useful suggestion came from Samantha:

"Conduct the best search you can in the house without tearing beneath the frames of the other pictures or taking apart the Sheraton and Hepplewhite. If that doesn't bring results, you might begin thinking about looking beneath the backings of the other works in the earl's *collezione*. And do try and find a record of its acquisition date."

~~~~

The following day at *Ca' Sospira*, Emma left the library and went up to the *altana*. Tintoretto, *Ca' Sospira's* red Irish setter, named for one of Venice's most revered painters, heard her footsteps, roused himself from his favorite napping spot on the kitchen hearthrug. He padded softly up the stairs in search of her. Resting his head on the chair arm, with gentle nudges aimed at her hand, he demanded to be stroked. She wondered about the dog's age, at first thinking he might have been the late earl's pet.

"No," Filiberto answered as he joined her, "Tintoretto is the pup of Titian, the late earl's setter. Lord Elmley adored that dog, and I must say, Tintoretto has turned out to be just as even tempered and affectionate as Titian. I had wondered when Tintoretto would add you to his string of admirers," Filiberto smiled at Emma. The dog fiercely wagged his plume of a tail.

Tintoretto became Emma's silent confidant. She pondered the missing painting over and over during her relaxing minutes in the rooftop garden, voicing disappointing results of her fruitless search to the animal beside her. His liquid brown eyes fixed on her face as though he understood every word she was whispering and would reveal his thoughts at the earliest opportunity.

Try as she might, however, Emma's mental gymnastics, the imagined theories about where the missing Carpaccio could be found, always returned to one person: Riccardo must know more than he was telling. But how to get him to confide? Especially as it might uncover facts causing him to lose face, or worse, reveal a lapse on his part.

Emma had a more satisfactory understanding of Riccardo than she did when she arrived. But their interaction remained awkward at best, and she wondered if Riccardo accepted her reasons for coming to Venice. What a doubting turn of mind he had! When she asked him about relatives, he told her he had none living. He had lost his father soon after his birth, his mother some years later. He was an only child. Was that a reason for his suspicious nature? If only he weren't so withdrawn. Still, he had invited Nigel Sleight to luncheon her first day so she could meet someone in her field; that was a kindness. And he left her strictly alone to complete her work, after that first day when he took her on a tour of the paintings. She appreciated that. Emma did not think she could tolerate interference. And the blissful library she had to work in. Yes, Riccardo was a good person.

The Bridge of Sighs

"I'll find out what he's hiding, and win him as a friend," she whispered, looking into the liquid depths of Tintoretto's velvety eyes. But this wasn't helping her get her research completed. She sighed, started for the stairway and found herself facing Riccardo.

"You've had a call from Nigel. He's asking you to ring him as soon as you can. Here is his number I've jotted down on the pad." The voice was quick, curt.

What could that be about? She hurried downstairs toward the hallway and picked up the antiquated telephone, amazingly one of only three in the whole house, a second one in the kitchen and another in a guest bedroom. Earlier Riccardo had told her the late earl disliked telephones and refused to have one in his library or his bedroom.

As she dialed the number, she was aware of a shadowy Riccardo hovering in the depths of the hallway. The closed shutters tinted everything dusky, and she could hardly see him.

"I've just had a visit from a *Signora* Violetta Puglio, and she is someone you should meet," Nigel began. "She's an old lady, hobbles about on two canes, comes in two or three times a year to sell us a few pictures from the remaining stock of the small art gallery she and her husband ran for a number of years before ill health forced him to close. He's been dead more than ten years. I believe she still lives in an apartment over the shop, in the Riva degli Schiavoni not far from the *Ponte di Sospiri*, Bridge of Sighs and the *Ponte della Paglia*. By the way, Emma, the

Ponte is one of the oldest bridges in Venice. Apparently they named it for the boats loaded with straw which were moored there around 1360 when it got its name. So much for today's history lesson!"

His chuckle floated over the wires and Emma could imagine his good-natured face smiling into the telephone. How even-tempered Nigel was.

"To get to the point, she mentioned something rather interesting," he continued. "She says they once owned a Carpaccio sketch which was their pride and joy until a wealthy British earl bought it for his collection. She did not name him, but let it drop he owned a house near the Fenice. I knew that would fix your attention, Emma. Would you like her telephone number?" He gave it to her, then rang off quickly. "Must go. Client. 'Bye."

Another confirmation, she thought. Not just the earl's handwriting on the scrap of paper, but also the revelation of this *Signora* Puglio to Nigel. There must have been a Carpaccio in the collection. Without hesitation she dialed the number.

"*Pronto!*" The voice sounded strong and firm. It could have been a young person, Emma thought as she responded.

"*Signora* Puglio? I am an art historian, Emma Darling, working at present for Lord Elmley at *Ca' Sospira*." she began. Returning the telephone to its cradle a few minutes later Emma felt elated. After listening to her credentials, *La Signora* invited Emma to her flat in the Riva degli Schiavoni the very next afternoon when she finished work.

Riccardo passed her in the hall with an innocent query, "Things going well with Nigel?" Had he been listening to scraps of her conversation?

"I heard you on the telephone earlier and guessed he might propose a visit. Why don't we go over to Vianello's when you finish up today and have Nigel show us his collections?" But Emma begged off, pleading a deadline she had set for herself which must be met. Truth be told, she did not wish to confide in Riccardo, not just yet, not until she had a chance to talk with *Signora* Puglio.

"Give me a day, Riccardo. Then I will have pushed on a bit more with my task. I've got such a little time to finish my job."

5

Signora Puglio Shines Some Light on the Puzzle

Emma walked leisurely toward the Riva degli Schiavoni after leaving *Ca' Sospira* at the close of work the following day. She had plenty of time, and she wished to collect her thoughts before meeting *Signora* Puglio. First she stopped in a little *pasticceria* behind *San Marco* where she selected a prettily wrapped box of delectable macaroons to present to her hostess. Then she made her way on one of the narrow streets leading west.

Most of the buildings along this part of the Riva, somewhat removed from the glittering San Marco, had seen better days. Past the still sumptuous façade of Hotel Danieli, where the English art critic John Ruskin had lived during his infatuation with Venice, she discovered the building which housed *Signora* Puglio's apartment. The ground floor was occupied by a shop selling posters, calendars and T-shirts, geared to day-trippers and school groups Emma noted, looking at the beautiful old walls and windows of the facade. Had this space once been occupied by the Puglio art gallery?

Higher, the view was more pleasing. She gazed at sparkling Gothic windows displaying beautiful examples of old Murano glass, glittering in the afternoon sun. What splendid sunsets these residents must enjoy, thought Emma, determined to look on the bright side. And they were near both *San Marco* and *San Zaccaria.* She recalled her wish to visit the Bellini altarpiece at *San Zaccaria.* That would have to wait.

A short distance away Emma remembered, was the *Scuola di San Georgio degli Schiavoni,* the ancient guild hall of the Dalmatians, where the Carpaccios hung. The fresco series told the legend of St. George slaying the dragon. Well, that too must wait. Her walk had been so leisurely time had evaporated. She was due at *La Signora's* in a few minutes. On the ink-faded list of tenants under glass hung beside the door, she found 'Antonio Puglio' written in a faint script. She rang the bell.

It was answered by a sharp buzzing releasing the lock, giving Emma plenty of time to slip inside. She took the lift to number seven. The door stood ajar.

"*Signora* Puglio? It's Emma. Emma Darling from *Ca' Sospira.* May I come in?"

"*Avanti!*" It was the ringing voice of the earlier telephone call. Emma walked into a small reception room furnished with a few good Venetian chairs of antique vintage, as well as two comfortable but worn armchairs. The walls held several Venetian street scenes, remaining paintings from the gallery, Emma imagined, and a prominently displayed crucifix. Sitting erect in one of the armchairs was a small, bird-like woman whose darting black eyes beneath modest but neat coiffure reminded Emma of the industrious house wren, the busybody of the avian world, hopping about on a mission of frantic nest building in the spring.

But this woman did no hurrying, not anymore. Cruel knots at the joints of her fingers marred the image of an active old age, along with the two stout canes resting beside her chair. The face however was serene, even beautiful. Here was someone who had come to terms with life, at least in spirit, Emma realized, yet one who suffered every time she rose from the chair to perform the movements necessary to get through each day. Emma believed she had observed the *Signora* once before, hobbling on canes into Saint Mark's, bound for the mid-morning mass.

What a nightmare Venice must be for the old: no handy buses or taxis available, narrow sidewalks along the network of small *rios*, arching bridges covered in steps which must be traversed. And the dampness everywhere, punishing to the arthritic.

Emma presented the small box of macaroons and sat down. As she looked into the alert black eyes, direct, brooking no nonsense, she was reminded of her professor of art history at the Uni in London. Maria Crawford possessed the same piercing eyes.

"*Signora*, Nigel Sleight of Gallery Vianello told me he believed you and your husband once sold a Carpaccio sketch to the late Lord Elmley of *Ca' Sospira,* near the Fenice. I am researching the collection for the present Lord Elmley in England, and I would like to find out more about it. I have been unsuccessful in obtaining any information in documents of the collection."

"You are not English, are you? Your accent is American. Are you from the South?"

Goodness, she is quick-witted, Emma thought, even if she is virtually immobilized. Nothing lacking upstairs. She smiled, giving details of her family; a professor father who left England for a post at the University of Virginia, an American mother, also a professor, a native of Virginia. Emma and her two younger brothers completed the family circle. She had been living in England several years, studying art history at the University of London. After completing her studies, she had lectured on art at London's Celia Drummond School.

"Thank you *Signorina*," the woman smiled, "Some people become impatient with the old and infirm when they won't get directly to the point. You have been generous in telling me a bit about yourself as a person. I find age has made *me* impatient. I feel I cannot spend lengthy amounts of time getting to know people. Now I will tell you what I know about the watercolor sketch."

She eased the shawl around her shoulders onto the chair arm. A small table beside her held spectacles, the morning *Gazzettino*, and what looked to Emma like a public library novel, judging from the code letters stamped on its cover. With a start she recognized the name of the author: Sherlock Holmes! The gift box of macaroons perched on the table's edge.

"Antonio, my husband, and I owned a small but select gallery in the shop below us for many years. Quality was our aim, and we collected the best we could within the limits our funds would permit. This meant late nineteenth and early twentieth century drawings and watercolors of Venice. Of course there were exceptions, and the greatest exception of all was the Carpaccio."

Emma drew a sigh of relief. She had begun to think the fabled Carpaccio she had allowed herself to dream of was only an imaginary family legend. But *Signora* Puglio had shone a beam of light under the closed door of hope. Emma leaned closer.

"Our clientele was made up mainly of affluent foreign visitors to Venice. They seemed to recognize the unique quality of our gallery, while many Venetians preferred highly rouged, voluptuous young women holding baskets of fruit as they rolled eyes heavenward, unaware of a swashbuckling dandy gawking in the background." Emma nodded. She knew money did not guarantee good taste.

"The Carpaccio sketch was inherited by Antonio when his uncle died. This uncle, who missed his calling as an academic, had been wealthy at one time and owned a prosperous gallery. Haunting the Correr and Accademia museums became more compelling to him, to the extent that his gallery suffered and ultimately closed. It was located in the Cannaregio district, removed from the bustle of *San Marco*, but at one time it had prospered. When he died, we did not expect anything because the gallery had been shut for years and he had been living on the sale of what was left. Just as I am doing now, actually." Lifting shapely brows she smiled, as though the thought amused her.

"He left us the Carpaccio; it was the jewel of both his and our collection. Some time before my husband died, it became necessary to sell it. I was put in touch with Lord Elmley by a kind gallery owner, a friend of my late husband."

"And when did your husband die, *Signora?*"

"In the nineteen fifties," she answered quickly, "He needed an operation when his health began to fail. He died soon after we had sold the Carpaccio." Her tone was matter-of-fact. Emma noted that the Carpaccio had come into the earl's collection in the fifties. Then why was it not listed in the catalogue at Elmley House?

"And can you tell me about the subject?" Emma begged. So much talk and rumor of the elusive work, and she had no idea what it looked like.

"You didn't know? Poor child. Venetians are so close-mouthed. Nobody trusts anybody." As Emma politely contradicted her hostess who had left the door wide open to her, sight unseen, *Signora* Puglio held up a hand to stop her.

"Never mind, Emma, I know what you are thinking. But the old must trust others, what else can they do? Besides, there is so little left." She glanced dispassionately around the room, "Who would want it?

"The Carpaccio is a watercolor sketch of two women, girls precisely, sitting on the *altana*, or rooftop garden, combing out their hair in the sunlight. They are wearing straw sun hats, with open crowns, blonde hair pulled through the crowns and spread out around the brims. At their feet is a lovely still life of a basket of lemons. The girls hold combs.

"As far back as the early 1500s women in Venice bleached their tresses with lemon juice. It was believed to be more efficacious if applied when sunlight could speed the lightening process. Blondes, even back then, were much preferred by gentlemen, you see." A teasing smile crept around the corners of her mouth. Emma nodded.

"The flowers and shrubs of the garden in decorative pots were appealing, and oh, yes, I believe there was a little dog sitting beside the girls.

"You know Carpaccio often placed similar animals in his paintings? Some art historians theorize it was Carpaccio's own little dog. How could they possibly know? I ask you! Complete fiction." Then, perhaps remembering she was addressing one of those creatures, an art historian, a guest in her own home, good manners hurried her past her remark.

"It was about twelve inches by sixteen, more or less standard size I recall. And in excellent condition. You understand one must be very careful of works on paper here, don't you?" Emma agreed, hoping to learn more. But *La Signora* had no idea why or when the sketch had disappeared from the Elmley collection. However, she offered to try to find the record of sale to Lord Elmley for Emma.

Emma's visit, while illuminating on one level, left her where she had begun on another. She had not really expected information from *Signora* Puglio concerning the whereabouts of the missing Carpaccio. To be able to confirm its existence meant great progress, however. As Emma made her way to Rosamund's flat in Dorsoduro, she knew she would have to confront Riccardo first thing in the morning. Hopefully she would soon have the record of sale in her hands.

But it was not Riccardo who greeted her the following morning at *Ca' Sospira*; it was Filiberto, as he brought her *caffelatte* to the library. *Santo Cielo!* For heaven's sake, Emma mused, inhaling the rich aroma of the coffee laced with hot milk, this job is spoiling me. As she sipped, she told him about her visit to *Signora* Puglio on Riva degli Schiavoni.

"Do you remember the Carpaccio painting, Filiberto? Did you ever see it?"

"Certainly. It was the late earl's favorite and always hung in his bedroom."

"Do you have any idea why it disappeared?"

"I believe it was sent back to England for some reason which I was never told. The late earl never talked about it. I thought perhaps because it was his favorite he was worried about the dampness here and wanted it in a safer climate. And we all knew he had plans to return to England at the end. Perhaps he wanted to die on his native soil. Maybe that was on his mind. As it happened, he died unexpectedly in his sleep, no time even to pack a bag. Of course the Carpaccio had gone long before that.

"Lady Sybil died first, you know. I am positive the late earl wouldn't have parted with that picture but for absolute necessity. And of course he had plenty of The Ready; there was no reason to sell it." He stroked his chin. Emma smiled at the familiar Cockney expression.

"And you never heard any of the family mention it, where it was hung in Elmley Castle for example?"

"No, I never did, nor do I know just when it was sent over. You do realize I was not privy to everything but I did hear a lot. Lord Elmley kept few secrets from me. I had been in his service too long, I suppose. He was lonely for someone who had known him in earlier years; he needed someone to talk with, especially after Lady Sybil's death."

Filiberto's comments rang true. His open face lacked guile. After all, he had given up his entire life in service to the Elmleys, and while the pay she was sure was quite good, Filiberto's service spanned the post World War I period when fewer and fewer men and women were willing to put themselves in a state of subjugation which domestic service entailed. The trend had continued. In the present world where equality was the mantra, there was little enthusiasm for the master-servant relationship on the servant side of the equation.

Emma sipped *caffelatte* as she sorted through Filiberto's revelations. If the Carpaccio was in England, why that was the end to it. She could put away her hopes and get on with her work. Had Riccardo misled her? Emma knew she could not forestall a conversation with him any longer. She made vague, tidying motions on her desk and prepared to tell him about her amazing visit with *Signora* Puglio. She hurried to his cubbyhole of an office and tapped lightly on the door.

"*Avanti!*" She walked inside and Tintoretto's tail began thumping. He lay comfortably curled on a small Turkey carpet in front of the desk. His eyes sparkled and he seemed to be giving her a welcome more effusive than Riccardo's, who stood up and motioned her to sit in the chair facing the desk.

"Good morning, Riccardo. And Tintoretto, you fickle-hearted creature. I thought you left the hearth rug in Cesara's kitchen only for me and our rooftop assignation. Shame, you faithless dog," and indeed, Tintoretto looked abashed and raised luminous eyes to Riccardo.

Riccardo laughed and replied, "Don't look to me, 'Tinto! You know you've thumped and slavered your way into everyone's affections. Emma might as well find out where she stands."

He smiled at Emma. Things seemed to be easing between them, and she didn't want to spoil it. He obviously felt a great affection for the dog. But she must tell him about her visit yesterday.

She plunged in, giving him a full account of *Signora* Puglio and the Carpaccio her late husband Antonio had sold to Lord Elmley. Riccardo sat silently, long tapering fingers forming a pyramid over his chest as he listened. A lengthy pause ensued. Tintoretto thumped his tail; Emma waited for Riccardo to speak.

"Well, you have caught me fairly. I hesitate to imagine what you must think of me, telling such a whopper. What you have just said is all true, that *Signor* Puglio sold the Carpaccio to the earl. It quickly became the favorite piece in his collection. Why I cannot imagine, it was only a watercolor, although I admit, a fetching one. He could have bought one of the last Canalettos remaining in Venice if he'd wished, possibly a small Tintoretto before they were all exported."

His eyes took on a far away gaze and he sighed. At the sound of his name, Tintoretto thumped the floor a few times, then put his head down over his front paws and looked longingly at Emma. Riccardo gave a little cough and continued.

"Then a strange thing occurred. Lady Sybil took a dislike to the sketch. The earl hung it in his bedroom, you see. She somehow got it into her head that he preferred the two girls in the picture to her. Silly, of course, not at all like her, but they were both in their final years at this stage after a lifetime together. She remained precise about social engagements, things she had a real interest in; other subjects bored her and rendered her vague and uncaring. Still, the late earl humored her whims up until the end. We all have our quirks." His dark eyes bored into Emma, seeking confirmation. Emma nodded.

"So the picture must have gone back to England along with all of the earl's papers and some of his personal effects. I was studying much of the time in Padua at the university before Lady Sybil died, you see. Lord Elmley was urging me to hurry and finish my studies. I honestly do not know what happened to it. But I am reasonably sure it went to England. The slip of paper in the book you showed me *was* his handwriting. The late earl certainly wrote it. But I saw no point in opening up a Pandora's box of distractions when you were just beginning a difficult assignment, researching the entire collection, with limited time in which to complete your task. And I knew the Carpaccio had been missing for years. So I tried to turn you toward your assignment, a more fruitful occupation I thought."

"I see. I appreciate your thoughtfulness. But let me assure you, Riccardo, I mapped out a timetable when I first arrived, and you will be pleased to know that I am right on schedule. As for the Carpaccio, there seems to be little doubt that it went back to Worcestershire, but I don't mind telling you, I have had the strangest feeling it is still somewhere in the house, ever since I found that scrap of paper; no facts you understand, merely intuition. Do you know the approximate date when it disappeared?"

"Ah, Emma. You are indeed *sympatico* where art is involved. I have seen your affection for those bits and pieces in the late earl's collection grow. Filiberto has noticed it as well. He mentioned it to me yesterday as you were pouring over those early twentieth century views of the Lido with the swimmers wearing the antiquated bathing costumes in fashion then. But seriously, Emma, I am uncertain of the date. You would be wise to forget the Carpaccio. Will you forgive my lack of transparency?" He said no more about the time of its disappearance.

"Of course. Riccardo." And she rose, giving Tintoretto, who quickly appeared at her side, a quick pat on the head. But thoughts persisted that the watercolor by Carpaccio, that most Venetian of painters, remained in Venice, hidden somewhere in *Ca' Sospira. And with Riccardo in charge, it is his responsibility to find it.*

~~~~

"Carpaccio, Vittore (circa 1460-1526), probably a pupil, certainly a follower, of Giovanni Bellini whose assistant he was in 1507. Excelled in paintings city scenes of his beloved Venice, rich with birds, animals and people, giving a wealth of detail on architecture, dress, customs and behavior of the period in whch he lived."

Emma read the entry in a worn Dictionary of Art and Artists by Linda and Peter Murray, a tattered but well-loved survivor from her London University booklist, written by two of her favorite professors. She always took it on her travels; it was invaluable. She sat at the desk, photographs of the Elmley collection spread out.

If in fact the late earl owned a Carpaccio, it would be the oldest picture in the *collezione*, indeed a pearl beyond price. It would lend great credence to the entire group of pictures assembled by a member of the English peerage. The collection might someday travel to museums and galleries world wide, and that would be a great honor. Emma knew she could not heed Riccardo's advice to forget it. She was more determined than ever now to find it.

6

A Picnic on the Lido

Nigel rang Emma, proposing a picnic the coming Saturday on the Lido, the beach of Venice on the barrier island between the Venetian Lagoon and the Adriatic Sea. Only seven miles long, less than a mile deep, the Lido's sandy beaches attracted crowds of Venetians and tourists alike in the warmer months. He suggested Emma bring Rosamund and Fiona Crawford from the consulate and Samantha Satchell from the Correr museum. Nigel promised to invite Riccardo, some Italian friends from the galleries, as well as Vittoria Dandolo, a coworker at Gallery Vianello.

"I'll speak with Riccardo, when I ring him, and perhaps he'll bring Tintoretto. He deserves an outing," he told her. "Can you plan a menu with the girls and let me know if there is anyone else you wish to invite? We'll meet at the Accademia Bridge at the *vaporetto* stop for the Lido, the men will bring beverages and carry all the heavier items. We'll have a great party."

Hotel on the Lido beach

The idea of a group picnic appealed to Emma. She had wanted to visit the Lido and now that summer had arrived so quickly, the coming Saturday seemed perfect. Rosamund helped Emma work out a simple menu, an *antipasti* platter of *prochiutti* and roasted vegetables, *panini*, the sandwich of Italy, filled with *mozzarella* and *provolone* cheeses, fresh fruit, and a sampling of Cesara's pastries for dessert, promised by Riccardo. The Venetian wine of choice, a *pinot grigio*, along with fruit juices would suit as beverages and if that couldn't be managed by Nigel and his friends, then the universal cola would serve.

Riccardo, with Filiberto's help, located a beautiful, old wicker picnic basket high on a shelf in the pantry of *Ca' Sospira*. Outfitted with small Wedgewood plates and table settings of silver with bone handles, it would turn the excursion into a very stylish picnic. For a brief minute Emma saw herself spreading the blue checked cloth covering the Virginia backyard table, red bandana napkins and paper plates set in place, watching as her father and brothers cooked hot dogs on the grill while she and her mother arranged bowls of special potato salad and baked beans on the table. She seemed to smell the sizzling hot dogs and a wave of homesickness washed over her.

After two p.m. the following Saturday the party got underway. The girls arrived in a group burdened like migrant nomads at the *vaporetto* stop, but the young men quickly snatched up bags and baskets as the boat shuddered into life and they hurried on board. Vittoria brought Guido, Luciano, and Massimo, the three young Venetian men Nigel had invited from art galleries near Gallery Vianello.

Only Nigel and Riccardo had not yet made an appearance, and Emma wondered if they would be left behind. But just as the gate was closing, Nigel, struggling with parcels, came running into view from the northbound *vaporetto* stop as fast as his short legs could propel him. Tintoretto strained on the leash.

"Where's Riccardo?" Emma asked as they bounded on board. Nigel held up a hand signaling lack of breath.

"*Momento,*" he whispered, breathing deeply.

Tintoretto waved his tail in anticipation, sniffing the bouquet of smells wafting in the air from baskets surrounding the little group standing in the open platform of the water bus. His attention was briefly drawn by the sweet smelling girls who clustered around him administering pats and strokes. He looked up at Emma, as though the limpid brown eyes were trying to tell her about Riccardo.

"Riccardo had a crisis with the kitchen plumbing at the last minute and couldn't leave," Nigel gasped, still winded from his sprint. "The plumber let them down—nobody will work on weekends here—and he and Filiberto were forced to get down to it themselves or face Cesara's undying wrath. A blocked drain."

"I imagine it won't take them long; the two of them know more about the workings of *Ca' Sospira* than a plumber," Emma said, observing Nigel's face wasn't quite so red and that his breathing was returning to normal.

A pity Riccardo was held up. But Nigel seemed certain he would arrive later. Emma let go worries about Riccardo, who seemed lonely and needed more gaiety in his life, and gave herself up to anticipation of the Lido's long strip of sandy, sun swept beach fringed by clear waters. Hugging the shore of the Venetian Lagoon, the waterbus passed a beautiful park covered with verdant trees and shrubs which seemed to tint even the air with lushness. Vittoria told Emma the *Biennale,* Venice's famous art show was held in the park every two years.

After a short journey to the Lido they struggled off the *vaporetto* burdened with trappings of the picnic. Making their way across an avenue clogged with cars and bicycles, they joined Venetians with their towels and beach bags, babies in perambulators and toddlers grasping toy ducks and sailboats, boarding the waiting coaches to take them the mile across the island to the Lido's fingerlike shoreline.

Cars were everywhere, Emma marveled. Just a few minutes from the Grand Canal, there were motors, buses and bicycles! Oh, the richness! She rejoiced inwardly, happy to be a part of it. Lush greenery, beds bursting with flowers of every imaginable hue echoed the national love of color. Emma saw busy shops and outdoor cafes along the route, people stopping at café tables to drink lemonade or eat *gelati* as they read the morning *Il Gazzettino* or simply met with friends to talk over the day's events. She must investigate this charming island more thoroughly another time.

Nigel's co-worker at Gallery Vianello, Vittoria Dandolo, was the spark igniting the party. She drew them together as a group, organizing water relays and games of tag on the deserted bit of beach the group claimed for its own. Sunbathers, taking notice of the sun's waning power, began the slow ritual of folding up lounges and towels and started back to the dock for the return journey, but the group stayed on. Emma organized a game of dodge ball with a large red ball brought by Fiona. Ample time remained to enjoy the long summer evening.

Nigel's friends, the handsome Italians, had beautiful manners and stylish shoulder length hair. Emma and Samantha were the only Americans; Fiona Crawford, Rosamund, and Peter Law, all from the British consulate, rounded out the guests. Fiona, who spoke with an accent of the Midlands, seemed to prefer the company of Peter, a serious-faced young man with short-cropped hair and extremely long legs. It was whispered he worked on "something highly secret" at the consulate. His owl-like glances behind horn-rimmed glasses most often swiveled toward Rosamund. Still, Vittoria remained the most vivacious girl in the group. Emma admired her long brown hair, carelessly scraped into a pony tail which swung and bounced with every movement of her head. She possessed a sunny personality, full of good will. Tintoretto moved through the gathering as might any privileged guest, winning new friends with each forceful wag of the magnificent tail.

Doge Venier, Sculpture, Fourteenth century

Vittoria was unaware she held center stage. Her soft blue bathing suit was frayed and faded but nobody noticed, captured by her effortless charm and sense of presence. Nigel earlier confided in Emma that while she came from one of Venice's oldest families, there was a Doge somewhere in the background, all the money had evaporated, little remained of the Dandolo's former wealth. A job was a necessity, and Vittoria cheerfully worked harder than anyone at Gallery Vianello. Her best friends, the cream of Venetian families of wealth and privilege, remained loyal and always turned up to enliven gallery receptions and openings, Nigel told her. No doubt, she brought business to Gallery Vianello he assured Emma as they sat watching the game.

Shadows lengthened, the *pinot grigio* was uncorked and handed round in small flutes from the wicker picnic basket. Fiona and Samantha unpacked the delicate plates and forks and served *antipasti* with sweet red peppers, artichokes and eggplant. Trays held mountains of *panini* and pastries. Drawn up in a congenial circle in the sand, the group did not break ranks until every macaroon had been eaten, with Tintoretto daintily accepting tidbits in the form of crusts and the odd nibble of cheese. Dusk hovered like a cloak over the Lido, pausing long enough for packing up belongings and brushing off the sand from arms and legs. An exodus to the beach bus began the homeward journey. Emma offered to return Tintoretto to *Ca' Sospira* with Nigel, so he could carry the picnic basket more easily. He protested but was overruled when Rosamund, Vittoria, and Samantha declared their intention of coming along to keep Emma company.

When the *vaporetto* drew up at the dock of San Marco the picnic ended with plans to meet for another outing later in the summer. Emma, Samantha, Vittoria and Rosamund followed Nigel toward *Ca' Sospira*. There was music at the Fenice that evening, a concert; the opera season would not resume until November. They walked across the brightly lit *Campo San Fantin* in front of the opera house, looking up at stately columns, the grand stairway and porch lit with glowing lamps. They could hear music, Offenbach Nigel suggested, floating on the air from the orchestra inside. As they walked on, at her first glimpse toward *Ca' Sospira*, Emma realized something was wrong.

"Look how dark it is! The outside lamps haven't been lit and inside it's black as a bat. That can't be right!" She felt twinges of unease as she peered at the shadows enveloping the house, outlined against the bright summer moon.

"It looks like somebody forgot to turn them on. Suppose the old butler's had an accident?" Nigel hurried toward the entrance.

"Good heavens! The door!" Vittoria pointed. It stood ajar.

"Something *is* wrong," Emma whispered.

Nigel hurried inside, fumbling for a light switch. Emma reached out and found the antiquated wall switch, unchanged since *Ca' Sospira* was wired for electricity at the time the late earl bought it, years ago. The dim glow of small sconces cast a pale light as they made their way into the *portego*, the large central hall, switching on lamps as they inched along.

Tintoretto's nose quivered and he strained at the leash, giving sharp staccato barks. Cautiously the little group moved toward the library. Everything seemed in order. Nothing had been disturbed in the *salone*.

"What could have happened? Where are Riccardo and Filiberto?" Emma asked herself as they approached the library. Suddenly they were startled by an insistent pounding. They moved closer together. Tintoretto barked furiously and set up a fearful whine. The pounding resumed, louder this time.

Nigel stepped forward and threw open the library door. Emma flicked on the switch and the chandelier overhead burst into light. They saw a room in complete disarray. Large books of art reproductions had been removed from shelves and carelessly thrown onto the Chesterfield sofa. Books were strewn on chairs, the desk top. Riccardo and Filiberto, bound and gagged, lay on a floor littered with books. Before Nigel could remove their gags, Tintoretto plunged between them and began licking their faces.

Riccardo bounded up, rubbing his hands together to restore circulation, his face a study in relief mingled with fear. Filiberto, joints creaking, heaved himself up with an assist from Nigel and sank, exhausted, into the wing chair.

"What's the meaning of all this? Have the police been called?" Emma asked after it was determined both of them were in good shape, no broken bones, only stiffness, sore muscles. Riccardo shook his head. Filiberto spoke.

"I went out to light the outdoor lanterns and close up the house. Two chaps came walking by. My first impression was they had left the opera house early. We don't get much traffic along here after nightfall," he explained, rubbing his chin.

"Before I realized what was happening they grabbed me. I shouted as loud as I could. That's when they decided to put the gag over my mouth. They certainly weren't from the Fenice. They were thugs." Filiberto sank down in his chair and Riccardo continued.

"I hurried to the library where the sound was coming from. I had been in the kitchen tidying up after we unblocked the drain. I bolted the rear door. Cesara had left sometime earlier. I found the pair had Filiberto tied up on the floor. They grabbed me and trussed me up in a matter of seconds. They were large men, but I must say, there was no excessive violence. They tied a gag over my mouth. I was sure they would begin carrying off silver and porcelain in the grand salon."

"As for calling the police, often it's more trouble than it's worth. I prefer to deal with this in my own way," he said curtly, daring Emma, or anyone else to protest.

"But surely . . ." Emma faltered, then lapsed into silence.

Emma's mind was busily processing information. Of course, Riccardo would immediately think of the precious furnishings of *Ca' Sospira*. Thieves would go for that first. However, those were heavy, bulky items. Hardly a job two men could get away with alone, unless there were others waiting on the water. But what if? Her thoughts raced to the Carpaccio. What if news of a valuable Carpaccio had leaked to the underworld? To the ears of unscrupulous art dealers in Venice? Then the library would be the likely room to search.

"Did they speak at all?" Vittoria asked.

"Yes, a few words," Filiberto answered, "in a Venetian dialect. I'd be willing to wager they were both born within sight of either the Murano glass blowing furnaces or the fishing docks at Torcello." He looked at Riccardo who nodded in confirmation.

"What did they look like?" Emma asked.

"Big heavy men, caps pulled over most of their hair. One had a very prominent hooked nose, the other a slight squint. But the thing I remember most is that *they did not look like thieves!* Not small and wiry, nor accustomed to slipping in and out of tight places. More like fishermen, or just plain workingmen. Their movements were slow rather than quick, they were relaxed in a rustic sort of way as though their thought processes moved along rather slowly," Filiberto said thoughtfully rubbing his chin.

"And what were you thinking, Riccardo?"

"I could hardly breathe I was so worried about the marble sculpture by Donatello of the five music-making cherubs on the table in the grand salon. It stood out like a neon sign, certainly to me!" He breathed deeply and continued.

"Lord Elmley never talked about it, but that sculpture's provenance goes straight as an arrow back to Donatello. He worked on it in Venice while completing major commissions at Padua nearby for the basilica there. There is also his sculpture of the *putti*, the cherubs in the Accademia, and the resemblance to our cherubs is no accident. They could be siblings, they are so similar. Both are priceless, of course."

Emma agreed, certainly the little group of *putti* by Donatello, the best Florentine sculptor of the Early Renaissance, would be high on every list. But was Riccardo deliberately steering them away from the painting? If so, why?

Emma observed that when Riccardo spoke of the furnishings of *Ca' Sospira,* his whole bearing underwent a change. His cheeks were flushed, his dark eyes alight with fervor. Clearly he deeply loved the beautiful things he had guided the late earl to acquire. There was no doubt of his sincerity about that. He seemed transformed, overjoyed they were unharmed, these precious objects. It obviously was responsible for his euphoria. But combined with it, Emma realized there was a reluctance to talk about the paintings, specifically the missing Carpaccio.

"So they didn't find whatever they were searching for?" Nigel's piercing look could have pushed through marble.

Filiberto smiled and shook his head. "No! They poked through every volume big enough to hold a fairly large sketch or drawing, and came up with nothing. I think the Hook Nose wanted to carry on with the smaller volumes but the Squint muttered something about an idiot would know they wouldn't fold anything so valuable and shove it in an ordinary book."

Riccardo abruptly walked over to Filiberto and helped him to his feet.

"Come, Filiberto. You look done in. After your ordeal, you need rest. We'll lock up as soon as our friends leave us. Then we'll go up to bed."

Time for us to go, thought Emma, reading the tea leaves. Was Riccardo motivated by concern for the aging butler or a desire to keep more information from escaping? A bit of both perhaps, Emma decided. She was relieved the two were safe, albeit exhausted. And she realized Riccardo's words, spoken politely, were a command. She understood that signal well enough. He was polite, but, not to put too fine a point on it, they were being ushered out. There was nothing more to be learned, at least not now. Riccardo, she noted, had not offered scraps of information like Filiberto. Why was he holding it back? Whom did he not trust in the group? He had not divulged so much as a smattering of what the break-in was about.

She rose and made for the front of the house, followed by the others. Opening wide the great door, Riccardo was especially charming to Rosamund, Samantha, and Vittoria, making apologies for the failure of his duties as a host to new friends and inviting them to return soon and take tea on the *altana* with him and Emma. However, she noticed he did not invite Nigel.

The girls and Nigel hurried to Rosamund's building on Dorsoduro, where Nigel took his leave quickly after bidding them all a cordial goodnight. Emma realized he was miffed at Riccardo's coolness. Riccardo was suspicious of Nigel. Could Riccardo blame him for the bizarre break-in at *Ca' Sospira*? Or was something else bothering Nigel? Something she knew nothing about?

As Rosamund inserted her key in the lock, Emma, Vittoria, and Samatha watched Nigel hurry toward the Rialto. His behavior seemed abrupt, not really in character, Emma thought. They were exhausted by this time. Emma could feel bits of sand sticking to her damp bathing suit underneath her clothes. Samantha and Vittoria must be longing for home and a bath just as she and Rosamund were. After a few minutes Samantha said goodnight and hurried off to her own flat nearby in Dorsoduro while Vittoria left for her parents' home near the *Miracoli* church.

7

Explicit Instructions on How to Cook a Goose

Emma hurried into work the following Monday, realizing her time in Venice was steadily trickling away. Sam was due to arrive in less than a month and she needed to press on with her evaluation of the collection. With careful planning, she knew she could finish on time.

It had been quiet at *Ca' Sospira*. Nothing more was said about the intrusion of the previous week; the art books had been returned to their shelves, the room tidied. Emma was grateful her notes and the stack of photographs she had painstakingly accumulated were left intact. Increasing her efforts to discover more about the painters in her research, she had little time to think of the Carpaccio, if indeed it remained in *Ca' Sospira*. However, an unexpected telephone call from Lord Elmley in England to inquire of her progress presented a chance to ask him about the missing painting. Did he know if it once had been an important piece in the collection? Had it perhaps been returned to England at some earlier date?

But he could shed no light on the puzzle. He had never heard of the work, certainly when Emma described it, he knew he had never seen anything like it. So progress on that path seemed mired in quicksand. The late earl's bedroom, not the library, was where the intruders should have been looking, Emma thought. It was lucky they chose the library instead. She put aside thoughts of the Carpaccio and got on with her work.

By midweek she had rewritten her evaluation of the collection in a first draft, based on additional material from biographical data she had dug out from the Accademia and the *Museo Correr* reference libraries. Samantha Satchell had proved to be invaluable, acquainting her with the wealth of material available at the nearby Correr, only a short distance from *Ca' Sospira*. It took only ten minutes to walk there.

Reassured her work was proceeding on schedule, Emma decided to take time off for the postponed visit to Nigel at Gallery Vianello. She invited Riccardo to accompany her. At first he begged off, pleading an overload of work, then appeared to reconsider and said he would come along.

While Nigel dealt with a customer, Emma and Riccardo were shown around by the vivacious Vittoria, looking radiant in a simple dark dress with a Peter Pan collar which cast her as an engaging *ingénue*. Hair and nails were beautifully cared for, and the black patent pumps encasing long, narrow feet were becoming and correct. Gallery Vianello was lucky to have her. She would attract people like a magnet Emma realized as she followed her around the exhibition rooms, noting Riccardo's delight in her presence.

Venetian girls of Vittoria's status seemed to take a lot more time in their grooming efforts than most English girls, who often could be indifferent to details. American girls dressed in a more casual, sporty style, yet managed to look well turned out. Venetian women looked at their best when she noticed them in the open air restaurants and in the shops in their court shoes, superbly cut dresses in darker colors and beautiful jewelry. But to wear stockings in this frightfully hot summer weather? Emma wondered how Vittoria and her compatriots managed it as she furtively glanced down at her tanned bare legs, feet encased in serviceable brown leather sandals.

Vittoria began by showing them the small collection of Bloomsbury artists. First a Duncan Grant painting of the garden at Charleston, the old Sussex farmhouse which Vanessa Bell had turned into a retreat for her artist friends. They saw a portrait by Vanessa of her sister, the writer Virginia Woolf, who had lived nearby at Rodmell with her husband, the Bloomsbury publisher Leonard Woolf. Lastly, there was a French landscape by Roger Fry, the unofficial leader of Bloomsbury who organized the Omega Workshops, where artists showcased their furniture, ceramics and fabrics for wealthy Britons with sophisticated tastes.

Emma immediately fell in love with the Fry landscape, its perspective tilted in the manner of Cezanne, using Provencal colors of terra cotta, green and blue. The price was startlingly low considering his stature as an artist. She knew Fry had served a brief stint as Curator of Paintings at the Metropolitan Museum of Art in New York. "Here is a lovely painting for some American or British collector," she whispered to Riccardo at her elbow.

"You and I should suggest to Lord Elmley that he consider the Bloomsbury artists for his collection in England. These are bargains he would never find in London. The Bloomsbury group are becoming more collectible every day, now that Duncan Grant is the only one of them left, and he is in his nineties. Charleston farmhouse is being restored. It's been taken over by a trust. When it is finally open to the public, people from around the world will flock to see it and Bloomsbury prices will soar!"

Riccardo gave a vague answer and they moved on to the earlier works with Vittoria as Nigel continued his circuit of the gallery, entrapped by a plump Venetian woman, complete with a trailing fox fur and a hat with a veil. She left the gallery presently, and Nigel joined them.

"I never can seem to provide what *Signora* Marachetti is looking for," he sighed. "If I show her a shepherdess with a crook and melting eyes, she is sure to want her to wear a red skirt, rather than a blue one. Even the flower tucked behind the ear of the gypsy sitting in a caravan is wrong. She decrees she should be wearing a gardenia rather than a rose." He threw up his hands in mock despair and Emma laughed, taking his arm and moving a little behind Vittoria and Riccardo.

"What are your thoughts about the break-in at *Ca' Sospira,* Nigel?" she asked in a low voice.

"Amazement was the first reaction I suppose. It all seemed so amateurish,as though the burglars seized Filiberto as an afterthought when they happened to be passing by."

His answer surprised her. She had thought it was a break-in carefully planned. It simply made things easier when the old butler had appeared to lock up for the night. Surely they had been prepared to pick a lock or gain entry through a lower window until Filiberto innocently provided access.

"Do you think they were looking for the missing Carpaccio?"

"Gracious no," Nigel replied smoothly. "How could they even have known about it? The Elmley Collection of paintings is one of the best kept secrets of Venice, Emma. Hardly anyone except a few reputable dealers knows anything about it; never have I heard a peep about a Carpaccio until recently when you mentioned the scrap of paper found in a book. Then, Signora Puglio came here on other business and mentioned Lord Elmley and her Carpaccio." He reached in his pocket and took out a roll of Polo mints from England. He offered one to Emma, but she shook her head. He popped one into his mouth.

"Frankly, the whole operation Saturday night seemed rather pathetic. Passing all those beautiful things in the Grand Salon to look through a few books in the library? For a valuable painting nobody has ever seen? It really seems improbable, doesn't it? I think Riccardo was extremely lucky to be visited by a couple of witless thieves!"

Emma said nothing, but something about Nigel's smooth reply rang false, some remark he made continued to nag at her, but she was unable to put her finger on just what it was.

They caught up with Vittoria and Riccardo in front of a selection of pen and ink drawings by Peter de Wint. Emma noticed they were standing very close to each other and Vittoria had a becoming blush to her face. Could Riccardo be a suitor of Vittoria?

She turned her attention to the Peter de Wint. A small cottage in a field, cows grazing, a tiny church at the edge of a cornfield, which Emma saw was not corn at all, but wheat; corn was what the English called it. The subtleties of language could be understood and expressed differently even in countries where a common tongue was spoken. The three works were framed in simple black frames with cream mats. Emma gazed at them long and hard. To her the drawings were beautiful and desirable in their expert hand and deceptive simplicity because they were so close to the pure, original idea of the artist. That is what drawings revealed, in their own quiet way. Bargains, all of them she realized.

As more visitors entered the gallery Vittoria left them. Obviously they were tourists and strangers, but her smile welcomed each one and immediately drew them inside with her expression of warmth. Riccardo followed her with his eyes. Emma had been told they had known each other since childhood. Had he romantic feelings for Vittoria Dandolo? He was so secretive she was sure it was unlikely he would ever confide in her.

Riccardo mumbled something about needing to return to *Ca' Sospira* and so they left a few minutes later. As Emma thanked Nigel for the tour, she realized Riccardo had hardly spoken a word to him. What could be the meaning of that?

They were leaving the area of the Rialto Bridge and walking along small canals on narrow passages in the San Marco *sestiere*, toward *Ca' Sospira*. It was a direct but obscure route which Emma could not yet have attempted on her own. How long did it take to master the shortcuts and hidden passageways of Venice?

Emma repeated Nigel's comments about the attempted burglary. Something Nigel had said was still nagging at her subconscious.

"His version of events that night fits his character. It is untrue," Riccardo snapped, a frown creasing his forehead.

"Whatever do you mean?"

The anger in his voice was something she had not noticed before. She knew Riccardo had few friends, but Nigel, she had believed, was one of the chosen. Then she remembered the hostility Riccardo had shown toward him on the night of the break-in at *Ca' Sospira*. In her determination to complete her work on the paintings, she had forgotten the displeasure and coolness toward him that night.

They were standing near the *Campo San Fantin*, looking up at the Fenice, absorbing the beauty of the fanciful architecture. He looked at her a long minute before replying. "Do you remember I had planned to come to the Lido outing at Nigel's invitation and bring Tintoretto?" She nodded.

"Then at the last minute I couldn't leave, because the plumber I expected failed to appear? When Nigel came along to collect me, I told him I could not possibly get away. Then he insisted on bringing Tintoretto. Well, now I believe that picnic was orchestrated to get me and the *Ca' Sospira* watchdog out of the house. To make it easy for his two henchmen to get inside, with only a frail old butler nearing eighty left to guard things."

"Riccardo, surely you cannot be serious. Why, Nigel is your friend! You invited him for luncheon the day I arrived. He tried to help us in tracking the Carpaccio by telling me about *Signora* Puglio. He wouldn't deceive you, try to rob you."

His temper flared up at her words as he spat out a reply.

"What if Nigel told you about *Signora* Puglio, hoping you would lead *him* to valuable information? Emma you simply do not understand, coming from America. You are too trusting, too sure of everyone's good intentions. I believe he told you about *Signora* Puglio for one reason: to ferret out information about the Carpaccio for his own purposes."

His dark eyes blazed. Emma's face felt as though she had been slapped. Incredulity mingled with humiliation at the rebuke.

"Listen," he continued, "Venice is an old city. Duplicity and double dealing go back hundreds of years into its history. Look at the influx of foreigners who have exploited Venice and Venetians. From east and west all through the centuries they have come, looking for plunder. Even Napoleon and his armies came to conquer us. Then the Austrians. More recently there has been the influx of certain groups from Sicily, Naples. Nobody talks about it, but that part of Italy harbors the *Mafioso*. Long before the mafia, however, in the time of the Doges, Venetians learned to be prudent. Being watchful meant being suspicious, in order to survive!"

She started to speak, but he held up his hand and carried on.

"Consider Vittoria, her people have been here for centuries and now they're virtually extinct and penniless. Poor financial advice and misplaced trust in false friends has whittled away at that family as anyone, including Vittoria, will tell you. Local legend has it the Dandolos knew only how to spend money, nothing about hanging on to it. The men of the family made the *ridotto,* the gambling house on the Grand Canal packed with unsavory characters, their nightly homes. Thieves at the gaming tables made short work of Dandolo money. Now she's got to work to put bread on her parents' table. Her job is not just something to keep her amused until she receives a good marriage proposal."

Breathless, feelings expended, he stepped back awaiting her reaction.

"But Nigel is a British gentleman," Emma blurted out. "Surely you cannot think he would be mixed up in anything dishonest!" Riccardo looked at her disdainfully.

"You think they're all perfect, don't you?" Riccardo's anger boiled over like an untended saucepan. "What about Rosamund's friend Cyril? Now there's a real prize for you! He should be strung up in chains for treating her so badly. Gentlemen, British gentlemen included, can be flawed humans, just like everybody else. Some are trustworthy, and some are not. After all Emma, human nature is both good and bad."

Emma, shocked at his outburst, realized there were deep running currents within the man she knew little about. And here he was, confiding in her as they walked down the narrow passageways toward *Ca' Sospira.* Worst of all, he believed Nigel was somehow mixed up in an attempt to steal a valuable panting gone missing at *Ca' Sospira.* It all seemed hopeless. She knew she could wait no longer to tell Riccardo of Lord Elmley's telephone call, what he said about the Carpaccio.

"When Lord Elmley rang last week to check my progress, I asked him if he had ever seen the Carpaccio. He replied he knew nothing about it, had never heard a word about any such painting by Carpaccio. Said as far as he knew, it had neither been in the collection nor sent to England. He reminded me the late earl went to great trouble to keep his collection intact in Venice. I should have told you immediately about this, but in the press of my work, I put the missing Carpaccio to the back of my mind. I'm sorry I did not mention it to you sooner, but I wonder, why did you mislead me?"

"That is something I have known for years, Emma. I knew it had not been sent to England. But I decided the best way to safeguard it was to say nothing at all. Then speculation might die down. If you could have seen how the late earl worshiped that painting, you would understand why he could never let it stray far from him. But what has happened to it? How can I find it without tearing up the house? It could be hidden in the walls, the floors, under the roof. Every lead has proved false."

His eyes, locked with Emma's, held frustration and fear.

"I simply do not know where it is, Emma, and whether you choose to believe me or not, I am telling the truth. If only he hadn't died so unexpectedly!"

Emma was shocked at the desperation in his voice. His eyes looked full, almost overflowing. Why, Riccardo was desperately trying to hide his feelings and keep control. She had not imagined the man was so burdened by the weight of failure to find the missing painting, or that he was so emotionally overwrought. How could she question his loyalty? He worked hard and was on duty twenty four hours a day. He lived simply, in one of the smallest rooms upstairs. His office was little more than a closet. But the nagging thought kept returning to her: *the Carpaccio disappeared while he was responsible for it. Did he take it?*

"We have more to worry about, now that we know persons unknown are looking for it, ready to steal it if given the chance," he continued as though talking to himself. They had resumed their walk and passed a modest bar at the street turning into the small *rio* beside *Ca' Sospira.*

"Believe me, Emma, they will succeed if we are not careful. It would be perilous to relax our vigilance. They will try again."

~~~

Unable to sleep on the daybed in her tiny room that night, Emma watched as moonlight flooded in the window roundel above her. Some submerged fact hidden deep in her mind nagged her, and she could not bring it to the surface. Swift moving clouds of the lightest gossamer spread seamlessly over the moon's gilded surface, passed by, and it burst again into brightness. Like everything else in this amazing place it was magic, nothing was as it seemed. What *was* it Nigel had said earlier?

As though summoned forth by that magic, Nigel's words at the Gallery Vianello jumped in Emma's mind. He said she had mentioned the Carpaccio and the scrap of paper at their first meeting when he came to *Ca' Sospira* for luncheon.

But I never told Nigel about the Carpaccio that day! At the table I sensed from Riccardo that I shouldn't be talking about it to anyone so I changed the subject. Then how had he learned about it? Certainly Riccardo hadn't told him. Was there an informant at *Ca' Sospira?* Who could it be?

She looked out of the window roundel and was struck by the quiet of the waters, unlike its cheerful busyness of daytime. As she watched the placid ripples, turned silver by the moonshine, a single gondola glided silently into her vision, the gondolier darkly outlined against the sky, bound on some secret journey in the cover of night. Who was the phantom figure? What was his mission? There were two passengers in the gondola, huddled close together, embracing perhaps, but she could not make them out in any detail. Or perhaps they were plotting something dishonest, evil. The boat glided quickly out of sight and her thoughts reverted to the Carpaccio.

If Riccardo was right, they were being drawn into a race against time to locate the missing painting before thieves carted it away. She had begun to realize that Nigel possibly could be involved in such a plan. Emma had been suspicious of Riccardo when she first arrived. As she began to understand him better, she knew that in Riccardo Montgano the Elmleys had a valuable employee with the fierce loyalty of a blood relative even though he was unrelated. But the vexing imp in her head whispered: then where is the Carpaccio?

~~~

At her desk the following morning, Emma reached into a lower drawer for the little leather notebook which held the handwritten record of trivia and social engagements of the late earl. An incongruity, his having such a notebook. From what she had learned from Riccardo and Filiberto, the late earl had preferred solitary evenings in this room pouring over books about art rather than presiding over dinners around the long mahogany table under the Murano chandelier. Lady Sybil had been the more social one. Emma idly sat turning the pages when her eyes fell on what seemed to be a recipe for one of those dinners.

"Get a fat duck from the market for dinner. One for eight will do, a brace if there are more than eight. Take plenty of butter to season it well. Only the best, made by the butter makers of the *merceria*, the market. Make a paste of herbs pounded fine. You will know when it is ground fine enough. Bake it slowly. Ever so slowly. Do not be impatient. Ring for help when basting as the pan will be too heavy to lift. Only someone strong. Only Filiberto can hold the pan properly while you baste. Make the skin wet with the butter dripping from the basting brush."

Emma put down the little book. Each sentence was begun on a new line, laid out to suggest a poem. Puzzled, she studied the words. These instructions were childlike in their simplicity. Meant for the *Ca' Sospira* cook? Not at all the style of the erudite connoisseur she had discovered the late Lord Elmley to be. Lady Sybil? Possibly. Her personality was somewhat more opaque. Emma had as yet formed an incomplete profile of the Elmley matriarch. What had she really been like?

Carefully set down, the beginning of each sentence had been outlined with flourishes and curves of the first letter. Why could he (or she) have bothered with such explicit instructions, instructions which seemed so child-like? Completely out of character with the late earl. He had not been a fussy sort of person. Or juvenile, come to that. Lady Sybil? Perhaps a more suitable suspect.

But arranged like a poem? Idly she glanced at the opposite page. A crude attempt at sketching covered the center. She could make out sprays of foliage and two summarily drawn figures in the park like setting. What could that be? She was faintly reminded of the sprays of greenery on the *altana* with its beautiful shrubs. The two figures? A subtle effort to suggest the two girls bleaching their blonde tresses? Quickly she took a piece of paper and copied out the words opposite exactly as they had been written, each new line begun with a capitalized letter of the first word. She looked at it intently then read aloud to herself the first letter of every line.

"GOTOMYBEDROOM". The letters jumped out at her. Go to my Bedroom. So it was meant to be a clue. Perhaps telling them how to find the missing painting? Frantically she paged through the notebook. Once, twice, a third time. But there were no more hidden instructions. That would have been too transparent. Somewhere, in another part of the house, there might be a new set of hints leading her to the painting. But where? In his bedroom, of course. She put the journal aside; she would show it to Riccardo. If only Sam were here to mull over the possibilities. She needed his patience and discretion to help her reason and consider. She must go to the late earl's bedroom and search! Someone in the house was possibly a spy. A tap at her door caused her to look up.

"Come in!" she called, quickly replacing the little book in the drawer.

"*Permesso, Signorina?*" Cesara stepped into the room. The patronizing tone irritated Emma, but she replied courteously. She could see someone behind the cook.

"We've had a visitor in the kitchen. Luisa, who was cook here before me for many years, has come to see us. I thought you might like to meet her. She was ever so interested to hear about you being here from England, working on the late earl's art collection."

Cesara lowered her eyes respectfully. Cool. Confident. She would not trifle with anything in her way, Emma guessed. Now she seemed self-effacing and would not meet Emma's eyes. An act, obviously. Once she had caught Cesara looking at her with a look that was positively malevolent. Emma had tried to be friendly; Cesara, although correct, was unwilling, determined to keep her distance. There was nothing comparable to the ease Emma felt around Filiberto.

The small, pale woman who stood behind Cesara twisted her hands nervously as she stepped forward. Luisa wore black; the dress hung limp on her skinny frame. A tired straw hat trimmed with a drooping rose rested on her small head. Someone else reminding me of a teacher Emma thought. Mrs. Perkins. World history. Tenth grade. It was the myopic gaze behind frameless spectacles they both possessed.

Timidly the woman spoke up in a low, nervous voice. "I don't want to disturb you, *Signorina*. When I worked at *Ca' Sospira* there was great goings on, not so quiet as it is now. Cesara invited me to meet you because she says you know about the pictures and have brought so much life back into the house. When I was cook, I loved looking at Lord Elmley's collection of paintings if I had time on my hands from my kitchen duties. He never minded, sent me right up to look at his special favorites, hanging in his bedroom.

"I was wondering, are the two girls bleaching their hair still at it? That one I loved to stand in front of." Her sudden smile revealed two gold teeth. Could Luisa prove to be worth her weight in gold? Emma, transfixed by Luisa's smile, quickly came to attention at the woman's words. So, Cesara had invited her to visit. But Luisa seemed guileless. Surely she had no ulterior motives, but Emma wondered about Cesara.

"No, I'm afraid the girls aren't on view, but I'll be happy to take you up and show you the *collezione*."

As they mounted the stairs Emma guessed Cesara could be hoping to glean more information for herself. Could she be the spy in the house who reported to Nigel? Someone obviously was funneling news to Nigel from *Ca' Sospira*.

Emma made the circuit of the late earl's bedroom. The former cook looked intently at each picture while Cesara hovered close by, not commenting. Emma observed she kept well within hearing distance. Luisa's admiration of the paintings brought an ethereal shine to her homely face. Emma found her obvious enjoyment touching. Hands stubby, reddened with work, the joints of her fingers showed beginnings of the cruel arthritic condition Emma had noticed so often in this damp city, surrounded by water. She was reminded of *Signora* Puglio's hands.

As Emma studied Luisa, she realized once more here was witness to the power of art to ennoble. The irregular mouth, scraggly eyebrows seemed softened, rendered almost beautiful, as the woman's weak eyes drank in the pictures. This was no ploy. Luisa's response was spontaneous and sincere; it transformed her.

"And where was the painting hung of the two girls sunning on the roof?" Emma asked nonchalantly, glancing around the room as Luisa finished viewing the *collezione*. "You said it was a favorite of yours I believe."

"Why *Signorina*, didn't you know? This wasn't Lord Elmley's bedroom. In those days his bedroom was the one across the hall. In my time, that is where the picture of the girls bleaching their hair hung." She pointed to the room across the hall. "That was the earl's bedroom."

Doges Palace, San Marco

8

Cyril's Charm Evaporates Rather Quickly

Emma, downstairs in the library sitting at her desk, struggled to come to grips with Luisa's revelation. It was a worry that Riccardo had not bothered to tell her this room directly above her head had not been Lord Elmley's bedroom, where he slept in the Elmley oak bed. Idly she wondered how many times the bed had been dismantled and moved about? When was the late earl's bedroom last moved?

Her thoughts returned to Riccardo. He had misled her again! Had let her think the present room with the Elmley Bed was the same one the late earl occupied during his lifetime. Why was it changed? Why hadn't he told her? In all of her thoughts and theories about the missing painting she had imagined it hung in the room overhead, for heavens sake! That was where the Elmley Bed stood, and the tapestry of Elmley Castle. She had spent time tapping along the walls, running her hand over the damask wall covering, searching for something hidden away. She had looked carefully at the tiles on the floor. Had they been disturbed? Were any of them slightly different, as though they had been broken, pried out and replaced? Once more the unwelcome thought surfaced that Riccardo concealed information to throw her off track. So he might keep the painting for himself? There, she had said it, after refusing to believe it all these weeks. And she had been so sure of his selflessness and loyalty when she recalled what she had learned from him.

Disappointed and deflated, she sat, wondering what to do next. Thwarted at every turn, learning nothing, should she settle down, complete her assigned task and forget about the Carpaccio? Collect her earnings at the end of two months and head back to London?

Of course yesterday when Cesara and Luisa had returned to the kitchen and she was alone, she had made a thorough search of the former bedroom which held a pair of watercolors of the Rialto and Accademia bridges along with a clutch of landscapes from Murano, the island across the lagoon famous for its glass blowers. One oil painting of the Doges Palace, and above the heavy chest a view of the Grand Canal bursting with water craft of every description, appropriate for a Venetian palazzo Emma thought, the Grand Canal being Venice's throbbing life line.

None of the pictures in the room aroused suspicion, not that she had expected it. No bulges under the backings to indicate something had been tucked underneath. She discovered nothing new, but she couldn't just ignore the bombshell dropped by Luisa, the cook.

Once again, she knew she must speak to Riccardo. She found him in the *salone*, directing the two maids, Giovanna and Dorabella, as they dusted. Emma took a moment to admire the sculpture by Donatello of the five cherubs and the collection of small bronze figures on tables against the wall and behind the sofas. Tables beside chairs held precious Murano glass, porcelain, and beautiful lamps which would add warmth to the room when lit for special occasions. Emma had never actually seen the room lighted at night. It must be one of the most sumptuous reception rooms in all of Venice.

The two maids seemed nervous. Riccardo was taking no chances on carelessness or inattention as he supervised. She had heard the pair on several occasions, chattering on the stairway and in the hall about film stars and fashions as they performed their duties. They were young and strong, essential to *Ca' Sospira* as Cesara and Filiberto aged. Dorabella tossed blond curls with a flourish. She was the most vivacious of the two.

"Will that be all, *Signor?*"

"Yes, yes," Riccardo answered absently, aware of Emma patiently waiting. "Go on up to the *altana*. Start on the terrazzo pathways and I'll join you soon. Careful of the orchid sprays now! The blooms last a long time if you do not touch them. Some of them will be arching over the paths. Do your mopping gently." He turned toward Emma who suggested they go to the library.

In a few seconds they reached her desk and Emma showed him what she had discovered in the notebook.

"You see, Riccardo, it looks as though the late earl was trying to give instructions to those left behind as to where he was leaving the painting."

Emma was prepared to hear him raise the usual roadblocks. However she was stopped by his quick reply.

"Nothing is mentioned about a painting in the recipe. The person who wrote it could have had in mind a piece of porcelain or glass, a rare book from the library, one of the bronze figures in the *collezione*.

"Yes, you are right," Emma grudgingly agreed. "But Riccardo, there isn't anything else *missing* in *Ca' Sospira* is there? Only the Carpaccio, if I am not mistaken?"

He admitted she was correct, but brushed off the disclosure with the usual vague disclaimers: the supposed painting had been missing for so long he feared there must be nothing supportable to prove it was still in the house.

"But that is impossible Riccardo, surely! Too much is known now," Emma blurted out. "There is no record of its sale; Lord William told me just a few days ago when he telephoned he had never seen it in England. We know the late earl loved his Venetian *collezione* and would never part with anything, but the Carpaccio he loved best! It must be here somewhere!"

Next Emma told him about Luisa's visit, asking him about changing the late earl's bedroom. At this news Riccardo's face stiffened into a mask.

"Luisa here? Yesterday? So she did not bother to pay her respects to me!" He bristled, assembling his thoughts, continuing a litany of Luisa's omissions.

"She was a poor excuse for a cook at best. Always muddling the recipes given her to prepare. Yesterday's rolls served with today's luncheon, hopeless at making the sweets. I was glad when she left.

"As for the change of rooms, yes, it was changed. The floor began to sag in the room where the Elmley Bed was, and it was decided to remove it to its present location, where the load bearing beams were stronger. She was right when she said that; it was before the earl's death, a year or so," he admitted, glaring at Emma.

Emma, who had learned to interpret some of the man's strange moods, realized that in Riccardo's lonely world, Luisa's only fault perhaps may have been making a visit to *Ca' Sospira* and failing to pay her respects to him. It was a small thing, but perhaps wounding to Riccardo because of the way he flared up. Emma accepted defeat once again. As long as he was angry like this, he would deflect her theories about the missing painting until doomsday and would not provide helpful information.

But things were changing. Sooner or later Riccardo would have to face an ever-growing roster of facts, however uncomfortable they might be. Emma knew the painting had been in the house at the time of Luisa's employment. The former cook remembered it. Its sale to the late earl had been confirmed by *Signora* Puglio, who had described it vividly. Lord William assured her a few days earlier the Carpaccio was not in England. There had been one attempt at robbery when thieves apparently were searching for a painting. These revelations suggested the Carpaccio was still somewhere inside *Ca' Sospira.*

~~~~

Emma unlocked the outside door of Rosamund's flat and slowly mounted the stairs. Venice was in the grip of a heat wave; she had hurried home, weaving among listless tourists burdened with rucksacks and camera bags. She planned to exchange her working uniform, a summer skirt in a Liberty print, white blouse and pumps, for a pair of linen trousers, sandals and a simple shirt. Rosamund would arrive soon; perhaps they would go for a cool lemon soda at the little bar on a small canal, deep in Dorsoduro. It was near the house where Ezra Pound, the American writer, had lived and also near Saint George's church, the Anglican church of Venice.

As the door to the flat came into view at the top of the stairway she saw it was already open. Rosamund must have left the consulate early. She hurried up and stepped inside, calling to her.

"Can you believe the heat? The pavements and cobblestones seem to be on fire all over Venice! Shall we seek out the bar with the vines?" The words died on her lips as she saw a strange man sitting on the sofa, giving every appearance of feeling right at home in Rosamund's comfortable reception room.

He sprang to his feet as quickly as long legs could unfold, a smile of dazzling brilliance spreading over a handsome face. His eyes, darkest blue and fringed by thick lashes, were remarkable for the intensity of their gaze. He waited expectantly, for the usual dazed reaction of females, Emma thought witheringly. She had already guessed who he was before he ever spoke a word.

"Cyril Meadowes, a friend of Rosamund, from out of town," he intoned and Emma felt her face turning red, furious with herself for advertising her anger.

"Don't I know you?" he spoke, blinking earnestly, misreading her blush for admiration.

"Emma Darling, Rosamund's friend. She has told me about you." Emma's words sounded toneless, her face bland. She refused to give him the slightest encouragement.

His countenance changed like a chameleon; a calculating look took over. Emma sketched out his thoughts in her mind. Colleagues at the consulate had taken Rosamund's broken heart personally. And now this girl. Why? What had he done? Simply extricated himself from a boring entanglement with the wrong woman and moved on to better things. The transfer to Prague came at a perfect time, perfect for him and Cassandra, perfect also to leave behind not only Rosamund but staid old fossils like Peter Law and other bores in the consulate office. This woman, an American judging from her accent, was obviously aligned with Rosamund's army of supporters.

The protagonists, stood facing each other, silence between them billowing to vampire like proportion. Cyril studied Emma's face. She looked at his. Was he thinking she was loyal to Rosamund? That she could be a dangerous enemy?

~~~~

When Cyril had left Cassandra earlier in the week to travel to Venice for a few days, she begged to accompany him. In their cramped bed-sitter in Prague, he'd had to dodge flying projectiles lobbed his way in the form of ridiculous high-heeled pumps. This most recent quarrel told him Cassandra's aim was improving. The shoe had barely missed his ear. And she was becoming lazy as well as intractable. Their living space was fast turning squalid, and she refused to go out and try to find a job. Had he made another mistake marrying such a beautiful, but volatile creature? He sighed. If indeed it had been an error of judgment, he would find a way to extricate himself soon enough.

~~~~

Basilica of San Marco, "Aqua Alta" (high water)

While Cyril nursed his thoughts, Emma wondered. What will Rosamund do? Rush into his arms? Burst into uncontrollable weeping? And she began planning ways to sustain her friend through a confrontation. She and Cyril were standing there, still facing each other, when she heard Rosamund's light step on the stairway. I must help her through this, Emma thought. More footsteps. Somewhere a dog barked. Rosamund's voice rang out.

"Emma, are you decent? Here are some people!" and without pause Rosamund sailed happily into the room chattering gaily.

"Look, I've brought Peter Law from the consulate and passing the Correr museum we ran into Samantha, then Riccardo walking Tintoretto so we've dragged them along too." Her words trailed off as she saw Cyril. Her voice wavered, uncertain.

"Hullo, Cyril."

There was a moment of silence, then Rosamund performed introductions as though her favorite people in all the world were meeting for the first time.

Her poise amazed Emma. Riccardo stood calmly, ignoring the undercurrents swirling about. Peter Law frowned as if he had swallowed a dubious oyster. He was trying hard to hide feelings of revulsion and distaste as though some undesirable reptile had slithered into the flat. Cyril put on a bland, assured mask and waited for his charm to take effect. Tintoretto stood alert, nose quivering at the unspoken hostility in the air. For once the dog did not wag his tail joyously at the sight of Emma.

"So you're back, Meadowes?" Peter Law's thinly disguised loathing made him rasp out the words. Cyril, the epicenter of their attention, nodded. Emma held her breath.

"It was necessary for me to be in Venice for business reasons," Cyril explained, looking a little indignant but smiling and waving his eyelashes at Samantha as the look of disgust deepened on Peter Law's open face. Glancing at Rosamund, Emma saw her brow was smooth, she was in command of her feelings.

"I thought I should return Rosamund's key I'd borrowed," Cyril, heedless of the signs, pushed on, confident his charm would carry the day.

"Clever of you to bypass the office, Cyril." Peter's thinly controlled anger stabbed again. The sarcasm was lost on nobody in the room, not even Tintoretto who unexpectedly emitted a rolling growl from deep within his throat. Riccardo quickly tightened his hand on the leash. So this was the scoundrel Vittoria had told him about, the bounder from the British Consulate who had behaved outrageously toward Rosamund.

Feeding Pigeons, Piazza San Marco

Cyril, picking up all the unfriendly currents swirling around him, decided to cut his losses and muttered something about "Getting on to the Rialto. Appointment, late already." He hurried out, leaving the keys on the console table in the foyer.

His departure was accomplished without comment, but Emma wondered silently what took him to the Rialto area. Fifteen minutes later, had she known, straight as a lemming he hurried through the ornate doors of Gallery Vianello which stood just beyond the *merceria*, now closed for the day, with all vestiges of the morning's frantic commerce in fruit and veg carefully swept away.

Inside Rosamund's apartment, calm was restored. "All at once your flat looks lovely, Rosamund," Peter Law commented as he gazed at her admiringly, approval shining in his eyes.

Emma silently applauded Rosamund's handling of Cyril. It was almost as though she had rehearsed the scene just played out. Knowing Cyril and his ways, Rosamund probably had imagined such a meeting and how she would react. Few could have guessed how difficult this confrontation would have been for her a few weeks earlier. Emma remembered all too well the sounds of crying coming from Rosamund's bedroom in the early days of her arrival.

Shadows began lengthening in Dorsoduro; cool evening breezes wafted along the *fondamenti*, pavements beside small *rios*, canals, as the group left Rosamund's flat, bound for the bar with the vine-covered terrace. Peter and Riccardo quickly arranged two tables pushed together outside the friendly little bar and soon the party was settled, looking out on Venice coming alive after the *riposo*. The previously deserted walkways swarmed with children; grandmothers wearing black dresses and lace shawls gossiped on benches, young couples gazed into each other's eyes as they strolled.

Talk flowed as the party sipped cooling *pinot grigio*. Emma noted that Peter Law seemed happy and at ease sitting beside Rosamund who told Samantha in matter-of-fact tones, that Cyril, had moved on to Prague from the consulate with a new bride and was, she imagined, busy spreading charm over everyone in that office. Tintoretto blissfully settled under the tables, velvety eyes trained on Emma as he occasionally lifted his head for a pat. Riccardo, relaxing, amused them with tales of his student days at the nearby University of Padua. He seemed to let go of all his worries.

"The thing about Cyril," Rosamund finished lightly, "is that his charm evaporates rather quickly when he doesn't get his way." A loud guffaw from Peter Law sitting beside her revealed his approval.

Peter seemed a worthy suitor for Rosamund, Emma thought idly, studying his open face on which laugh lines gathered at the corners of kindly brown eyes. Much more suitable than the vain peacock Cyril. If only the missing Carpaccio could be found as easily as affairs of the heart were set right.

San Zaccaria (late fifteenth century)

Emma received a call later that evening from *Signora* Puglio who rang to propose tea the following afternoon at a little neighborhood bar across the *campo* from *San Zaccaria.*

"But *Signora,* I would like to take *you* for tea. Remember, I visited you. Now it is my turn."

"Nonsense. They would not give you *lo sconto!*" Followed by, "Be there at four promptly." There was a click. The call was finished.

Emma, smiled as she replaced the *telefono* in its cradle, having become accustomed to *La Signora's* brevity. What was she talking about, *lo sconto?*

The following afternoon Emma found *La Signora* comfortably seated at a small table outside the deserted bar on *Campo San Zaccaria.* The man behind the bar inside hastened toward them when Emma arrived on the stroke of four.

"*Prego, Signora* Puglio?"

"Tea with lemon, Giuseppe," she answered, smiling as he hurried off.

"They are especially good to me here," she told Emma after greetings had been exchanged. Emma asked her about *lo sconto.*

"Why it is the discount, of course. They don't talk about it, but merchants in Venice discount to locals, about thirty percent, have done for years. It is completely unofficial, of course, but they all do it. Some tourists would be furious if they knew, but it helps Venetians, many of whom live on subsistence wages or fixed incomes."

Emma mulled over this information. There was not a scrap of self pity in her voice. An image sprang up of narrow passageways clogged with gawking tourists snapping away with cameras, students striding mindlessly along the center of the *fondamenti* like untrained puppies. Visitors were necessary for the survival of Venice, but they made the business of getting around more difficult, especially for the old.

Even feeding all the pigeons at *Piazza San Marco,* perhaps the most sacred rite performed by travelers to Venice, created sanitary problems for the city. She had read articles about this problem in *Il Gazzettino.* Sightseers were a mixed blessing. More of a problem perhaps than *aqua alta,* or high water, the flooding which had plagued Venice intermittently in winter months for years. Emma felt a new appreciation of her friend sitting beside her.

Emma and her hostess next spent several minutes in polite inquires of each other and exchanged comments on the news. Emma related details of a Vivaldi concert she and Rosamund had attended at the church of *San Vidal,* across the Accademia Bridge, in San Marco.

Doorway, Campo San Provolo near San Zaccaria

Emma had been in Venice long enough to know that the reason for the invitation from *La Signora*, if indeed there was one, would be revealed in due time and would not be brought up until preliminary polite talk was finished. She nibbled one of the little meringue confections shaped like a swan and filled with cream, so popular at tea time in Venice. At last *La Signora* opened a small handbag strapped to her shoulder and took out an envelope.

"I spend considerable time going over papers my late husband Antonio saved from business at our gallery," she explained. "In a strange way I feel he is very close to me at those times. Almost as though he were here. Do you think I am crazy?" The bright eyes fastened on Emma and again she was reminded of the industry of a little brown house wren.

"No *Signora*, certainly not. I spent several precious summers with my grandmother in England. It was the same with her, she missed my grandfather, whom I hardly remember, I was so young when he died. Keeping his memory close brought her great comfort."

"Do you miss her?"

"Very much. Grandmother Matilda was a link to the country of my father's birth, his home before he came to America. Partly because of her, I decided to study art history in England when I finished my degree at the University of Virginia."

There was a quiet moment while *Signora* Puglio nursed her thoughts and swallowed a tiny sip of tea. She summoned a fresh pot by indicating the teapot to the attentive Giuseppe, who kept her in his sights as he served stand-up customers at the bar inside. Teacups refilled, she handed the envelope to Emma.

"Yesterday as I was looking through my husband's papers I found this. It is a letter written to him by Lord Elmley a year or so after he had received the painting he purchased from us. He wanted another copy of its provenance which he asked us to sign, and to keep a copy for our records, in case something happened to the original," I think those were his words."

"Was this a strange request?" Emma asked, accepting the envelope.

"Not particularly," she replied. "It would have been strange coming from a typical Venetian, who never bothers with records of any kind. But we did business with continentals, Germans, for instance, who liked everything, such as a picture's provenance, tied up neatly.

"Our British clients were often like that. Lord Elmley certainly wanted it, or he would not have asked. Really, I imagine it is nothing very important. *Ca' Sospira* must have a copy of the same letter somewhere on file. But I thought you might not have seen it. You can read it when you get back to your office. I wish I could have found something more exciting, perhaps leading you to the missing painting."

As the teapot emptied and office workers began hurrying across the *campo,* Giuseppe appeared with *Signora's* coat and the two stout canes. "Beppe is here from school now to escort you, *Signora Puglio*," he said in a deferential tone tinged with concern. A little boy with enormous brown eyes and a shy smile peeped out from behind his papa's white apron.

"Good! Then I will not keep my escort waiting." She fixed a sweet smile of surprising softness on the child and rose, accepting a kiss on her cheek from Emma who had quickly risen. Beppe was introduced to Emma and the child with the solemn face dutifully offered his hand to be shaken.

Emma watched as the pair slowly left the *campo San Zaccaria* and disappeared in the crowd, walking toward the Riva degli Schiavoni. Beppe was gazing up respectfully at the old lady. Emma watched until they moved out of sight.

She strolled toward the church across the small *campo*. In the quiet of *San Zaccaria* she would read the letter in her purse as she admired her favorite altarpiece. *Signora* Puglio disdained sympathy for her pitiable physical condition, Emma reflected. Venice was a difficult city for the aged, but she had a will of steel and there were people who cared for her, Emma thought, as she looked toward the Riva.

Before entering the church, Emma stopped a moment to study the ordered façade, knowing *San Zaccaria* was one of the most famous Renaissance churches in Venice, designed by Mario Codussi and completed around 1500. An earlier church, dating back to the ninth century previously stood on the site.

The interior was ablaze with votive candles burning on small tables in the side chapels. Emma went directly to the chapel containing the painting of the Madonna and Four Saints by Giovanni Bellini. She took a few minutes to study the calm beauty and balance of the little group. Bellini had created a spatially perfect apse, a semicircle with a vaulted ceiling, the Madonna enthroned at the center. Bellini's grouping seemed wrapped in silence yet aware of each other, as though experiencing some spiritual rather than spoken communion. A small angel sat below the Madonna playing a stringed instrument. The altarpiece was an early example of the *sacra conversazione* genre. Emma had shown a slide of it to her students many times. Color was of the greatest importance to all Venetian painters, certainly to Giovanni Bellini. Emma drank in soft tones of pink, orange, acid green and dark blue. Seated comfortably in an empty pew in front of the painting, she opened her purse and took out the letter.

20 May, 1965

My Dear *Signora* Puglio:

Some years back I purchased from your late husband a Carpaccio sketch of two Venetian young women seated on an *altana* bleaching their hair. I am very pleased with this work and feel grateful to you and *Signor* Puglio for agreeing to my purchase.

At the time, you handed over the provenance along with the picture. Now, however I find I need another, somewhat altered copy to give to my son for his records

137

so that its disposition will be secured at my death. Please indicate on the provenance that the watercolor will go to my son Richard at the time of my death. As the owner of the gallery, please affix your signature and date to this copy.

Thanking you in advance for your trouble I remain,

Yours faithfully,
ELMLEY. *Ca' Sospira*

Emma let the letter slide to her lap as she gazed trance-like at Bellini's harmony of color and design. She was not thinking of the painting at all. How could she, when she knew Lord Elmley died, unexpectedly, on May 22, 1965? It was likely his sudden death occurred before the provenance he requested was ever received! Quickly she reread the letter. How could she be aware of the Bellini or think of anything but his reference to his son "Richard"? William was the name of the present earl! *Who was Richard?* The handwriting of the letter was wavy and fragile, as though written by a shaking hand, yet it certainly seemed authentic.

Replacing the letter in her handbag, she walked as though dreaming toward the San Marco *vaporetto* stop and stepped aboard a number one just leaving for the Accademia Bridge. Gazing out at the churning waters as she stood with her fellow passengers, she reflected. Young Lord Elmley was named in the letter as 'my son, Richard'. Never had she heard him called

Richard before. Also, how strange it seemed that Lord William in England had known nothing about the watercolor of the two girls on the *altana* bleaching their hair when she asked him about a Carpaccio during their recent telephone conversation. This letter stated the picture would be left to "my son Richard".

How could this be? The young earl, of course, as the oldest male, inherited the bulk of the money, the property, and the title under English Common Law. Venice, however, ever since being conquered by Napoleon in 1797, had been ruled by the Napoleonic, or Civil Code. It made a difference as to who inherited: Under English law, all went to the eldest son. In Venice, siblings shared equally when a parent died.

Emma knew there were three daughters older than the young earl, in addition to a second son, James, the youngest child of the late earl and Lady Sybil. The late earl, Emma knew, was Lord William. She had heard both Riccardo and Filiberto refer to him in that way. And she had known the present earl bore the name of his father. Young Lord William.

There had surely been a reading of the will in the presence of all the heirs sometime after his death This letter, *Signora* Puglio's copy, should have cropped up at that time, if not before. Emma could not figure why the young earl seemed so surprised when she told him about a Carpaccio when they spoke by telephone. Recalling his honest, unassuming manner, Emma could hardly believe he had deceived her. He had not known of its existence.

Later the following day, on the *altana* with Tintoretto, it occurred to Emma that like many aristocrats, the present earl probably possessed a string of names given at birth. Four were not unusual. Perhaps one of them was Richard. He must have assumed the name William after the death of his father. But for what reason?

This might explain the confusing use of Richard rather than William in the letter written by the late earl shortly before he died. There were two references to his death in the second paragraph. It was obvious his demise weighed heavily on his mind. In only two days he was dead.

Did these revelations have anything to do with what happened to the Carpaccio? Emma was certain they did. She looked around her at the beauty of the property the late earl loved so much. Who could perpetuate life here after he was gone?

Suddenly everything had become too complicated. The revelations in the letter had puzzling implications to be unraveled. She must proceed cautiously. She closed her eyes and let the cool breezes of the *altana* ease away feelings of frustration.

9

Vittoria Engages in Some Sleuthing on Her Own

Following the encounter in Rosamund's flat earlier the past week, Cyril Meadowes had breezed into Gallery Vianello toward the second exhibition room where Vittoria Dandolo sat at a small desk inlaid with *pietra dura,* marble of varied colors, as she poured over a current exhibition catalogue. The gallery was almost deserted. The afternoon *riposo* had scarcely ended and there were only a few tourists braving the temperature, listlessly hanging on to cameras dangling from their shoulders or from straps around their wrists. One or two had ventured inside to escape the heat a few minutes and were shuffling around, dazed looks on their faces.

Vittoria looked up from her reading as Cyril's shadow fell across the page. Immediately she rose, murmuring "May I help you, *Signor?*" in her calm, beautifully modulated voice.

She knew who he was, of course. By this time everyone in Venice had heard the story of his departure for Prague from the consulate taking with him a beautiful young Venetian clerk. In many ways, the city was like a small town; its citizens loved gossip.

What could this disgraceful man be doing back in Venice, she wondered, but she made sure her eyes didn't reveal that she recognized him.

"I don't believe we have met, have we?" Cyril began, eyelashes waving like a flag in high breeze as he trained blue eyes on her. He is full of himself, Vittoria thought scornfully. No doubt this minute he is wondering how he can make a pass at me, or any girl he happens to see. Disgraceful man! Poor wife!

Vittoria's reply was brief, ignoring his question. "Did you have an appointment, *Signor*?"

"Why yes, I believe so," he began. "But first, if you could show me around your lovely gallery . . ." His voice trailed off, rendered silent by her withering glance. Suddenly Nigel materialized at his elbow, quick as a genie out of a bottle.

"Never mind, Cyril! This way," he commanded, leading him abruptly to the small cubbyhole of an office he shared with Vittoria and another employee. Had the man been a puppy, Vittoria thought, Nigel would have picked him up by the scruff of his neck. Vittoria followed them as long she could with her eyes. The office door banged shut.

Nigel began speaking before the door closed. "The people you recommended for the *Ca' Sospira* job were hopeless. Made a complete botch of it and were lucky to escape before the alarm was raised. I thought you said they were art thieves!"

"I said they worked in galleries," Cyril replied sulking. He did not add that they were only members of a cleaning crew who serviced several framing businesses, distant cousins in fact, of his bride Cassandra.

"Well, that pair didn't find a thing, and we are still trying to lay hands on the Carpaccio. We cannot afford another bungle! Next time I'll recruit someone to do the job!" Nigel sank back in his chair and paused a few seconds, letting his temper cool.

"Look, if you want to be a part of this scheme, you had better look sharp. And you'd best leave off new distractions now that you're married. I've heard Cassandra has quite a temper."

"And," he added, glaring, to be sure Cyril took the point, "as for the lady in this gallery, forget it. She is a Venetian blue blood, not interested in the likes of you." Or me either, he reflected glumly, no matter how polite she is. He reached for one of the rolls of Polo mints on his desk, quickly opened it and popped one into his mouth.

"What have you come to tell me?" His voice bored into Cyril.

"Calm down, Nigel. I promised I would find you a buyer and I have. His name is Jan Hussaye, a Czech entrepreneur, a lover of opera and paintings, especially the latter. He is prepared to pay. A most cultured man, and a wizard in his business dealings."

"How much?" Nigel demanded. He crunched another Polo.

"More than you proposed, I can tell you that." Cyril's blue eyes were flashing as he met his gaze. "He mentioned US five hundred thousand, but that isn't firm. He's got to see it first." Cyril's look told Nigel he resented the treatment he was undergoing. Probably thinking he's a pompous diplomat and I'm only a bloody salesman, Nigel reflected.

"All right. For the present, you're in. But don't mess up again, I warn you. And whatever you do, don't blab to 'Sandra!" Nigel let his voice boil over with displeasure as Cyril prepared to leave.

"By the way, what's Hussaye's business?"

"He brews beer, surely you've heard of the Cesky-Krumlov magnate who owns a world famous brewery in the mountains above Prague at Cesky-Krumlov? And don't call her 'Sandra. Cassandra is her proper name," he fussed, closing the door with a slam and hastily departing Gallery Vianello.

~~~~

Vittoria Dandolo never lifted her eyes from the catalogue page she was inspecting as Cyril Meadowes hurried by, ignoring her presence, his face unnaturally red. But she missed nothing. There had been some kind of quarrel between him and Nigel, she was certain of it. What could their business have been?

Nigel Sleight was welcoming a number of strange visitors lately into the tiny office that served them both. The two boatmen types looked like rustics from the Venetian island of Torcello when they shuffled in, hats in hand, a fortnight back. Their temerity told her visiting an art gallery was a rarity. They seemed overwhelmed, clearly out of their depth. What business had Nigel with those two? And this disgraced Englishman, Cyril, transferred to Prague for goodness sake, and now returned to Venice so hastily, why was he beating a path to Nigel's door?

A month earlier, Vittoria had observed as Nigel checked out one of the gallery's leather folios, presumably bound for a visit to a wealthy client in the Castello district. The woman had requested some Piranesi etchings of Rome on approval from Gallery Vianello. Giovanni Battista Piranesi, a Venetian architect, went to Rome in the 1740s and recorded the antiquities of the city in hundreds of etchings which had become highly popular.

The receipt book noted the time the folio left the gallery, the identification number of each etching it contained and who checked it out, duly signed and dated in the space provided. She gazed thoughtfully at the folio. Piranesi, the poetic engraver of eighteenth century ruins and antiquities of Rome was eminently collectible. On a hunch she secretly inspected the folio when Nigel returned. He had left it on the desk they shared as he hurried to a waiting customer in the main exhibition room.

The five Piranesi views of ruins were missing, yet there was no receipt for any sale. Vittoria absorbed the discrepancy quickly. She understood it could mean theft, and she waited for an explanation. But Nigel never explained.

The gallery owned a wealth of Piranesi etchings. Had Nigel counted on the easy, trustful attitude at Gallery Vianello that nothing would be missed and sold them for his own gain? In a few days Vittoria discovered the entry of the approval visit had been removed from the records. Nigel had taken possession of the missing etchings, disposed of them, and there was no record of his having checked them out!

Five authentic Piranesi etchings with an impeccable provenance would easily be worth ten thousand pounds, Vittoria drew in a quick breath as she did the math. The sum was so much quicker to calculate in pounds, she thought, even for an Italian. The brain could hardly contain the noughts necessary to work it out in *lira*. Italy's monster inflation, rising each minute, encompassed everything, from a tin of olive oil to an expensive Murano vase.

Was this Nigel's first attempt at stealing? Or had he been at it for some time? Warily she left the little cubbyhole of an office, deciding to keep her secret at present until she observed more before reporting him to her superiors. Now he was working on some scheme with Cyril Meadowes. What could that be about? She would continue watching Nigel Sleight very carefully.

~~~~

The youngest Vianello son, an errand boy at the gallery during the school holidays, deposited several envelopes addressed in beautiful hand-lettered script in front of Vittoria.

"The post, *Signorina*."

"Thank you, Piero." Invitations, she was certain. Venetians loved to entertain and any excuse provided a reason for a party. The largest one looked more interesting, written in a large flowing script retaining vestiges of a child's penmanship lessons. On the back was the address of the Correr Museum and Gallery.

> "Dear Vittoria,
>
> We are opening a traveling exhibition of Venetian Sketches of Canaletto and Guardi. The event is really a vehicle for an evening party. I am sending an invitation to Emma and Rosamund of course. Do come! And bring whomever you wish. Friday, the tenth, at eight. Hope to see you then!
>
> > Cordially,
> > Samantha Satchell

The *Museo* Correr housed among its treasures paintings of the Venetian school from the fourteenth to sixteenth centuries.

It blazed with lights as Emma and Rosamund climbed the grand stairway leading to the *piano nobile*, magnificent reception rooms of the principal floor of the old palazzo, now a museum. Presumably the party was meant to show off the refurbished rooms as well as the traveling paintings on exhibit; one reason was as good as any other for a party. And a new experience for me, Emma thought in anticipation, slowly ascending the noble stairway.

She had never been to an evening such as this, with many local luminaries present. Most Venetians were fiercely loyal to their own painters, notwithstanding the *Collezione* Peggy Guggenheim, a museum of contemporary art housed in the historic, unfinished *Palazzo Venier dei Leoni* on Dorsoduro, facing the Grand Canal.

A few inspired guests had come in costume and Emma and Rosamund walked among bewigged ladies and gentlemen wearing clothing of eighteenth century Venice. Emma saw men wearing waistcoats, powdered wigs and lace collars like Filiberto, who, decked out in the Elmley livery, would have fitted perfectly into the setting, Emma thought as she and Rosamund viewed the guests.

Emma saw Riccardo at the buffet table, looking pleased as he escorted Vittoria Dandolo. So Vittoria invited Riccardo. But where was Nigel?

The pair moved easily in step, and Emma wondered why she had not seen the two together before. She recalled the picnic at the Lido, which Riccardo had missed, remaining on duty at *Ca' Sospira* on the fateful day of the break-in.

Vittoria had arrived straight from the gallery Vianello, wearing a simple black dress of superb cut and a single strand of beautiful old pearls which focused attention on her marvelous posture. Her eyes sparkled as Emma moved toward them.

"Before you dash away from us to have a look at the pictures, Emma, let me point out some of the notables here tonight. You will have heard the names before, I imagine." Vittoria disengaged her arm and took Emma aside while Rosamund and Riccardo moved together toward the paintings.

"I also wanted to chat with you a moment about Riccardo," she said in low tones as they avoided the crush of the buffet table. "He has confided in me just a little about that Carpaccio watercolor, and he is so worried about it he can hardly think of anything else."

"Worried?" Emma answered, surprise written on her face. "He never speaks to me about it at all. He seems unconcerned, hardly believing what I continue to learn, advising me to forget it existed, if indeed it really does. I have searched everywhere, racked my brain to find that painting. I am beginning to think it is a complete myth. Riccardo acts as if I am crazy, thinking it is hidden somewhere in *Ca' Sospira.*"

"*Exactamente,* he is in such a state about the Carpaccio's whereabouts as you. Keeping silent is his way." The look of skepticism on Emma's face told Vittoria exactly what she thought of that.

"Listen, Emma, you are wrong about Riccardo. Believe me, he is as upset about the disappearance of that watercolor as you are. He feels responsible, don't you see, because he was left in charge after the old earl died. The will made that very clear. It is humiliating to him, not being able to find it. He fears that if its disappearance becomes common knowledge, it will destroy him and cost him his position. That seems to me a powerful incentive for trying to locate it, don't you think?"

"Well, forgive me," Emma offered in a soft voice, "but if one plays the devil's advocate, it also seems a handy position to take if he has the painting tucked away somewhere safe and is not planning to reveal it at all. What if his intent is to sell it himself and keep the money? He does not make a tremendous amount in his job. He is a caretaker, really, hardly a curator, not to put too fine a point on it. He is guarding the house and its contents for the Elmleys in England. He never is allowed to buy anything at auction or at galleries to enhance the collection. I am sorry, Vittoria, but that is how it could appear to an observer, trying to be fair minded." The surprise on Vittoria's face gave Emma a jolt, as though Emma had lost her senses to harbor such thoughts.

"I have known him for years," Vittoria protested. "He is loyal and honest to a fault, that is his makeup. Believe me, Emma, Riccardo can be boringly loyal! I have known him since we were children. He has a very sad family history, raised by a single mother, and now he is completely alone. He felt an amazing bond with the late earl. I can vouch for their mutual regard. Almost as though he belonged to the Elmley family."

"What was his mother like?"

Vittoria's hands fluttered, as though to hide a moment's confusion. "I didn't actually know her well. She was kind, very beautiful, a quiet, private sort of person. Even when she was young she was spoken of as a recluse. She lavished all of her time and attention on Riccardo. When she died, Riccardo began working at *Ca' Sospira*, even though he was still studying at Padua at the university several days a week. The good train service we have allowed him to do that. He finished a degree in art history he had begun earlier. The curator of furniture and *ogetti d'arte* at *Ca' Sospira* is the only position he has ever held. The late Lord Richard could not have been kinder to him."

"Did you say Lord Richard? The late earl's name was William, was it not?" Emma had a funny prickling at the back of her neck again. Lord William or Lord Richard? What was going on in this crazy Elmley family? Suddenly she felt out of patience with it all.

She studied Vittoria's face, her cheeks afire in the light of the candles as she mumbled an apology.

"William, I meant. Forgive me. Shall we have a flute of *prosecco?*" she quickly asked, turning abruptly to a bewigged waiter circulating with a tray of the Veneto's famous champagne.

Café Florian (eighteenth century engraving)

Conversation *finito,* Emma realized. Vittoria was in love with him, that seemed obvious. Naturally, Riccardo could do no wrong in her eyes. Why had she chosen him? He hardly made enough to support a wife. But Emma discarded her unspoken doubts. Who could possibly explain the attractions humans developed for one another? She certainly would not attempt it. But calling the late earl "Lord Richard?" What did that mean?

There would be no more discussion that evening of the missing Carpaccio and Riccardo. In her gentle way, Vittoria had conveyed this deftly, but it was not a worry. Emma was too busy processing the insight she had gained: Vittoria was fiercely loyal to Riccardo Montgano and convinced beyond doubt of his honesty. The late earl had been his mentor, almost a father figure. Another thing: the will Vittoria had mentioned. What will did she mean? Was there another will? Perhaps one left at *Ca' Sospira?*

"Vittoria," she asked as they sipped flutes of sparkling *prosecco,* "The will you mentioned, was that one left in Venice? If so, would Riccardo have a copy?" But Vittoria had no idea of the whereabouts of such a document, saying she had assumed the will was read in England after the earl's death.

"We haven't seen Nigel tonight. Is he here?" Emma turned to another puzzle.

"He received an invitation, just as I did," she answered. "He said he could not make it. 'A prior engagement' I believe were his words." Did her reply sound cynical? Or frosty? Both, Emma decided.

~~~

Samantha Satchell bore down on them, brimming with enthusiasm. "At last I have found you two! What do you think of our little summer *festa?* Emma, I'd like to borrow you to introduce you to one of my colleagues at the Correr. She spent a summer in Charlottesville at the University of Virginia."

Emma's face lit up. She was enveloped in a wave of homesickness she always felt when home in Virginia came to mind. Over Vittoria's shoulder she saw Riccardo and Rosamund had returned and were making their way toward Vittoria. She followed Samantha into the exhibition rooms.

Iolanda Alberti had the thin, almost brittle elegance ladies of wealth and family seemed to carry in their genes in Venice. Emma could imagine Vittoria resembling this type twenty years on. Taking the pleasant-faced woman's proffered hand, Emma thought that these women were clever enough to charm their way over any obstacle, if they wished.

Introductions complete, *Signora* Alberti quickly spoke, "Tell me, is Virginia still a paradise in the spring on Mr. Jefferson's campus, with all of the Judas trees, Red Bud you call it, and azaleas in bloom? And what is that spectacular native tree one sees blossoming white everywhere? Named for an animal I seem to remember. How could I forget? Pupwood?" Her brow wrinkled just a moment. "No, no. DOGwood!"

Pleased that she had come up with the name, she smiled. Emma assured her that Virginia's beauty remained pristine as she remembered it in the springtime. She guided Emma around the exhibition rooms, revealing nuggets of information about each painting as they made their perambulations.

"But I am sure you know all about our collection. I myself have seen you here several times in early afternoon when most tourists and all Venetians observe the *riposo,* or siesta as the Spanish so musically refer to it."

"No, *Signora,*" Emma protested, "I have much to learn about Venetian painters. I am afraid many of my art history professors barely scratched the surface; they were seduced completely by the greatest names, Titian, Giorgione, Tintoretto. A shortage of time to complete their prospectus had to be factored in as well of course. During my stay in Venice, I am putting what free moments I can snatch to good use by studying the Correr collection carefully."

They paused to look at a painting by Carpaccio which Emma had seen before. Similar in setting to the missing watercolor in the Elmley collection, it contained two Venetian courtesans sitting on the *altana,* accompanied by two dogs, two doves, a peacock and an attendant dwarf. The aging women seemed to be suffering blackest despair as they sat slumped in their chairs.

No straw hats nor bleaching of tresses, no basket of lemons nor the lightheartedness of the lovely girls in the Elmley Carpaccio, if Emma could rely on *Signora* Puglio's earlier description of it.

"Carpaccio was our television news reporter of the period," *Signora* Alberti remarked as they stood before the painting. "He went everywhere looking, and like most Venetians he loved gossip. What a story he paints of these old, worn out crones in their rich dresses and jewels, sadly contemplating a bleak future. Carpaccio recorded with his brush in the same way Dickens immortalized with his pen in the nineteenth century, looking at life in Victorian England. In the Renaissance, Carpaccio saved for all time the look and flavor of Venice. Is not his wealth of detail simply delicious?"

"Indeed yes." Emma replied. "In the *Ca' Sospira* collection there apparently was once a delightful watercolor by Carpaccio of two young girls sitting on the *altana* bleaching their hair with lemons. They wore straw hats without crowns, I believe. Did you ever hear of it?"

"Why no, I did not," the woman answered pleasantly. "What happened? Was it sold?"

"There is no record of its sale. Riccardo Montgano, the curator of furniture and *ogetti d'arte* has been unable to trace its whereabouts. I had hoped perhaps you might have heard what happened to it, a gift to some Venetian institute or religious order perhaps?" *Signora* Alberti shook her head, but offered no explanations.

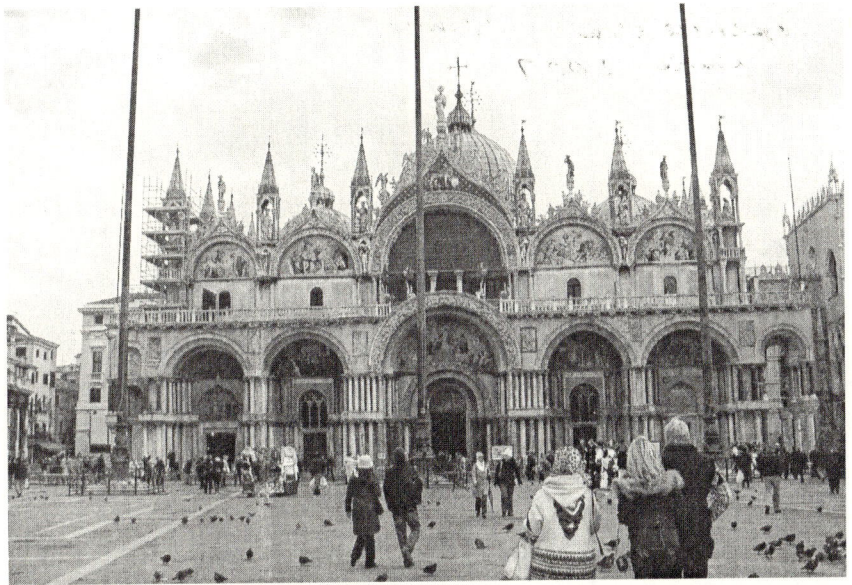

Basilica Of San Marco

"So how have you been getting on with Riccardo Montgano? I see he is here tonight and I am so glad! He is entirely too much to himself at *Ca' Sospira!*"

Iolanda Alberti waited expectantly as Emma hesitated.

"You know Riccardo?" Emma asked, determined to learn what she could from this new acquaintance, while at the same time remaining loyal to Riccardo.

"*Si,* he was a classmate at the same school as my son Bruno when they were young sprigs," she said. "I shall never forget that child's appetite! Occasionally Bruno would bring him home from school, but I could never fill him up, even with bowls of *pappa col pomodoro,* the hearty Tuscan porridge we make of ripe tomatoes stewed with olive oil and yesterday's bread. Do you know it?" She laughed at the memory. Emma shook her head.

"Well, Riccardo's appetite has not changed, at least at the daily luncheon at *Ca' Sospira.* I can vouch for his enjoyment of food. To answer your question, Riccardo and I get on very well. He has been extremely helpful in introducing me to the collection of the late Lord William Elmley. Did you know Riccardo's parents, the Montganos?"

Iolanda Alberti quickly looked at Emma, as if she were searching out some hidden meaning. Was she surprised to hear the late earl called William, not Richard?

"No *Signorina* Darling, I did not know his father at all. I was not a friend, but an acquaintance of the mother as I said earlier. She was quite young when she died. The father had been dead much longer, I believe. I never met him."

"So the late *Signora* Montgano had a strong influence on her son?" Emma asked, studying her companion.

Iolanda Alberti accepted the name William of the late Lord Elmley with no confusion. William not Richard, and also the name of Montgano for Riccardo's father. Why had Riccardo been so secretive about his parents? Had it been politeness on *Signora* Alberti's part not to correct Emma? Or had Riccardo deceived her? She supposed she might have misunderstood Riccardo, but thought it unlikely. How like Riccardo to shroud his upbringing in mystery!

"Yes, she was a strong influence. And it was a positive influence. She adored her son. He was devastated when he lost her. I remember that. She was a caring mother and a person of the highest character, you may be sure." Whew, thought Emma. Such emphasis. Was she a saint? Could Riccardo's father have been a bounder?

They moved on to a painting of the Madonna and Child by Alvise Vivarini, a member of the Vivarini painting dynasty from Murano working in the fifteenth century and well represented in the Correr. There were Vivarini drawings in the late earl's collection which Emma was researching at *Ca' Sospira*.

"Vivarinis are extremely rare," *La Signora* told her. "Anyone having similar sketches in their possession is lucky indeed. There were not many to begin with and you know, works on paper are very fragile here." She smiled winningly at Emma.

Ah yes, there it was again. Works on paper and their fragility. Could this be a subliminal invitation to remember the Correr when the time came to disperse the Elmley collection? These Venetians were almost too subtle in their all-encompassing charm. She looked at the Vivarini sketches in front of her. What *Signora* Alberti said was true. They were uncannily like those in the Elmley collection. Old friends. And so beautiful.

Each day Emma was becoming more aware of the discernment which had built the late earl's collection. She felt his passion and applauded his choices. Emma also knew his careful selections meant the collection was becoming more valuable each day.

Returning to Dorsoduro with Rosamund after the party, Emma felt too restless to read a chapter in the John Julius Norwich book on Venice on the little bookshelf above her head. She lay in her bed looking out the low window. Both Vittoria and Signora Alberti were lavish in their praise of Riccardo, but some of his statements did not prove out, either about his family background or his duties at *Ca' Sospira*. She went over her conversation with Vittoria Dandolo, knowing that in some way, important information had been revealed, even though she was unable at present to know how everything fit together. Like a bruise under the skin it was there, tender as one touched it, but nothing more. It would be revealed later, she thought drowsily.

She gazed on the silent waters of the Grand Canal, just in time to see the black gondola skimming the waters. It was the same gondolier guiding the graceful craft. His figure was tall; the shirt, tucked into dark trousers, followed the contours of powerful arms. This time he was not carrying a couple. A single passenger was leaning back on cushions, a hand trailing idly in the moonlit waters. Lord Byron swam in these waters, she thought dreamily. And the moon he saw is shining down on Venice tonight. Am I dreaming? Emma sat up in her bed for a better look. No. She watched as the phantom gondola drifted out of sight, unsure whether the passenger was man or woman. Who could it be? And who was the mysterious gondolier? What was their business, riding in a gondola at this hour on the Grand Canal?

~~~~

Vittoria Dandolo also entered a period of reflection in her bedroom in the modest apartment her parents owned in the Cannaregio district near the Church of *Santa Maria dei Miracoli*. She had loved Riccardo for so long, and she knew in her heart he loved her too. But how could they manage to live if indeed he ever posed the all-important question? He was uncertain of his position at *Ca' Sospira*. It depended on the present Lord Elmley. He could decide to sell *Ca' Sospira* at a moment's whim. He could bestow the favor of the curatorial post of the house and its many treasures on someone else.

Vittoria believed Emma Darling was an intelligent, honest person. She liked her very much. Should she trust Emma with her hopes for marriage to Riccardo? Why not? Emma could perhaps throw new ideas into play; she might actually help them. She knew Riccardo harbored fears Emma might replace him, despite Emma's telling him repeatedly of her plans to marry the young surgeon Sam McGregor and settle in London. If only Riccardo weren't so fearful, so unsure of himself! He had so many winning qualities. He should exhibit them more often. She would try to persuade Riccardo to be more cooperative. Ultimately she must help him see that Emma was steering the boat in the same direction as he. Their goals were the same.

Vittoria Dandolo had long ago put aside the dreams cherished by young girls for a Prince Charming to appear riding a white horse. She knew she could never love anyone but Riccardo. She held tightly to the conviction that she could make Riccardo happy should they become husband and wife. And she resolved to turn that possibility into reality. Perhaps she would entrust her dreams, her hopes to Emma; maybe she could help Riccardo along in making his position more secure. She resolved to confide in Emma.

10

Under the Awnings at Florian

Before the week was out, Emma received a telephone call from Vittoria, proposing tea after work the following day. Vittoria suggested Florian on the *Piazza San Marco*, convenient to them on their homeward journeys.

The conversation with Vittoria at the Correr evening resurfaced in Emma's mind. It was that bit when she spoke of "Lord Richard" and said he could not have been kinder to Riccardo when his mother died. The fact that Lord William Richard Elmley and Riccardo, shared the name of Richard probably was coincidental, but Emma knew the late earl had enabled Riccardo to complete his degree from the university at Padua after his mother's death. Also, he was given a job as curator of *Ca Sospira's* furnishings. Had the late earl been kind enough to finance all of Riccardo's education at the University? If so, it was kindness of a very generous sort. That Riccardo was the

Italian name for Richard persisted in her thoughts, something unexplored yet precious she must hold on to for future use, in the same way Tintoretto clung greedily to a favorite bone.

Over the teacups under the awnings at Florian, she found Vittoria disarmingly frank in answering her questions about Riccardo. Straight away she declared that she admired him, had done so since childhood. But, Vittoria added, she had not known Riccardo's mother well.

"I remember her as a gentle presence, shy and retiring when I saw her at birthday parties. Always in the background, but never far from her son. Many in Venice regarded her as a recluse." She paused, taking a small sip of tea.

"Her reputation in Venice, a city often wallowing in pettiness and gossip, to say nothing of questionable morals, was of the highest, absolutely unblemished and above reproach. It was Riccardo's late father, whom he barely remembers, who was the rogue. He had a reputation of chasing after women, and for shamelessly neglecting his wife and child. He also went through inherited wealth quickly, I've heard." She looked thoughtful.

"Well, I am hardly one to criticize there. Surely you know about the Dandolos, and it is true, every word! We are poor as church mice, hopeless at hanging on to money, always have been, for centuries. Even one year in England at Roedean School proved almost too much for my parents, the cost of tuition, I mean. But it got me the job at Vianello's, you see, and I must have a job. I've always been grateful for my year in England," she finished, looking thoughtfully at Emma.

So she had gone to the prestigious Roedean, a finishing school for girls in rural England. Emma nodded, not commenting on Vittoria's somewhat embarrassing financial disclosures. Instead she put another question forward.

"I had always thought the late earl was called 'William.' Several people lately have referred to him as 'Richard'. You did at the Correr evening. What do you know about that?" Emma noticed that Vittoria shifted in her chair, fidgeted with the teapot; her cheeks turned slightly red.

"Now Emma," she said at last, "I am going to repeat some things I have heard which do not have a factual basis, certainly nothing like proof. And they were not told to me by Riccardo. I seldom get him to say anything at all about the Elmleys." She took a tiny sip of tea.

"You know by now that the late earl was bewitched by Venice when he first came over as a young man. Later, after marriage to Lady Sybil and a succession of children, his admiration for Venice and its people did not wither away. It became even stronger with the passing of the years. He bought *Ca' Sospira*. His final capitulation to Venice occurred one might say, when he made the decision to live here, rather than in England.

"Some people wondered about this. Of those skeptics, some dug deeper and ferreted out, or stumbled upon, a reason. The reason it seems, was a widow with a child: Esperanza Farsetti, who bore the surname of one of the oldest families in Venice. *Ca' Farsetti*, their home, or *casa*, as we say, was built in the *quattrocento*. It still exists on the Grand Canal, and now serves as the Town Hall of Venice. Young Esperanza married a Montgano. It had been an arranged marriage I heard; the Montgano family came from Lucerne." Emma blinked in amazement as Vittoria raised a hand and continued.

"There's more. This, attraction, rapport, I hardly know how to describe the relationship between Esperanza and the late Lord Elmley, was not sexual. Apparently it was rather a meeting of similar minds on a much higher plane, and eventually it brought the earl, along with a wife and a house full of children who were near maturity at this point, to Venice to live. Permanently. The late earl simply gave up England as a residence.

"I think it is fair to say the children weren't around much by that time, a few weeks in summer with their parents for those still in university. They were grown ups, adults really. The young earl, the oldest male, would inherit and had been well trained for his duty: to marry, produce an heir to carry on the title, the English estates and responsibilities after his father's demise. 'An heir and a spare,' as the English refer to the oldest son's obligation to produce. Charming, don't you think? At any rate, the young earl assumed his charge early, with good grace, from what I have heard.

"One can find plenty of skeptics here, probably in England too, who pooh-pooh the idea of course, that such a platonic friendship between a man and a woman can exist." Vittoria studied the slice of lemon floating in her teacup with the greatest concentration.

"Sigmund Freud naturally would have been one of them, and certainly Venice would be obvious as one of the world's more tolerant locations to conduct an extra-marital arrangement. But to the contrary, the late earl seemed to have more interest in matters of the mind rather than of the flesh, notwithstanding fathering a houseful of children with Lady Sybil." Vittoria paused.

"It was well known in Venice that his wife, Lady Sybil, was not a particularly deep thinker. She did not read books nor did she relish serious discussions. She was a conscientious mother, hostess, an expert needlewoman and horsewoman, the latter accomplishment not earning her much purchase among Venetians, however, water-surrounded as we are." She paused for Emma's smile before continuing.

"You know that ambitious tapestry worked in petit point of Elmley Castle, the manor house in Worcestershire, in one of the bedrooms at *Ca' Sospira*? Well, every stitch she worked with her own hands. Can you believe it? Also, I should mention, the late earl's title meant a lot to him. He was a serious student of history. He had an understanding of his responsibilities to the title and his obligations to his family history, as well as to his wife and children."

Here Vittoria took a macaroon and thoughtfully bit into it as she looked out on the tourist ritual of feeding obese pigeons waddling around the Piazza San Marco. One young boy with a look of bliss covering his face, open palms of his hands holding crumbs, had attracted three or four birds perched on his dark, curly head and more crowded onto his outstretched arms as a proud mother snapped his picture.

"It was rumored around Venice that Lady Sybil had slight interest in reading anything beyond the covers of the current issue of *Vogue* or *Country Life,* and she was not quite so *sympatico* about the move to Venice as her husband. That notwithstanding, she apparently kept her unhappiness to herself and got on with her duties, as wives usually did in those days.

"It was during this time that Riccardo and the late earl became very close. And the late earl began asking his Italian friends and dinner guests to call him Richard rather than William. It was one of a string of given names he was burdened with at birth, one which he had never used before. This bizarre request we heard, strictly gossip of course, was another irritant to poor Lady Sybil, who sorely missed her house and homeland, her friends and horses it was rumored. To cap it all, her husband changed his name in his declining years. It was almost too much."

So Richard had been another in the string of suitable Elmley names. And he preferred being called that in Venice, at least by those closest to him. Emma filed the facts she heard away in her head.

Emma was reminded of the incident Riccardo had mentioned to her in a rare moment of confidence, when he revealed Lady

Sybil's apparent jealousy of the two girls in the watercolor by Carpaccio. It had seemed ridiculous and child-like to Emma at the time. But had Lady Sybil suspected her husband's so called friendship with the widow, Esperanza Montgano? Any wife would hate that. Or would pouting and petulance have been a part of Lady Sybil's make up? Had she been something of a diva? Surely not. Much more likely it was jealousy, or possibly just one of the manifestations of old age along with the attendant aches and pains, as Riccardo had suggested.

But the thought persisted that it could have been based on something more serious, a husband's divided loyalty, which could threaten the well being of her own children sometime in the future. For the first time, Emma felt sympathy rather than impatience toward poor Lady Sybil.

The Florian string orchestra began playing opera arias and familiar folk songs as the girls sat quietly reflecting on what Vittoria had said. Emma sketched out new insights as she listened while violins, violas and cellos floated Mozart over the patrons as well as the humble pigeons and energetic sightseers on *San Marco*.

"And what did Riccardo think of all of this?" Emma asked.

"Riccardo never discussed it. He was extremely close to the late earl; there was a real bond there. I am sure about that. Mind you, after such a disastrous father, Riccardo was ripe for the appearance of a kindly mentor. A father figure if you like, interested in his welfare, especially after his mother died. But

I think it is fair to say the late earl took an interest in him long before Esperanza passed away. I am certain he helped prepare Riccardo for his curatorial job at *Ca' Sospira*. By financing his study, I mean. And he was responsible for the entire cost of putting him through the University of Padua. It is one of Italy's oldest and most revered places of learning, you know," she added, the earnestness of her dark eyes claiming Emma's attention. "Close by, with many daily train connections, so he could remain a day student."

Lingering another half hour, the two parted; Emma hurried to board the *vaporetto* for Dorsoduro and the Accademia Bridge while Vittoria walked in the opposite direction toward the Cannaregio District near *Santa Maria dei Miracoli* and her parents' apartment.

The visit had given Emma new insights into Riccardo's behavior, and a better understanding of his loyalty to the Elmley family, in particular to the late earl. There was also the startling possibility of a fissure in the united front of wealth and prestige presented to the world by the Elmleys in the form of dark, unexplained secrets.

11

Might Sherlock Holmes Lend a Hand?

The following Monday Emma reached *Ca' Sospira* a few minutes after ten o'clock, breathless after what amounted to a trot from the wide steps of the opera house to her destination. She hated being late, even a minute or so. She hurried up the marble steps and pulled the chain beside the massive door and waited. Whatever could be the matter? It was strange she had not been greeted immediately by Filiberto's cheerful *Buongiorno Signorina,* and the frenzied wagging of Tintoretto's plume of a tail. She heard his bark from deep within the house and at last, footsteps shuffling toward the entrance.

"Thank heavens you are here." Filiberto stood before her minus his satin waistcoat with its gold embellishments, his ruffled shirt sleeves rolled up to the elbow. A kitchen apron tied tightly at the waist fell almost to the buckles of his black shoes and his hair, uncombed, rose in snowy tufts around his face, pushed forward by his pillow. A grey stubble sprouted on his cheeks. The collective impression Emma received was one of interrupted slumber, hasty dressing and no time for the customary daily ablutions.

"Whatever is the matter?" His disheveled appearance was so unlikely it frightened Emma.

"Quickly, follow me!" Filiberto reversed course and sped behind a racing Tintoretto, mindful of the *portego* furnishings as he loped from the central hall toward the kitchen.

Beyond the swinging door Emma could see Riccardo sprawled in the cook's chair with his eyes closed, elbows propped on the table, palms turned outward. Emma gasped when she saw the ugly raised blisters covering his hands. The smell of charred wood and smoke filled the air.

"Riccardo, are you all right?" She recoiled from the acrid smell permeating the room and her eyes began to smart. "Where was the fire?" Emma looked about in disbelief as Riccardo's eyes fluttered open then closed as he seemed to drift out of consciousness.

"Here in the kitchen, *Signorina* Emma," Filiberto confirmed. "Burning in a rubbish bin. Riccardo found it when he made his early rounds this morning. It was a fire, all right, deliberately set to smolder a long time before bursting into flame. When Riccardo reached the kitchen this morning a blaze had broken out in the bin. He grasped the barrel with both hands, dragged it to the outside door and rolled it into the canal as quickly as he could, but the damage had been done. Look at his hands!"

"They must be bandaged carefully," Emma said, shocked by the swollen welts. She noticed the roll of gauze and a basin of clean water on the table beside Riccardo. Filiberto had begun to dress the burns.

Oh Riccardo, Emma's thoughts were tinged with self-loathing. How could I ever have thought you were dishonest?

"Are his hands clean?" Her voice was barely a whisper, she was so overcome with remorse.

"Yes, I've seen to that, and he wants a homeopathic salve applied. Won't hear of calling the doctor, or the police either, for that matter. I was just getting down to it when you rang the bell."

Filiberto took up a tube of salve and gently began applying it to Riccardo's hands.

"This is a healing formula of calendula flowers, made especially for burns. We keep it in the kitchen. They sell it at the *farmacia* near the Fenice. It's very good."

"But police?" Emma whispered. "Why should you call the police? It was an accident, only a horrible accident?"

Sculpture, Treasury of San Marco, Fourth century

"The fire was set." Filberto spat out the words from drawn lips. "It wasn't an accident. It is a miracle Riccardo found it soon after it burst into flame. But he paid a high cost!"

Emma's heart began beating a tattoo in her chest. "But who, why? Are you sure? Couldn't a spark from the range have popped out, igniting the rubbish in the bin?"

"The bin had been carefully packed with kindling and larger pieces of wood. The fire had been laid." Filiberto replied as he wound more gauze around the hands. Riccardo had not spoken.

"Surely then, if the fire was set, we must notify the police," Emma said to Filiberto.

Suddenly Riccardo opened his eyes and looked directly at Emma.

"Do not call the police!" He closed his eyes and once more seemed to drift out of consciousness.

"Of course not, Riccardo. Not if you say so." Emma answered.

"He is right," Filiberto whispered to her. "You can never be certain of their loyalties! Some of them have been tainted by the *Mafioso*, moving up from the South. Riccardo asked for my word, *Signorina*."

The South. She shivered. The mafia. So that was why they did not trust the police! She had never lived anywhere, knowing what it was like to fear the police.

Filiberto finished his task and set aside the gauze.

"We must get him to a comfortable place to rest, a bed, where we can keep watch over him. If he develops anything like fever, we shall have to disobey him and call for the doctor." He spoke barely above a whisper.

"The Chesterfield in the library would be comfortable," Emma suggested. "He can rest there quietly He will want to be on this floor, not in his bedroom or his office, both so far away from the busy part of the house. We can keep an eye on him and attend to his needs."

"But where will you work, *Signorina?*"

"I can work there. My desk is some distance away from the sofa. I work quietly, mainly reading and jotting down notes. We can monitor how he recovers and if he objects, we can find a more private space. I have a feeling Riccardo, if he is able, will get to his feet in short order, as soon as the pain eases a bit."

Emma was feeling anxious, and a very long way not only from Sam, but from her family in Virginia. Fears for the safety of everyone at *Ca' Sospira* engulfed her; she felt apprehensive and worried.

"He'll recover, don't worry. You have been a great help," Filiberto said, giving her a reassuring smile.

Riccardo slept through the morning as Emma and Filiberto discussed the fire in whispers. There apparently had been no forced entry, Filiberto had checked all the windows on the ground floor after they moved Riccardo to the library and settled him with pillows and a wool throw. All were secure except for the kitchen window where the bars had been neatly sawn open in preparation to enter. But no evidence of entry had been found. Emma wondered aloud about Cesara. Why had she not arrived by this time? But Filiberto had no answers. He shrugged.

"She marches to her own beat." Filiberto added, careful of Riccardo's heavily wrapped hands resting on his chest as he tucked the throw over him.

He brought in a carafe of water and a glass, taking up his post in a nearby chair.

With Tintoretto near the sofa, his eyes never leaving the sleeping Riccardo, Emma and the valet continued to puzzle over the scanty details of the fire. In Emma's mind, the most important thing she had learned was the depth of Riccardo's loyalty to *Ca' Sospira*, its possessions and its owners, the Elmleys. It bordered on the obsessive. He behaved like a member of the family in his struggle to put out the fire, even though he suffered cruel burns on his hands in the attempt. The fact that the fire had been set was a puzzle which made no sense whatsoever.

Why would thieves destroy what they hoped to steal? A ruse, perhaps, to learn the whereabouts of the Carpaccio painting, hoping Riccardo would rush to save it from the flames? It reminded her of the plot she had read long ago in a Sherlock Holmes story. But which one? The information eluded her.

Idly Emma gazed at the soft colors of the beautiful leather bound books lining the walls of the library. The late earl possessed wide-ranging interests. Apparently he had favored classics of the great thinkers and philosophers through the ages, English authors, a limited number of biographies. It was principally a scholar's collection, with a few selected works of fiction.

Her eyes fell on the novels of Sir Arthur Conan Doyle. Emma recalled her feeling of pleasure when she saw the books for the first time on the shelf. How many happy hours she had spent growing up in Virginia, reading on the cushions of the window seat in the sunny dining room, lost in the exploits of Holmes and the faithful Dr. Watson as they brought thieves, swindlers and murderers to justice. Sherlock Holmes had been her hero. And it was true what her mother and father often said about their daughter: She preferred reading mysteries to reading romance novels.

Santa Maria della Salute on Dorsoduro

It pleased Emma to know the late earl had enjoyed an occasional excursion into the world of Baker Street. Emma searched in her mind for the elusive title of the Sherlock Holmes mystery. A beautiful actress had hidden away a love letter, a letter from a monarch of a small European kingdom, she recalled. The letter could cause trouble and embarrassment should it ever be revealed when his forthcoming marriage to a princess was announced. The actress refused to give the letter up, however.

Emma's recall was put on hold as Riccardo awakened asking for water. He will be asking for food soon. Where was the cook? She held the glass as he drank.

~~~~

By eleven o'clock Emma was missing the morning *caffelatte*. "What about Cesara?" she whispered to Filiberto.

"I've been thinking. She has no telephone. But I can ring the daughter in Dorsoduro. I have her number. I'll go to the *telefono* in the hallway."

He returned a few minutes later to report that nobody answered.

"It seems strange. I am positive Cesara told me the daughter could not go out to work at present, as her children are very small. She said the daughter took care of other children in the neighborhood at her home, a sort of nursery, bringing in a few *lira* to help with expenses."

"If she keeps children, she would have to answer. Mothers could be calling. Are they purposely not answering? We have no one on hand to cook luncheon. Riccardo must have good, nourishing food for a quick recovery. What can we do, Filiberto?" Emma struggled to keep anxiety out of her voice. Guiltily she recalled all the opportunities she had ignored to learn her way about in the kitchen. On several occasions her mother had met her indifference with some advice.

"When the time comes, you can learn. Anyone who can read can learn to cook. Just get a reliable cookbook." As that need had not yet arisen, Emma remained untutored in the culinary arts.

She sat quietly as Riccardo dozed on the sofa. She recalled frankfurters toasted on a stick, peanut butter and jelly sandwiches, the smoky campfire scrambled eggs of Girl Scout days, the breakfast bowl of cold cereal. None of it seemed suitable for *Ca' Sospira's* more evolved cuisine. She did not enjoy feeling helpless. It was against her principles. The unease surfaced once again.

"I can order a tray sent up from the *Ristorante Fenice* a few doors down from the Fenice when we are ready for luncheon. I have done it on occasion through the years in an emergency such as this," Filiberto, who had joined her to keep watch, offered.

There was a slight stirring on the Chesterfield. Riccardo's voice, barely audible, floated toward them.

"Call Luisa. She will come. Tell her Cesara won't be coming back. Tell her I need her help." As if to punctuate Riccardo's words, Tintoretto gave a sharp bark, looking directly at Emma.

"Of course, Riccardo. I have her number," Emma replied. "She gave it to me when she visited recently. I told her I would let her know when my work on the *collezione* was finished."

"*Va bene*, good," Riccardo answered, wearily closing his eyes again. "Ring at once, please."

She hurried to the telephone in the back hallway. In a moment found the number in her small address book. Riccardo had seemed certain Cesara would not be coming back. When he recovered, she must ask him how he could be sure.

Emma returned to the library with the good news that Luisa had saved them. She was fulsome in her outpourings of sympathy for *Signor* Riccardo. She promised to be on her way within the hour, bringing *piselli*, fresh picked green peas from her own garden. There would be a *risotto* with *piselli* and *prosciutto* for luncheon she promised. In spite of herself, Emma felt her mouth water at the prospect of creamy rice studded with fresh green peas and tangy bits of ham.

Emma realized as she looked at Filiberto whose wrinkled features were fighting a losing battle with old age and Riccardo, on the sofa sleeping in spite of horrible burns on his hands, that in the space of an hour her involvement in the affairs of *Ca' Sospira* had deepened considerably. She knew now Riccardo's loyalty to the Elmleys was above dispute. The burns on his hands proved it. He had not taken the Carpaccio.

~~~

Riccardo took luncheon on a tray sitting at Emma's desk while Filiberto stood by. Emma watched Riccardo delicately guide the fork to his mouth grasping it by his thumb and index finger which had escaped the burns. That he was able to feed himself and do justice to the excellent *risotto* seemed hopeful. A spoon replaced the fork and he tucked into a delicate egg custard to finish the meal.

Riccardo, a little color in his cheeks, seemed to have no trouble regaining a healthy appetite Emma noticed from her post in the old wing chair. She rejoiced inwardly as Tintoretto's tail began its fulsome thump of the floor while he sat at attention beside the sofa. Filiberto cleared away and departed with the tray, followed by Tintoretto who would beg for tidbits as Filiberto ate in the kitchen. When Filiberto returned, Emma would have her luncheon on a tray in front of the bay window of the dining room. Luisa had resumed her former post as though she had been absent a week rather than several years. When she had presented Riccardo with a pretty little nosegay from her own garden as she brought in his tray, Emma was certain she saw tears well up in Riccardo's eyes.

Figure of Fame atop Dogana (Customs House)

Thank goodness there was no more resentment there, Emma thought, remembering his earlier anger which she attributed to Riccardo's sensitive, easily wounded nature. All because Luisa had failed to pay her respects to him. Emma could find nothing to criticize in the delicious dishes the woman had prepared so efficiently. How sensitive Riccardo could be about following his somewhat stilted ideas of correct behavior. This was true of other Venetians she had noticed. Turning toward Riccardo, she asked if she could bring anything to the library from his office.

"No, thank you. I plan to go up and do some work in a few minutes."

"Are you sure?" she began, but glancing at his face, she realized he wanted no more fussing. The pain in his hands obviously had lessened. There was nothing wrong with his feet. He wanted to be off.

Hoping to forestall his departure she asked, "Riccardo, what did you mean when you said Cesara will not be coming back?" His dark eyes flashed like lightening bolts.

"She realized I knew she was in on the plan to steal the Carpaccio by starting a fire in the kitchen," he said, but observing the concentration of Emma's brows he knew she would not be content until she received all of the pertinent facts. He sighed and continued.

"You know her duties: she prepares luncheon. Later she prepares supper on a tray for Filiberto and me, puts it in the cold box and does all the washing up. Then she goes home. Yesterday I came in a few minutes early to see her off and she was on the *telefono*. Quite by accident I heard every word she was saying."

Emma leaned forward. "And what was it, Riccardo?"

"She said she had seen to the window in the kitchen. She had unbolted it, just as they ordered, but how anybody could get around the iron bars was beyond her!"

Emma gasped. Cesara, the respectable cook had proved corruptible! Was nobody able to withstand temptation in this city? She looked at Riccardo who was studying her reactions carefully.

"For your information Emma, I saw the open window this morning when I smelled smoke as I entered the kitchen. I noticed the bars had been sawn through, easily enough I imagine from the looks of them. An experienced burglar could have done it in a few minutes with the proper tools. When I overheard Cesara on the telephone yesterday I had no idea that anything would occur so soon, only a few hours later.

"That was my mistake. I had put in a call to the ironmonger of course, and he was to come today to install new bars. You remember, I told you the thieves would certainly try again. The plan must have been set to go forward immediately. I didn't dream they would try last night." He looked down at his bandaged hands.

"But why did they choose the kitchen? So far from everything of any real value in *Ca' Sospira!*" He muttered the words, shaking his head in disbelief.

"Cesara could not be sure you heard her speaking on the telephone yesterday, but nonetheless, I am sure she would have turned and fled if she had seen all the frenzied activity at *Ca' Sospira* this morning when she arrived. There was the open window at the back door where she normally entered, sawn bars lying beneath the windows, perhaps cinders on the passageway from the burning rubbish bin you earlier flung into the canal. The sight of that alone would have frightened her away. She knew her part in the plan would come to light sooner rather than later when you put things together. She must have scarpered quickly when she saw what was going on in the kitchen. She left for good, fearing the authorities would be looking for her."

Emma's mind was racing furiously as she once again recalled the mystery of Sherlock Holmes. She went to the bookshelves and took down the Conan Doyle mysteries. After a few minutes searching she found the one she was looking for, "A Scandal in Bohemia." That was the name. She told Riccardo the story quickly, that the locale was in London, not in a lonely haunted castle on the moors as were so many of Conan Doyle's tales.

"The fire scheme was actually planned by Sherlock Holmes himself, so that it would flush out a love letter to a beautiful London actress, a letter which, if made public, would destroy a monarch's hope for an advantageous marriage. Holmes realized the woman would hurry first to protect this valuable letter when a bogus fire broke out."

Riccardo, wearing a look of incredulity, gave a wan smile, "You must memorize whatever you read, Emma. You seem to have total recall at your fingertips. Do carry on." Emma blushed and continued with the story.

"It was successful, of course. Holmes and Dr. Watson and the police were concealed outside in the shrubbery, watching from a window while the woman hurried to a wall safe. At *Ca' Sospira*, as it happened, nothing was hidden away in the kitchen as the thieves had thought. You did not try to rescue anything stowed secretly away when you saw the fire. You focused on putting out the fire in the rubbish bin. But what made them think it was hidden in the kitchen?"

"Perhaps Cesara told them of the earl's notebook with instructions about cooking a goose. Instead of the bedroom, they concentrated on the kitchen." Riccardo looked down at his bandaged hands.

"But who could have known about Sherlock Holmes?" Riccardo mused thinking aloud. "Surely not Cesara or the two rustics, if they were helping her."

"You are right of course," Emma answered quickly. "But Nigel certainly would have read Sherlock Holmes, Cyril too. English and American kids who loved to read would have discovered

Holmes by the time they reached their teens." She sat for a moment twisting a strand of hair, deep in thought.

"Riccardo, you really should consider calling in the police. All of them can't be corrupt. They could give us much needed protection here. It's possible they might put the perpetrators behind bars." He gave her a thoughtful look.

"Riccardo, just suppose the person who wanted to steal the Carpaccio had reason to think the picture *was* hidden somewhere in the kitchen? And having searched there previously, probably with Cesara's help, he failed to ferret it out. Perhaps a fire, something set in secret before Cesara left for the night, would serve as a decoy. One person who surely knew where the Carpaccio was hidden and would hurry there to try to save it was you, Riccardo." Emma paused to catch her breath. He sat calmly looking at her, his dark eyes narrowed.

"You know, Emma, you may be right. I recall now something strange that happened, the day of the picnic at the Lido. That was the day, you remember I couldn't go and Nigel took Tintoretto and told everyone at the *vaporetto* stop I would come along later." Emma nodded. Deliver us from conspirators, she thought.

"Well, that's another example of Nigel's trickery. I never told anyone that. Nigel simply invented my words. I knew I couldn't possibly leave Filiberto alone guarding the house, especially after Tintoretto had been taken away.

"Nigel was so smooth. He arranged the plans to his satisfaction, plans of which we were absolutely unaware. It's true, I thought I might perhaps join you at the Lido when he suggested it. However, thinking it over, I realized it wouldn't have been wise, leaving only Filiberto in charge. He is loyal to a fault, but not terribly strong, not anymore. As things turned out, the thieves took care of both of us, didn't they?" Sadly he shook his head.

"But that wasn't all you were going to tell me, was it, Riccardo? What else happened on that day?"

"It was in your office, Emma. I had forgotten, but just now, when you said something about Cesara helping the thieves, it came flying back to me. I suppose I'd not thought of her before in the role of accomplice. That afternoon, I went to your office to have a look at the auction coming up from Ditchfield's current London catalogue, the one you keep on your desk. I'd wanted to check out some old Murano glass they were selling, similar to pieces in our collection. I hurried inside, the door was shut I remember, and there was Cesara, bold as you please, and she had the little leather notebook belonging to the late earl in her hands." Emma gasped.

"She got quite red in the face and mumbled something about looking for an old receipt of Lady Sybil's for cooking a goose she had seen years ago in this little notebook, and she was just putting it back. I didn't think much about it, I had no reason to suspect her then. Now that I recall the incident, it was obviously a cover up. She was snooping, plain and simple, laying the groundwork for the break-in." Anger clouded his features.

"It sounds so plausible, I am positive you are right, Riccardo. Cesara must be in on the plan to steal the Carpaccio. What if she believed that the recipe itself, not the earl's bedroom, was the clue, meant to lead to the picture hidden in the kitchen! What if she thought the kitchen, not the bedroom, was the actual hiding place? Yes, that must be it," Emma finished triumphantly.

"It saved her a lot of trouble if she failed to work on the bedroom clue," Riccardo answered somewhat bitterly. "The picture didn't turn up there, did it?"

"No, it didn't," Emma agreed. "Neither bedroom nor kitchen, come to that." The two looked at each other glumly.

Emma saw however what Nigel, Cyril and Cesara did not realize, that poor Riccardo was as much in the dark as they were. He had no idea where the Carpaccio was hidden. Emma understood now, beyond all doubt. She looked at Riccardo's swollen, bandaged hands. What a long time it has taken her to discover the honesty and loyalty of this man. She shook her head in disbelief. How wrong early judgments of another's intent could be.

Neither she nor the evildoers who were plotting to steal from *Ca' Sospira* had counted on someone with Riccardo's courage. At great cost to himself he first undertook to extinguish the fire. He had made no move whatsoever to hurry to save a precious picture. And the reason, Emma knew now beyond all doubt: *He had no idea where the Carpaccio was hidden!*

12

Spying at Santa Maria della Salute

Emma was walking in the *sestieri* of Dorsoduro, one of the six districts of Venice running along either side of the Grand Canal. She had just seen Nigel Sleight and Cyril Meadowes get off the *vaporetto* at the Accademia Bridge and was determined to follow them to see just where they were going. Luckily she was twenty minutes early for a meeting with Rosamund and Vittoria at the flat.

Vittoria Dandolo had offered to take them to a little dressmaker she knew, a gifted seamstress who had an eye for cut and design. Dorsoduro, Emma thought, hurrying along to keep the two men in her sights, was more appealing than Cannaregio with its excess of new, rectangular buildings, looking like cornflake boxes. The San Marco district was more beautiful still, with its centerpiece of *San Marco* and the Doges Palace, but forever clogged with tourists, even on the back streets.

She moved rapidly, keeping Nigel and Cyril in view. They seemed to know exactly where they were going. Vittoria had told Emma over tea at Florian about Cyril Meadowes' surprise appearance at Gallery Vianello to meet with Nigel. They must be working together in some underhand way to rob *Ca' Sospira* of its Carpaccio.

Further and further away from Rosamund's flat, she followed the pair. Past the garden entrance to the Peggy Guggenheim Museum of Modern Art and, as she crossed the bridge over the next canal, she could see they were getting quite close to *Santa Maria della Salute*, the huge church on the point of Dorsoduro, adjoining the *dogana*, the customs house. Dedicated to the Virgin Mary in thanks from a grateful citizenry for deliverance from the plague, the Salute rose, a dominating landmark. Could they be going there? It looked as though they were. *Santa Maria della Salute*!

She crossed the tiny *Campo San Vio* where Saint George's, the English church stood. Past the lush greenery of back gardens behind high walls and entrance gates of *palazzi* facing the Grand Canal. They surely cannot be going in to pray. The thought amused Emma, that either of these men might get down on their knees. Their actions and their interests seemed a world away from prayer.

She recalled how when she first arrived in Venice, she had viewed Nigel in a favorable light. He had been friendly and outgoing. Riccardo, on the other hand had seemed suspicious, grudging and withdrawn. Now her ideas were reversed.

Impressed by Riccardo's faithfulness to the family who employed him, she knew he chose friends slowly, but once decided, Riccardo offered long-lasting loyalty and friendship. The image of him, hands covered with burns after putting out the fire at *Ca' Sospira*, floated before her eyes.

Riccardo's suspicions about Nigel had firmly taken root in her thinking. What was Nigel plotting? Cyril of course was another matter. Since first learning of his shabby treatment of Rosamund, she had loathed him. His boundaries apparently knew no limits. And now she found herself following the two as they hurried toward the church on some secret mission. Perhaps they were meeting someone. Emma crossed a bridge over another small canal and walked toward an open area in front of the church where a few tourists milled about, cameras snapping.

The pair stopped in front. Emma knew she could not draw closer, it was too risky. She ducked into a little green area beside the church where small trees gave welcome shade and a few benches provided a cool place to view the wide walk leading to the entrance. She sat down, partly obscured by a large oleander bush in a tub, and waited. She still could see where the men stood talking. They had picked a good time for their meeting. Hardly any Venetians stirred during the *riposo,* the rest time after lunch. Only a few dispirited tourists braved the heat.

Emma longed for some form of disguise, perhaps a flowing red wig, sunglasses, a large floppy hat. Then she could ease closer without fear of being recognized and overhear something important. The men stood patiently, occasionally glancing toward the entrance to the church. Were they going in? Emma reached in her string bag for a fresh handkerchief to mop her forehead. The paving stones and bulk of the great church radiated heat. She put away the handkerchief, closed her purse and looked up.

In the space of the few seconds, Nigel and Cyril had been joined by a woman and the three of them were walking toward the meager shade offered by her bench! With speed worthy of Pegasus she eased behind the luxuriant oleander bush as they approached and took seats on the deserted bench.

Emma strained to hear as it occurred to her this was the perfect time for the unlikely trio to meet. How could anyone stir in this heat? Venetians would come out later, when the sun was down and breezes had begun, as they did every evening near sunset. Now however, there would be little chance anyone save tourists would observe them. The three could plot and plan freely. Cesara was speaking.

Emma caught phrases like "I know he heard what I said to you on the telephone," and "When I got there I was afraid to go inside."

There were words she could not pick up, then, 'I saw what happened when I looked in the window. There the three of them were, Riccardo holding up his hands and sitting with his eyes closed, Filiberto rushing about and the American girl standing there gawping. Neither he nor the old butler made a move go to a cupboard or pantry to find it."

Emma flinched at the unflattering description of herself as she reflected on Cesara's, words: neither Riccardo or Filiberto made any attempt to rescue anything from the fire.

"I think *Signor* Riccardo must have got burned putting out the fire. Nothing in the kitchen was out of place. All the fuss going on was about his hands. I hurried away real quick." Cesara dabbed nervously at her brow.

"So much for our plans to smoke out the picture." Nigel, peevish, mopped his face with a limp handkerchief and glared at Cyril. "It *was* a bit over the top, trying an old Sherlock Holmes trick. Surely you could have thought of something a little more original and up to date. We are not in Victorian England, for pity's sake!"

"Calm yourself, Nigel. You wouldn't be complaining if it had worked. I can make Riccardo reveal the Carpaccio's whereabouts all right, with a little encouragement of another sort."

Cyril spoke softly, in honeyed tones, but Emma caught the threat implicit in his words. Her heart pounded. Forceful persuasion, torture. She knew what he meant. Riccardo, Filiberto, even she might be vulnerable. It wasn't difficult to work out what Cyril had in mind. She felt rivulets of sweat running down her arms and legs.

"Bet the old fossil of a valet would have a bit to tell us, with some proper encouragement," Cyril grinned.

Emma shivered, feeling a frisson of fear as Cyril rambled on, saying what a pleasure it would be to wipe that superior, look-down-her-nose-at-one stare off Miss Yankee Doodle's smug face. The comment rang out like a slap. How could any female think Cyril attractive? Compared to the kindly smile, measured poise and intelligent face of Sam McGregor, Cyril was the devil incarnate, Emma reflected.

Wake up, you, the watchful imp in her brain hissed. You realize he is talking about you, Miss Yankee Doodle? Emma gulped, as a bolt of fear of fear shot down her spine.

"How about Filiberto? Cesara, you could pump something out of him, easily," Nigel began, but she quickly interrupted.

"I can't go back now. I know *Signor* Montgano heard me talking on the telephone to you. He knows I am on your side. He would call the police.

"And now I am out of a job." Cesara sniffed.

"Oh, he'll be calling you again. You are too good a cook to give up, and you know how he loves his food! Give him a couple of days, and he will be ringing. He'll be begging you to come back, I assure you." Nigel patted her arm and babbled on.

How soothing Nigel could sound, Emma thought in disgust. He is just as good a con man as Cyril. He understands nothing about trust and loyalty. Cesara is right to worry. Riccardo will never hire her back, not in a million years.

Water Gates, Window Boxes on a Small Canal

"Here, Cesara. Take something to tide you over." Nigel reached inside his pocket and pulled out a roll of bills.

"Remember the bonus I gave you for finding the earl's notebook and showing it to me? They did not even notice it was missing, remember? We need you. Your help is very valuable." He slipped folded bills into the woman's hand. Emma's face showed her surprise. So it was true! Cesara had taken the notebook.

"We are getting so close to finding the picture. By the law of averages it's bound to turn up soon and then you will be paid a real bonus. You won't have to worry with cooking ever again."

"So you found nothing in the kitchen?" Cesara asked, quickly pocketing the bills. She did not look at either of the men but kept her eyes lowered.

"Well, no," Nigel answered. "The timing was a bit off and we could not actually go inside. We were at the window just after he put out the fire and rolled the rubbish bin into the canal. We saw Riccardo didn't feel like doing anything but sitting, nursing his burns. He wasn't fit enough to look around anywhere, to go to something hidden as we had hoped. He simply flopped down and held up his hands. The chap seemed quite undone so we left."

You would be undone too, if you had burned your hands badly in such a courageous, heroic act. Emma raged in silence. She thought how unlikely it was that Nigel might ever commit such a selfless act. Oh, how she longed to see the three of them led off in chains.

It took all of her will power to keep silent as the meeting ended and the three parted, quickly blending into the trickle of tourists trudging to and from the church. Emma saw them turn down a small side street knowing she must not follow them, but hurry instead to Rosamund's flat. She had caused her friends to be late already for the appointment to visit the dressmaker.

Walking rapidly, she thought over what she had learned at the *Salute.* How determined Nigel Sleight could be when he didn't achieve his purpose. He would not give up, even when pressure escalated. So Cesara had shown Nigel the leather notebook from the library. She must have taken it away from the house. Perhaps most important of all, Emma had learned they were now considering the use of force to discover the picture's hiding place.

~~~~

"Whatever is the matter?" Rosamund exclaimed, reading Emma's worried expression as she entered the flat.

"Sorry I'm a little late. I've just been a witness to something rather amazing and I am trying to process what I've just seen in front of *Santa Maria della Salute.*"

"So far out of the way! What were you doing there?" Rosamund's voice sounded cross as she studied Emma. "You didn't forget our appointment with Vittoria, did you?"

"No, of course not," Emma answered, nodding to Vittoria, perched calmly on Rosamund's sofa. Venetians seemed to have little awareness of time, she had noticed.

"I saw Cyril and Nigel get off the *vaporetto* at the Accademia Bridge, and I followed them. That is where they led me." Vittoria and Rosamund looked at her in amazement.

Rosamund's frown deepened. "Those two! Whatever could they have to talk about? Cyril seems to be spending a lot of time in Venice, away from Prague. Vittoria just told me he called in at Gallery Vianello some time back because he had an appointment with Nigel."

"Just when was that?" Emma asked quickly.

""Soon after the Lido picnic, a few days later, the Tuesday or Wednesday after, I recall," Vittoria replied. "I thought I told you about that, Emma." Emma shook her head; it was a later meeting she had mentioned.

"Perhaps it was the day I found him here, waiting for Rosamund, to return her key. I know for a fact he and Nigel are working together," Emma said softly. "When he left that day, he said he had business in the Rialto. At the time I supposed he meant consulate business."

"When he arrived at Gallery Vianello, Nigel bundled him right off into the office we share and shut the door," Vittoria remarked. "I couldn't hear anything from my little desk. But I imagine it was something underhand they were plotting." The two girls looked at her.

"Why would you think that?" Emma asked.

Vittoria told them she had seen Nigel weeks earlier check out Piranesi etchings on approval to take to a client and return without them or any record of sale. Apparently he had sold them for himself and pocketed the money. Later Vittoria found the record of the withdrawal had disappeared from the receipt book.

"So Riccardo has been right all along. Nigel Sleight cannot be trusted," Emma said softly.

"Not a shred of trust!" Vittoria agreed.

As they mulled over Vittoria's revelation, Rosamund spoke up.

"There's a rumor going around the consulate that Cyril has been given the sack."

"You mean, he is not working at the consulate in Prague anymore?" Emma said quickly. Rosamund nodded.

Emma could hardly believe Cyril had lost his job. How did people cope with a crook in the family? She saw the figure of a careworn mother in a kitchen somewhere in England, sitting at a table in tears, reading a letter from her son Cyril containing nothing but bad news. How did such unfortunate parents cope? Her thoughts swerved to Pen Browning, Robert and Elizabeth's son, a near cipher when he grew up. Yet he had managed to acquire *Ca' Rezzonico,* the beautiful Grand Canal *palazzo* nearby, thanks to his wife's money, of course. Emma passed by it almost every day. At least Pen had provided a beautiful home in Venice for his aged, widowed father's final days. And had managed to stay out of jail. She doubted Cyril was capable of such filial or any other type of devotion.

"Fiona told me. It may be just a rumor. But he is definitely spending a lot more time in Venice," Rosamund was saying. "Scads of people have mentioned it to me. It's not embarrassing anymore."

Poor Rosamund. Emma shifted in her chair. She hadn't managed to shake off completely the association with Cyril. She began telling them what she had learned after following the men to the church.

"Cesara, the cook at *Ca' Sospira* is working with both of them. I managed to hear enough to learn she was partly responsible for setting the kitchen fire last week at *Ca' Sospira.* She was the one they persuaded to lay the kindling in the rubbish bin.

"Still, the attempt failed, Riccardo is recovering. The burn scars on Riccardo's hands are beginning to heal." Emma looked thoughtful.

"You think Riccardo is overly suspicious, Emma. I know you do. But many times his caution is well placed. Look at Nigel. Riccardo was right about him, wasn't he? And Riccardo is brave and honest as well," Vittoria declared with great passion.

Vittoria, who had been spending a lot of time at *Ca' Sospira* while Riccardo recovered from the burns, seemed determined to help search out the missing Carpaccio. She was proving to be a valuable ally, Emma realized. She was wise enough to realize that finding it could play an important role in her future with Riccardo. Vittoria looked at her watch and suggested they visit the seamstress at once.

"Cesara lives quite near *Signora* Zambelli. I saw her one day a while back after I had tea with Riccardo at *Ca' Sospira.* I was hurrying to her house for a fitting, and I saw Cesara walk into the street near the Zambelli cottage. Shall I show you the house?"

Emma was on her feet in an instant, the visit to the dressmaker overshadowed by the possibility of locating the house where Cesara lived. Led by Vittoria, the girls hurried down the stairs and made their way in the direction of the Salute church, turning down a *rio* near the Peggy Guggenheim Museum. From the canal it was only a few steps to *Calle Querini,* the street where Rosamund led them.

"Here is number 252, Hidden Nest, the little house owned by Olga Rudge, the violinist, whose companion of over fifty years was Ezra Pound, the American poet. He spent ten years in a psychiatric institution, did you know?" Vittoria pointed to a plaque over the door. A set of blue bed sheets flapped in the breeze on a line stretching from an upper floor window. A wireless inside was playing classical music.

Emma told them the violinist Olga Rudge specialized in the works of Antonio Vivaldi.

"She is an American too, you know. From Ohio, I believe. I read in an article just the other day; she is still alive. Pound died a few years back."

"He was buried on the island of *San Michele*, a great honor accorded only to a few non-Venetians," Vittoria said. Emma and Rosamund knew it was the burial island of Venice.

The three stood for a moment looking at the tiny house which had welcomed so many authors, painters and musicians during the couples' occupancy. It seemed more like a doll's house than a space for humans, Emma thought. Impossibly small for anything but the simplest gatherings with tiny rooms on three floors.

They continued walking toward a cottage nearby, painted grey with weatherbeaten red shutters which had faded to a pale tone. It was not unattractive, Emma thought, surrounded by a few rose bushes tumbling about in a rambling manner. So this is where Cesara lived.

As they walked by, two men came toward them from the opposite direction, making their way to the front door of the house. Strangers to Emma, they looked like workmen. She knew she had never seen them before. Both were tall, one had a large hooked nose, the other with a pronounced squint to his left eye. They hurried inside as the door opened and shut quickly.

Emma was startled by Vittoria's sharp intake of breath.

"What is it?" she asked.

"Those men!" Vittoria said. "I just realized they are the same ones who came to the gallery, asking to see Nigel ages ago."

"You're sure?" Emma asked. "And when was that?"

"Why, before the Lido picnic I believe," Vittoria answered.

"Goodness!" Emma looked at the two. "Could these be the men Filiberto and Riccardo described when we went with Nigel to *Ca' Sospira* that night, after the picnic? Remember Rosamund? Didn't Filiberto call them Hook Nose and Squint Eye?"

"The pair who overpowered them and tied them up?" Rosamund whispered. "Clever, Emma! They surely are the ones who turned the library into such a mess searching for the Carpaccio. One had a hooked nose and the other a squint, just as Filiberto said. I remember now. Someone said they were distant relatives of Cyril's wife. Could they be related to Cesara as well?"

They hurried away, not wanting to be discovered should Cesara be peering out behind a curtain at the tiny window. They made their way to the dressmaker's house on a small pathway behind *Calle Querini*. There was no street sign, nor were there house numbers. Venetians had so many places to keep track of, Emma reflected. No wonder the city seemed like a village in so many ways.

Signora Zambelli, barely five feet tall, seemed to blend into the flower-infused wallpaper which covered the walls of her cottage. She spoke with a lisp, white hair arranged in a bun which threw into prominence her regular but faded features. The eyes shone with black fire as nimble fingers roamed the surface of her work table, picking up stray pins which she plunged with fierce jabs into a blue satin pincushion shaped like a giant plum at her elbow and held in place by an elastic band. Another smaller pad at her wrist sprouted needles. In a friendly voice, she welcomed them.

Rosamund and Vittoria ordered new frocks on the spot. Emma however, busily mulling over in her mind the increasing role Cesara was playing in the drama of the missing Carpaccio, paid scant attention to the swatches of fabric and patterns. She could not focus on her wardrobe when she had discovered so much about dangers looming at *Ca' Sospira*. She longed for time alone to piece together events of the afternoon into some sort of pattern.

From observations at the church to the appearance of the two men who apparently had earlier strong-armed their way into *Ca' Sospira,* Emma sensed a correlation. She needed time and quiet to work it out. Before leaving the seamstress however, she redirected her thoughts and ordered two fine lawn stoles for evening wear as gifts and promised to collect them before leaving Venice.

13

A Mighty Leap onto the Great Elmley Bed

That night, as Emma lay on the daybed in her small room, she felt herself a prisoner of the sticky midsummer heat as never before. Venice seemed airless as she tossed and turned on the narrow bed, unable to rest. As the night wore on, she could hear Rosamund's even breathing through the open doors of their rooms.

At last falling into slumber, Emma dreamed she was walking toward Accademia *vaporetto* stop, bound on some nameless journey. It was an inky, moonless night when she was suddenly seized from behind by Nigel Sleight and Cyril Meadowes. Tightly grasping her arms, they marched her quickly to the dock and bundled her into a shadowy gondola moored alongside.

She opened her mouth to cry out in alarm and felt something cold and hard, like the barrel of a revolver, boring into her back. Caught up in the reality of the dream, she gasped, almost choking with fear, as the cry died in her throat. Where were they taking her?

She recognized the figure of the gondolier she had seen before as she looked from her little roundel window in Rosamund's flat, only this time in her dream she was pushed into his boat, being borne away. So the gondolier was working with Nigel. Where were they taking her? Silently she cried out repeatedly in her deep slumber. The dream seemed so real she felt cold drops of perspiration on her forehead, tremors of her hands clutching frantically at the covers.

"We are taking you to *San Michele*, Emma," Nigel told her, all pretense stripped away. Lips drawn tight in an unyielding line, he bore little resemblance to the relaxed, friendly young man she had met at luncheon her first day at *Ca' Sospira*. She cowered under the gaze of those cold eyes, wondering how she had ever thought of him as a friend. *San Michele*, the burial island of Venice! A desolate place, no houses, only headstones. She trembled.

"We're leaving you there alone unless you tell us where Riccardo has hidden the Carpaccio." Cyril smiled at the warning, looking giddy with anticipation. He clearly wanted the worst to happen, she thought fearfully.

She felt the cold spray from the canal on her face as the gondola moved faster through the inky quiet of the waters. Her knees were like jelly. Her voice had deserted her. And if she couldn't speak, tell them, she did not know where the

Carpaccio was hidden, would they shoot her, leave her to die on that island of death? Amazingly she found her voice and began to scream.

She awoke, bathed in perspiration, with Rosamund's hands shaking her shoulders and calling to her.

"Emma, Emma! Wake up! Wake up! You're having a nightmare!" Her pillow and hair were damp and her legs were tangled in the rumpled covers of her bed. Slowly, almost drunkenly she swam into consciousness, sat up and allowed Rosamund to lead her to the kitchen. Sipping hot tea with plenty of sugar, Emma recounted the awful dream.

"I was terrified; I am so afraid something like this will actually happen to me, or to Riccardo, or to poor, dear Filiberto."

Clucking with sympathy like a mother hen yet reminding her it was only a bad dream, Rosamund took away the teacup and brought her digestive biscuits and a cup of warm milk. Then she helped Emma back into a freshly tidied bed, where she drifted into a calming sleep.

~~~~

The following morning Emma found herself at *Ca' Sospira,* the nightmare remembered but no longer an obsession. She decided to visit the room where the great Elmley bed stood, even though she knew it had not been the late earl's sleeping room during his final years.

When she had questioned Riccardo about this bit of information picked up quite by accident during Luisa's visit, Riccardo had muttered something about the sagging floor due to the extreme weight of the great Elmley Bed. It was decided to set up the bed in the room across the hall, which had stronger load-bearing beams. The move had occurred at one of the rare times when Riccardo had been absent, during the term examination week at the University; he had taken a short leave to study.

Now that sounds like some convenient explanation, Emma thought. Could something more important than a sagging floor have caused them to move the earl's bed? And hadn't he told her it occurred a couple of years before the earl's demise?

She entered the room and was again struck by the cold feeling it always brought to her, dominated as it was by grays and blues of Lady Sybil's needlepoint hanging at the head of the bed. She bent closer to inspect it.

Elmley Castle, the manor house, home to the family since the sixteenth century, stood in an imposing landscape of carefully edited trees and hillocks leading up to the building. It had been given a balanced classical façade in the eighteenth century by an unknown architect at the same time the fabled landscape expert Capability Brown was called in to impose the stamp of his Arcadian, idealized style on the parkland surrounding the house.

Medieval parterres had been ripped out and confining garden walls knocked down to present all-encompassing vistas of nature, carefully edited by Capability, and brought up close to the windows of the house. Gothic was banished. Perhaps that is why the overwhelming effect of the needlework over the giant bed seemed cold and out of place at *Ca' Sospira*. After all, Venice, clothed in glorious medieval architecture, proclaimed itself the most Gothic of cities.

She perched on the edge of the bed, studying the work in greater detail. Why there was even a moat around the castle. Had that been a reconstruction by Lady Sybil of a former moat, discovered in some research on her part into the history of the house? More likely it was a suggestion from her husband, she decided, recalling Lady Sybil's indifference to serious reading such as history, her preferences firmly lodged somewhere between *Country Life* and *The Lady* magazines, by all accounts.

A scratching noise at the door made her start, and she peered around the bedpost in time to see Tintoretto nose his way inside the room. He padded softly toward her, nails of his paws clicking on the highly polished tile floor. Emma leaned over to put her arms around him and hugged his neck, careful to avoid the swinging tail. As she straightened up, Tintoretto suddenly sprang onto the bed. He settled himself and the tail began its rhythmic thumping of the coverlet.

"Hop down at once, 'Tinto! Riccardo would be livid if he knew you were up here!"

But her warning came too late. An ominous sound of splitting wood filled the room and Emma felt the mattress beneath her sag as a falling slat struck the floor with a clatter.

Now we're in trouble, Emma thought as she slid hastily off the bed to the floor, leaned over and looked underneath to survey the damage. Lifting the edge of the bed skirt, she saw a splintered slat, perhaps one of the original timbers hewn from the mighty Elmley oak which fell during a fierce storm, a disaster which had done great damage in the county of Worcestershire. Emma had read about it in one of several family histories in the library.

She knew about the building of the bed from perusing another of those books. The Elmleys had decided to fashion a bed built from the fallen oak timbers as a symbol of survival. Emma gleaned more details about the bed from Filiberto, whose brain was a bulging warehouse of legend and incident about Elmleys through the ages.

She remembered reading in one book that Charles I, stopping in the nearby Royalist town of Oxford during England's Civil War, had been forced to flee the approaching Roundheads and paused for a cool drink of water offered by an earlier Lord Elmley, under the Elmley Oak, then a much younger tree. What a lovely family legend Emma thought as she recalled from English history that the Stuart monarch, in spite of possessing great elegance and charm, was unable to keep his head.

There had been more to the story. The same Elmley who proffered the cool water to his king had later taken shelter in a secret room upstairs when the Roundheads eventually reached Worcestershire, hunting for the missing monarch. The sovereign was long gone, but this Elmley, perhaps realizing King Charles with his dwindling Royalist forces would not escape capture, had remained at home on leave a little longer, prudence forcing him to hide when the Roundheads, led by Oliver Cromwell, appeared at his gates.

Legend recorded that Lady Elmley entertained the uninvited Roundheads that night with a sumptuous banquet; so much wine was drunk the enemy spent the night groggily drowsing under the banquet tables and slunk off in great shame and humiliation the next morning without searching for valuables, King Charles, or the Earl of Elmley. This noblewoman's perspicacity saved the house from being raided and torched; she also saved her husband's head.

Nothing however, could save the doomed King. At his beheading in 1649, England lost the greatest collector of art it has ever known; his collection formed the beginnings of the present Royal Collection. Emma gave a sad little sigh at the ironies of fate history served up in interesting detail to anyone who bothered to look for it.

She took a moment to reflect on the layers of meaning which had inspired the Elmley family for so many years. Each recorded memory, each legend, retold and passed on to upcoming generations, wove a gossamer net stronger than steel around the Elmleys, clothing them in loyalty. No wonder duty and responsibility were so ingrained. Legends like this one had been drummed into heads of all the little Elmleys from the cradle.

"This day dreaming of the Elmleys isn't helping me fix this disaster," she muttered to Tintoretto in the silent room. "What shall I do now?"

14

Knocked Breathless by a Fall off Cupcake

Emma touched the fallen slat with the toe of her shoe as she continued to stand by the bed. Tintoretto was looking up at her, waiting expectantly. What now? She dreaded telling Riccardo what had happened. He was sure to be upset. Could she possibly fit the slat back into the bed frame? But as her toe pushed it in another exploratory prod, the end of the slat protruded from bed coverings which reached to the floor. Carefully she bent down and grasped the end of the board.

She tugged as it slid easily into sight, a piece about two feet long where it had splintered. The splintered slat had been wrapped in the center with heavy linen cloth tied around it where it had given way. But why use cloth for such an obvious carpenter's job? Strong wood was what was needed. It made no sense.

Unwinding the linen was easy. The binding twine securing it fell into shreds at her touch. A piece of parchment bearing the Elmley crest slid away. It was not a splint after all, rather a hiding place for a secret letter! She picked it up and began to read. As her fingers unrolled the scroll of paper, she came to the heading, "My Dear Son:

Emma paused, raised her eyes and gazed, unseeing, at the dog. If this was parchment from the time of the Royalists and Roundheads, wouldn't it have decomposed before the linen covering? No! Wait! It had to be something much more recent! Understanding, like an electric charge, surged through her. She felt her heart beating furiously under the simple blouse. Heavens! What had she found? She looked down at Tintoretto, alert and observing her actions.

"'Tinto! 'Tinto! What have you stumbled upon?" Emma felt the peculiar tingling sensation at the back of her neck. Something of far greater import was about to be revealed. She read on.

"This is a difficult time, beginning preparations for what I am sure will be my demise, but certain things must be put in order before I leave this earth and you must take care of them for me. First of all, I must have the Elmley Bed sent back to England along with the needlepoint tapestry of Elmley Castle worked by my wife Lady Sibyl. Those two items must be returned to the place where they belong, and that is, of course, Elmley Castle. The second charge which I leave in your hands is this: You are to have for your own the Carpaccio painting of the two girls on the *altana* bleaching their hair which is the prize of my entire collection. It was your mother's favorite and she always claimed that, like Venice, it belonged closest to my heart. I do believe she was right."

Whatever could this mean? Emma looked up from the letter, gazing at, yet not seeing, the needlepoint hanging above her of faraway Worcestershire. Surely the late earl could not have meant the Carpaccio? He mentioned the needlepoint tapestry earlier, worked by the present Lord Elmley's mother, Lady Sybil, did he not? The letter was, after all, addressed to 'My Dear Son.' However, both Filiberto and Riccardo had told her Lady Sybil had disliked the Carpaccio intensely, loathed it would be more accurate. But the letter did not specify 'Lady Sybil'. It only described 'your mother's favorite' in referencing the Carpaccio, and described it carefully, leaving no room for doubt.

She read it again. The letter was addressed to 'My Dear Son'. Could it be meant for someone else? Not the son who would supervise the setting up of the Elmley Oak bed when it arrived in England. Rather, a son in Venice who would be sure to find the letter when he supervised the dismantling of the bed and sealing up the crate which would be shipped back to England? *This was a letter for Riccardo!*

Long ago, as a small child, Emma had been knocked breathless by a fall off the back of her pony Cupcake while riding in the Blue Ridge mountains of Virginia. The same sudden shock of breathlessness overwhelmed her as she looked down at the faded ink of the parchment in her hands. What she had secretly wondered about and turned over and over in her innermost thoughts was true. Riccardo Montgano was the son of Lord Elmley.

So, the veiled rumors about Riccardo's parentage were right. There had been a Montgano husband, a bounder, if her informants were correct, but Riccardo's father was none other than the late Lord Elmley, Lord William Richard Elmley! The Earl's friendship with the shadowy Esperanza Farsetti Montgano had indeed been a friendship of the most tangible kind. It had produced an heir.

She stood there, absently stroking the dog standing at attention beside her. Furiously she tried working out dates. If Riccardo were in his late thirties, his birth date would have been around 1940 perhaps even a few years earlier. The present earl had to be several years older. The letter was written in the late earl's faint but regular hand Emma had come to recognize in her research. No doubt about that. She was certain it matched. She read on.

> "Perhaps you have wondered about my reticence in speaking to you of this, but I can assure you, having the privilege of seeing you grow to maturity so close to me has been one of the greatest joys of my life. Not telling you of my feelings has been the cruelest punishment I could ever have imagined; I hope you will understand and forgive me. I cannot heap disgrace on my late wife, Lady Sybil, and the children of our marriage.

They also weigh heavily on me, those responsibilities to my children in England, who must be dealt with fairly. It is how they will judge me, their father, which frightens me. The title will be handed down to my eldest son William. I believe he is a man of honor and integrity. I will explain the situation to William when I reach England, for it is my intention to leave for Worcestershire at once; my days are dwindling and I feel a great compulsion to end this earthly life on my native soil. Uppermost in my mind is my wish to set things right with you and with William. My hope is that you will be not only friends, but true brothers.

"To you, I am leaving *Ca Sospira* and its contents. Its best chance for survival lies under your ownership. Your love and affection for the property has been evident in your inspired stewardship here. I have set aside funds in trust for its maintenance and upkeep which are awaiting you at the time of my death at *Banco d'Italia* on the Piazza San Marco. Also in the trust are funds to provide for you amply during your lifetime. At your demise they will revert to the Elmley trust which was created specifically in Venice to handle expenses of *Ca' Sospira*. Should you decide to marry, then your heirs will receive your property and assets of course.

"The furnishings from the Venice house should remain in Venice, and they belong to you, except for the Elmley oak bed and Lady Sybil's tapestry hanging above the bed. Both the tapestry and the bed belong in England as I am certain you would agree. I request that you personally oversee the dismantling of the bed and the crating of the tapestry. Before sending off the tapestry you must remove it from its frame and make an assessment as to its condition. Vittoria Dandolo will assist you in this. She recently received training in England at Roedean School in needlework preservation. She will be of great assistance to you. Her family is both honorable and trustworthy. It is important that you contact her to help with the packing of the tapestry for its journey home to England, along with the Elmley bed."

Emma reread the closing lines. What could it mean? Was the old man hinting that Vittoria would be a suitable wife? Or had he merely known of her expertise, gained in England at the private school Roedean and knew it would be a great help to Riccardo? Was Vittoria somehow the key to finding the missing Carpaccio?

Emma sank into the nearest chair, her head spinning. Whatever else the implications were, this news meant that Riccardo and Vittoria could be married. Finally, after years of selfless service, the rewards were at hand for Riccardo.

Minutes later, contemplating the enormity of what she had read, she wondered why the late earl's orders had not been carried out? The Elmley bed and the tapestry were still in Venice. Why? Riccardo was as yet unaware of his good fortune contained in this letter, and surely the Elmley bed should have gone back to England years ago, accompanied by Lady Sybil's tapestry of Elmley Castle.

A Freight Boat on Dorsoduro

Next her thoughts flew to the personal tragedy of the seventh earl of Elmley. His unconventional life had perhaps led him to great happiness, but what a price he had paid! She was reminded of the sad little lines by the poet Edgar Allan Poe which he had placed in the catalogue of paintings, on the same page where the pressed rose was inserted. How terribly poignant those lines, she thought, after discovering this letter.

"In visions of the dark night
I have dreamed of joys departed,
But a waking dream of life and light
Hath left me broken hearted."

It was clear to her that Poe's lines were recalled by the earl as he awaited his death. Emma's eyes filled with tears, and it was some time later before she was able to compose herself and return to the library with Tintoretto.

She left the splintered slat where it lay under the sagging bed as she crept out of the room with the dog, carefully closing the door. Tintoretto failed to understand why his mistress had suddenly become so quiet as he padded behind her to the library. Emma quickly went over the notes she had made after her most recent meeting with *Signora* Puglio. May 22, 1965 was the date of the late earl's death, two days after the letter of provenance concerning the Carpaccio had been sent by the Puglios. The letter Emma was holding in her hands had been dated May 21, *one day before he died!* Hardly time for the earl to make the letter and its contents known to Riccardo if he had been away, visiting those distant cousins in Switzerland. Had the man some forewarning of imminent death? It seemed likely.

There had been no opportunity to confer with the heir, young Elmley in England. The old earl died unexpectedly in his sleep, before the bed could be dismantled and sent off on the long journey. Young Elmley knew nothing of his father's wish to return the bed and the needlepoint, nor did Riccardo. And neither son knew the old man's intention to leave the Venetian house and its contents to Riccardo, complete with a trust for its perpetuation and upkeep.

The late earl, desperate to get the letter to his natural son, must have gotten help, perhaps from Filiberto, to affix the parchment to the slat. But it was unlikely he would have confided in his servant telling him the contents of the letter. It would not have been seemly in that proud family, Emma realized, no matter how loyal a servant Filiberto had been. No, the late earl must have trusted only Riccardo's tact and discretion to handle matters in the most discreet manner possible. But things had not worked out that way. Riccardo was absent when he died. Emma twisted a strand of hair around her finger.

When the time came to dismantle the bed and tapestry, Riccardo would surely find the letter. But that had not occurred. Why did the bed remain in Venice, along with the tapestry? The oversight, if that is what it was, had delayed the revelation of his parentage, and deprived him of what was rightfully his. And the heir, William? Probably, if he thought of the bed and tapestry at all, it had been one of many pressing duties, and he filed it far back in his mind, overwhelmed when the old earl died so suddenly. And the amazing letter revealed nothing whatsoever of the whereabouts of the missing Carpaccio. Where was it?

Letter in hand, Emma made her way to Riccardo.

Entering his office Emma noticed that his hands had recovered almost completely from the burns. The bandages were small now, insignificant unless he opened his palms. Emma knew later that morning he was expecting Vittoria, who would accompany him to a luncheon at the Accademia in honor of a visiting lecturer from Rome speaking on baroque and renaissance silver. She wondered how best to present the letter. Dread of the approaching moment made her decide to discharge the matter quickly, as tactfully as she could.

In a few carefully chosen words, Emma told him of the broken slat and what she had discovered wrapped around it after it fell to the floor. Without further explanation she handed over the sheet of parchment, still rolled up like a scroll.

"The bindings gave way when I touched it. I am afraid I unwittingly read a very private letter, meant for your eyes alone, but I had no idea of what it contained." She turned to go as he beckoned her back with a wave of his hand. He was in a very good mood, she guessed, anticipating the luncheon and lecture with Vittoria, at the Accademia.

"When I first saw you Emma, little did I realize 'Tinto would become Dr. Watson to your Sherlock Holmes," he said, a smile playing about the corners of his mouth.

"The broken slat is nothing. Please do not distress yourself. It can easily be mended."

The leaden weight on Emma's chest lifted a little. He certainly felt better. Would his good feelings withstand the shock of what he was about to discover? How might he react? Would he be angry, frustrated at a secret kept far too long? As he unrolled the letter and began to read, she tiptoed out, closing the door and giving him the privacy such news demanded. Emma returned to the library.

~~~~

Riccardo sat motionless. Seconds became minutes. He remained still, eyes never leaving the page. Then he began absently stroking Tintoretto's head with the back of his hand. Riccardo looked away from the sheet of heavy paper, lost in his private thoughts. What he had often allowed himself to dream about had at last come true in the few seconds it had taken to read the letter. It was a sobering thought and he set his eyes again on the words in front of him.

Tintoretto gave a soft whine.

"Forgive me, old boy . . . . I just can't seem to take it in. How could this have happened? His mind reached back to the bleak time when the earl had died. Confusion, sadness, hurrying home from the Swiss relatives, shock at *Ca' Sospira*. And somehow, in the tumult, the bed had not been dismantled, crated up and shipped to England. Had he known it was what his father had wanted . . . but he should have sensed it, realized, without being told! But for the numbness, the emptiness, the shock of it all, he would have known. Who would have paid attention to him? Nobody. If there was no word from the earl. When the sharp pangs of grief subsided, he simply had let matters take their course. After all, he was only one of the employees, more elevated than a servant perhaps, but an employee, nonetheless. He shook his head. He heard Vittoria climbing the stairs.

"*Caro*, are you ready? We must not be late!" Her voice trailed off as she saw his face, a study in contrasts. Sadness, joy, mingled with doubt, surprise.

"I thought you'd never come, Vittoria. *Carissima*. I have wonderful news." He rose and folded her in his arms. "Pardon me, *Cara*. I am afraid I am going to need a few moments to recover from this. Would you read it aloud please?" His eyes looked suspiciously moist as he held out the letter.

"Of course, Riccardo." Vittoria took the letter from him and began to read.

~~~~

In the library Emma sat at her desk, dazed, thinking a walk would clear her head. She wished she had brought Tintoretto down with her. It was so hard not sharing the good news with somebody.

Before she could straighten papers and tidy her desk, however, Vittoria sailed into the room followed by Riccardo.

"Darling, how marvelous you look! We've come to say how pleased we are you and Tintoretto brought us such good news. Your eyes are sparkling and, look at you, your cheeks are blushing!"

If an angel had suddenly flown into the room Emma could not have been happier. Vittoria was the best person in all the world to receive this news with Riccardo; Vittoria would see that he accepted it and didn't worry about what might go wrong. She hurried to greet them.

"It is very good news," she smiled, taking their hands. "Just the kind of marvelous news that begs for a celebration lunch."

And making plans for meeting her later in the afternoon, Riccardo and Vittoria embraced her and then floated off toward the Accademia for their lecture and luncheon.

~~~~

She heard the heavy door at the front of the house close as she shifted papers on her desk half-heartedly, her mind soaring leagues beyond the walls of the library, mulling over the astounding letter. It took her to Worcestershire for a few imagined vignettes when the news arrived at Elmley Castle. There was no way of being sure how it would be received. She collected her handbag and straw hat along with Tintoretto's leash and eased out of *Ca' Sospira,* firmly closing it behind her. Following a short stroll with Tintoretto, window shopping in some of the designer boutiques along *Via Venezia,* she returned to the house. Emma would have been unable to describe a single gown, or handbag, or pair of shoes or even a very small scarf that she had gazed at fixedly for five minutes in one of the glittering shop windows. Tintoretto, accustomed to these lapses, seemed not to mind, as though he understood her thoughts were firmly engaged elsewhere.

Lucia brought in a sandwich on a tray for her and took Tintoretto to the kitchen for a snack. After eating, Emma drifted upstairs to the room where the Elmley Bed stood under the needlepoint hanging above the headboard.

She thought furiously about the Carpaccio. Its disappearance must have occurred about the time of the earl's death. It had stayed in Venice when the coffin had begun the long sea journey to England. The bed's removal had been postponed. Was the delay because of the stress and shock of the earl's unexpected demise? Had the late earl asked one of the servants to tie the letter, carefully wrapped in linen, to the bed slat just before he died? She had read of amazing accomplishments of people who knew they were dying. Could he have managed it alone?

The return of the bed and tapestry to England likely had been overlooked in the shock of the earl's sudden death. It was true, the young earl had faced a mountain of responsibilities when he arrived to take charge. Yes, everything must have been thrown into confusion both in Venice and in Worcestershire. She saw the earl, overwhelmed with grief at his father's passing, multiple duties raining down on him: accompanying the body home, arranging for the management of *Ca' Sospira,* keeping on the loyal staff who had served the late earl in Venice. Days drifted into weeks, months, years and the bed remained in place. Emma was beginning to understand how the unthinkable had occurred. Not only was the letter undiscovered, but the hiding place of the Carpaccio was still a secret.

The careful instructions and startling revelations contained in the letter were never brought to light, unlikely as that seemed. They lay untouched and unopened, tied to a slat under the bed.

We may never know exactly how it occurred, she reasoned. Or maybe, if we put our minds to work, we'll come up with a plausible explanation. She found herself wishing for Sam's understanding and patience. His steady surgeon's hands were guided by logic and deliberation. What a great help he would be, if only he were in Venice.

Yes, logic had been a guiding force of the late earl's life. But no. Emma reined in her thoughts. That wasn't entirely true.

What about Riccardo and Esperanza Farsetti? Here was glaring evidence of one instance in the earl's life when logic did not rule. In spite of what the Elmley patriarch may have believed were his highest intentions, passion broke free in his long relationship with Esperanza and he had to deal with the attendant complications as best he could. Emma pondered this quietly for some minutes. His imperfections rendered him human after all, like the rest of us walking the planet, plodding along day by day. She liked him the better for it, somehow. Mankind's shared threads of goodness and weakness wove humanity together in the final analysis. It had ever been so. Redemption lay in how we met evil, a drop of poison in the aquifer of purity. It surely brought us all, at some time, to the brink.

15

What Is A Wahoo? An Indian War Cry?

Approaching footsteps and the melodious peal of Vittoria's laugh alerted Emma to Riccardo and Vittoria's approach. Good grief, Emma thought, glancing at her watch. Have I been up here all this time? They were back from the Accademia, coming down the corridor toward the bedroom.

"We guessed we might find you here," Vittoria called as she and Riccardo entered, walking arm in arm.

"How was the luncheon?"

"Luncheon?" Riccardo looked blank.

"We never got there," Vittoria confessed, flushing prettily. "Guess what!"

"Impossible," Emma smiled. "You mean you and Riccardo skipped that lunch? I cannot believe it!"

"The truth is, we did. And best of all, we're engaged! We're going to be married!" Emma gave a great "Wahoo!," and hurried to embrace Vittoria.

"*Dio Mio!* Whatever was that?" Riccardo, startled, took a backward step. "An Indian war cry?"

"Something along those lines," Emma grinned. "We learn it in Virginia when we're papooses, strapped to our mothers' backs. Riccardo, it's a Virginia hooray. Now, just tell me, how did this splendid news come about?" Vittoria's eyes sparkled.

"Riccardo proposed to me in Tommaso Migliori's gondola, smack in front of the *Palazzo Barbaro* right on the Grand Canal." Her words rang out like an aria; her face could only be described as radiant. Riccardo looked adoringly at her, reflecting on the amazing events of the day. Vittoria confided.

"We happened upon Tommaso soon after we left *Ca' Sospira*. He offered to take us to the Accademia. Then when he heard about the letter, he insisted on a longer ride. It was then that Riccardo whispered in my ear, proposed I mean." Vittoria lowered her eyes like a school girl.

Riccardo beamed and took up the account in a voice complementing the shine in his eyes. "Emma will not be satisfied until she knows every scrap there is to be learned.

"Tommaso and I have been friends since we were kids you see; he's always been willing to treat us to the visual pleasures of Venice from the comfort of his gondola, mostly after tourist hours, of course. Often late at night when the moon is at its most beguiling, shining on the waters he invites us. Today was an exception. He insisted we celebrate at once."

"So you never even got to the Accademia luncheon?" The pair stood in front of her like mischievous children, holding hands. She marveled at the unthinkable: Riccardo foregoing a meal.

"What a celebration there will be when you make your vows if this romantic interlude is any sign," Emma sighed. She thought of her mysterious gondolier poling the waters at night, visible from her bedroom window. He might well be Tommaso, Riccardo's generous and law-abiding friend. Perhaps there was nothing sinister after all in those moonlight gondola excursions she had looked down upon. Why Riccardo and Vittoria could have been his passengers! What a city! Would Venice ever run out of surprises?

Would she and Sam take a turn floating down the Grand Canal enjoying the moonlight from the viewpoint of one of the beautiful black *gondole*? She doubted dear, sensible Sam would see it as she did—or yearn for the enchantment she craved. He possessed a more logical turn of mind. Logic or no, she ached for his arrival.

"Just where and when will the big event take place? Or is the date set?"

"Later, later, when there is more time to reflect," Vittoria answered, coy yet practical, moving into business mode. She drew shapely brows into a frown.

"Now, there is work to be done. I propose to begin to carry out my duty as outlined in the late earl's letter and examine the tapestry. I think he must have had me picked out all along as the right person for Riccardo to marry, don't you, Emma? Such foresight, don't you agree?" Her eyes and her smile revealed she was joking.

"I barely knew him, of course. I met him once or twice when I was with my parents at big parties, probably during *carnivale*. Thinking back, I do remember one occasion when I had just finished my studies at Roedean and was glad to be back home. He asked me several questions about Roedean at some social occasion when we first met."

The three of them were in such high spirits, it was difficult to settle down. Laughing about their gondola ride, Riccardo recounted how Tommaso had to be prevailed upon in the strongest terms not to burst into the chorus of *O Sole Mio* as they sailed blissfully down the Canal in bright sunshine, oblivious to cameras trained on them from tourist laden *vaporetti*.

"Tommaso has invited us for another ride, when the moon rises, and he'll have champagne flutes and a bottle of *prosecco* on the little table covered by a tiny Persian carpet. We'll have a celebratory glass. He swears he'll bring three flutes so he can drink with us, and Riccardo is already worrying if we'll end up in the water with a tipsy gondolier in charge. Ugh! Those murky depths!" Vittoria laugh sounded like tinkling bells spilling from her lips.

Riccardo hugged her, impulsively, careful to keep his hands from clasping her too tightly. His fingers were still tender. She moved to the great bed, motioning Riccardo to a chair. Vittoria positioned herself on one side of the headboard.

"Help me, Emma. Riccardo must pamper his precious hands and watch our progress comfortably seated in that chair while you and I are going to lift that behemoth of a tapestry down from the wall."

Emma hurried to the other side of the bed. The wall hanging was heavy, but they managed to lower it gently onto the large bed, face down, without incident. The front had been scrupulously dusted; the back sprouted cobwebs which they quickly brushed aside.

"Now Emma, don't fret. I know what I'm about!" she began, catching the look of apprehension on Emma's face as she began tugging to unloose the backing. However the surface of the bed proved too soft for the work to proceed.

Vittoria thought for a moment then decided they should move it to the round table handily located in the center of the room.

Garden View of Grand Canal Palazzo

"Have no fear, Emma! I do know what I am doing. A luminary from the British Needlewoman's Society from London came to us at Roedean to give the art majors a course on conservation practices for old tapestries and needlework such as this. She was an expert, and I paid careful attention.

"You know the reverence our English friends have for old needlework. Well, in Venice we also have a lot of it on old furniture, bed coverings, casement hangings and so forth. Old Fortuny upholsteries, like those downstairs are lovely, don't you agree? Fabric restoration is a new sideline at Vianello's which I set up for them, and it makes a good profit in addition to selling pictures," she added, chattering as she worked.

Her strong fingers probed gently and at last she slipped the backing board out of its groove. Underneath, a large, blank sheet of heavy paper Emma guessed must be parchment or vellum, slightly smaller than the tapestry, lay face side down. Turning it over, Vittoria and Emma found themselves looking at a watercolor. Two young women in sun hats were sitting in the open air of the *altana* bleaching their blonde tresses. They wore dresses of the Renaissance in the Venetian style. They were silent as they admired the sparkling color, then turned to each other and began shrieking like peacocks, bringing Riccardo out of his chair.

"I say, Riccardo, oh Riccardo, do look!" Emma was laughing and tears were spilling down her cheeks at the same moment. She hugged Vittoria and then threw her arms around Riccardo's neck.

"Look what we've found!"

Emma's face held a few tears, a broad smile. Her thoughts flew to Sam, Maria Crawford, her professor at London University, *Signora* Puglio, Samantha Satchell at the Correr. Next, thoughts of her family crowded into her head. They would understand. Something precious, a long lost painting, had been found! Her heart pounded, her head was spinning. She seized Vittoria's hands and began waltzing around the room.

"*Bella, Bella, Bellissima,* so that's where it has been hiding," Riccardo murmured softly, bending over the painting, his face drinking in Carpaccio's colors and the two young girls bleaching their blonde tresses.

Emma looked at him and saw a man like Atlas, from whom a great burden had slid away. He knew *he* hadn't stolen the Carpaccio, but not being able to find it had cast a shadow over him.

At last he turned away from it and, locking arms with the two, mindful of his hands, he led them in an impromptu promenade round and round the room until they collapsed on the edge of the great bed laughing.

"Best we don't roost here," he said, quickly easing off. "We don't want a total collapse. The picture must have been placed behind the tapestry shortly before the earl died." As he gazed, a faraway look came into his eyes.

"I was away, in Switzerland, one of the few times I left him. If only I had realized . . ." His voice trailed off, becoming incoherent.

"Now, Riccardo, it wasn't anything you did. Don't say what if . . ." Quickly Vittoria stroked his cheek, placing an arm around his waist.

"His health had been failing, more than anyone imagined I suspect, but his Spartan upbringing meant he did not discuss such weaknesses as illness and decline. He was making hasty preparations to leave for England when he died. He realized it, but nobody else did, and he certainly wasn't going to tell anyone." Vittoria made the comforting sounds of affection, refusing to let him carry any burden of guilt.

"He was certain you would be the one in charge of dismantling and packing up the bed and the tapestry. That was revealed in the letter. I think he meant you to contact me because he thought I would be able to protect it. And I just might discover the Carpaccio underneath," she added primly as Riccardo and Emma burst into laughter.

"I agree completely with Vittoria," Emma said. "That was what I read into his directive to call her in to examine it. And if you and she wanted romance, well, so much the better. Sound advice it proved, since she led us right to the picture after fruitless searches, Riccardo."

"The colors are so much more vivid than I remember," Riccardo said dreamily. "I really find it most attractive, a very desirable Carpaccio."

Emma, near bursting point in her euphoria, hooted.

"A very desirable Carpaccio," is it? Don't be lukewarm, Riccardo. We've just found the most beautiful Renaissance watercolor in Venice, that's all! Wahoo!" And she and Vittoria circled the room again dancing a victory dance.

Breathless, they sank into chairs.

"Riccardo, who could the late earl have got to affix the letter to the bed slat in such a way? He wasn't physically able to do that. I suppose he could have slipped the picture into the tapestry earlier, when he was stronger. But the letter at the end, he knew it had to be hidden, quickly." Vittoria's ivory forehead wrinkled ever so slightly.

"Filiberto would have been the obvious choice," Riccardo replied. "He would have done anything the earl asked. He adored him and was faithful in every way. Surely you can see that, Vittoria."

"Yes," Emma spoke up, inserting herself into the exchange, "But surely Filiberto would have spoken, especially after the break-ins began. I was as determined to find the Carpaccio as you, remember? I have asked Filiberto several pertinent questions about the Carpaccio and the late earl. He pleaded ignorance each time."

"Would you reveal something so private to someone who was not a member of the family, Emma? Something so serious as, say, a stain on his master's character? To have revealed that would have been a violation of a lifetime of loyalty to his revered family. Emma, Emma, we Venetians will never be as open and trusting as you and your countrymen, but the English also can avoid ah, transparency, when it is deemed necessary."

Vittoria spoke up in a thoughtful voice. "I believe the picture was hidden earlier, before the earl lost his strength. He could have asked the tapestry to be taken down to inspect it, then done the insertion himself, when he was alone. But the letter was at the end."

Riccardo looked over the Carpaccio as Emma spoke up. "You are right, he would not have confided to a stranger, or even to a trusted servant, but you, Riccardo, after all, you *were* family, he would have told you. Surely Filiberto sensed it. Or perhaps it was somebody else, maybe even a nurse who helped out part-time when his health began to fail, or one of the maids, anybody who saw him on a daily basis whom he could ask privately to lend a hand. Surely the person who helped him had no idea what the letter contained, nor the tapestry either, for that matter."

"My guess is, the picture has been in its place here for many years. Remember, Filiberto considered himself 'family'; he knew the earl wanted the painting to be found by me," Riccardo replied. "Filiberto did not know exactly why, I imagine, but he had his suspicions, and he understood his job was to carry out his master's wishes. He did it without question, you may be sure of that. Trust and silence were an unspoken part of their perfect understanding of each other. He also knew I would be in charge when the bed and tapestry were ready to be sent home. Pleading ignorance to your inquiries was the only solution he could choose to keep from compromising his loyalty to the family. I hope you will not judge him too harshly, Emma."

"Of course not, Riccardo, you know I would not," Emma murmured, her tone thoughtful. "But why didn't he tell you?"

"Timing, Emma, timing. Filiberto was waiting for orders from the new earl, of course. His loyalty to both of them was seamless. He would never disappoint either."

"I once had a brilliant history professor at the Uni in London," Emma said, as she considered Riccardo's words. "He told us there was never a possibility for revolution in England such as the French experienced because the English aristocracy lived in such close harmony with their servants the need would never arise. In other words they trusted them, treating them as equals in many respects. Not so close the master-servant relationship apparently, in France."

"He was principled in his thinking about everything, the late earl," Vittoria said thoughtfully.

"But how could he have foreseen the new earl would put off the moving of the Elmley bed back to England? Poor young man! He had all he could do to make arrangements for Lord Elmley's coffin to be sent back, more arrangements ahead for the mammoth funeral in Worcestershire Cathedral. Nobody suspected that the old earl would expire before his wish to die in England could be fulfilled. It came as a shock to everyone." Vittoria sighed.

"And sending off the Elmley Bed and tapestry? What happened there, Riccardo? It is still here after all these years." Emma reminded him.

"I imagine it slipped to the end of a long list of things to be done when the young earl took over. Most pressing of course, was to turn around the vast estate in England, left for years without a resident owner and bring it back into a revenue-producing property. That must have looked like the labors of Hercules to Lord William." Riccardo looked down at his hands. "Ironic that the letter, the key to it all, should remain undiscovered all this time.

"And I didn't even suggest crating up the bed and the tapestry," Riccardo admitted, "Even though I thought of it often. You see, in a strange way, that bed was my last, tangible link to the earl. For reasons I did not understand at the time, I didn't want to part with it. In the end, bed and tapestry stayed."

"And the painting and the letter remained undiscovered," Vittoria murmured.

"I read in the library all of the clippings of the funeral in Worcester cathedral," Emma said, her thoughts turning to that sad time in the Elmley family.

"I expect you, Riccardo, were responsible for placing them there. The newspaper accounts are complete, listing everything one could possibly want to know about the cathedral service, the music played, which readings from the Bible were chosen, which quotations offered from Shakespeare and William Blake, two most English of authors. It even listed who attended from the aristocracy and the royal family. It makes fascinating reading.

"I learned that during World War II, for example, the king and queen decided that if Windsor Castle and Buckingham Palace became unsafe for the two little princesses, they would be taken to the country, to Elmley Castle, where they would be protected and cared for by their loyal subjects, the Elmleys. London did suffer terribly under the German blitz, of course."

"I cannot take credit, Emma. Filiberto saved the papers and the clippings. You see? It is his loyalty," Riccardo sighed. "I understand, because that is exactly how I felt."

"When I think of how close Lord Elmley's careful planning to reveal the whereabouts of the Carpaccio came to going undiscovered, it makes me quite faint and weak in the knees," Vittoria said.

"You have no idea, Vittoria," Riccardo answered. "Wondering, sensing how things might be about my parentage, yet I never heard a word. I had given up all hope."

"And what about the *Banco d'Italia*? Why did you never receive any letter from them? Or the lawyer in Venice? Surely the late earl had legal counsel in Venice ?" It seemed unbelievable to Emma the silence about Riccardo had dragged on for so many years.

"I think I know the reason for the bank's failure to act," Riccardo said. "The earl did not give instructions to them. He simply stored instructions in the safety deposit box there. They were marked *privato* and left in place, to be claimed at some future date by the new earl. I believe the trust officers had not a clue what they contained.

"As for the lawyer, I suppose the same thing again: the earl did not entrust his secret to anybody. The lawyer who handled matters concerning *Ca' Sospira*, was unaware, like everyone else. He was charged only with matters pertaining to the house, not carrying out any terms of a will or bequests."

"How difficult will that be, facing the bank and the lawyers?" Emma asked.

"I doubt if it will present any difficulty at all," Vittoria answered brightly. "Riccardo and I will go to see the trust officer first thing Monday morning at *Banco d'Italia* on San Marco.

He happens to be a Dandolo, a distant cousin of mine, a fine, responsible trust officer, in spite of some outrageous gamblers in his ancestral line."

She flashed a smile, looking Emma thought, extremely pleased that she had produced a relative, albeit a distant one, who could be counted on to smooth the way in implementing the late earl's wishes.

16

An Unexpected Visitor at the Water Gate

Emma sat at her desk making final corrections to the new catalogue of the Elmley collection of Venetian paintings. It was almost ready for Lord William's approval, after which it would be printed. She felt a tremendous rush of happiness and satisfaction; she knew she had done a good job.

The entries, every one of the seventy-five works, had been photographed by a professional photographer, the text expanded with newly discovered information about the artists, brought to light by Emma's patient research. She had discovered art history scholars had busily been widening their nets, researching many names among the secondary rank of Venetian painters which made up the bulk of the collection. Reference libraries at the Accademia and Correr Museums were a great help to her in gathering information.

She also made an unexpected discovery: she had thoroughly enjoyed the project. It had given her a taste of what a different path from lecturing as an art historian could offer, the researching and cataloguing of art collections in private hands. She would welcome a similar assignment, although she could hardly expect a return to the place she had grown to adore, *La Serenissima,* Venice most serene. But the prospect of an assignment in England of a similar type intrigued her.

Of course, not to put too fine a point on it, the *collezione* was actually Riccardo's collection now. But after discussing it with Riccardo and Vittoria, they both insisted that she should proceed as instructed by Lord Elmley. He would learn soon enough the startling revelations about his father when he arrived for his scheduled visit; meanwhile everything should remain unchanged.

After the tumultuous week just past, she welcomed the calm of her neatly arranged desk as she poured over proofs. Was Antonio the father or the son of the Vivarini painting dynasty? The son. Yes, that was right. She moved on to the next entry. Finishing her task, she reached high with both arms and gave a mighty stretch. Now she could give herself to the anticipation of Sam's arrival. Soon Sam would be in Venice. She had so much to tell him, show him, and so many new friends he must meet.

The house seemed quiet. Tintoretto was keeping her company. Riccardo and Vittoria were at the *Banco d'Italia* for another appointment with Vittoria's cousin, the trust officer. Emma knew big changes were coming at *Ca' Sospira.* She looked up at the sparkling Carpaccio watercolor of the two girls bleaching their blonde tresses on the *altana*. Riccardo had placed it on the top shelf of one of the book-lined walls so she could admire it as she worked, but every evening it went into the large wall safe concealed in the library. H was taking no chances.

"After all," he had said, "you are the one, with Vittoria of course, who found it. What a magnificent Carpaccio! The earl knew what he was about when he penned the warning not to sell it and slipped the scrap of paper into the last page of the catalogue." Emma smiled to herself, remembering Riccardo's coolness toward her when she first arrived. Driven by fears he could not find the Carpaccio, he seemed unlike the warm, generous person he had become in recent days. She understood now.

Luckily she had found that notation written by the late earl on her first day at *Ca' Sospira*. He had obviously meant it as another reminder for Riccardo, should the instructions hidden under the Elmley bed not be found. But Riccardo was too close to it to act. So many secrets had remained undiscovered for so many years. Life was funny. No matter how carefully men planned and plotted, fate could, and often did, steal a march.

Now, she reasoned, under Riccardo's caring ownership, life would go on at *Ca' Sospira*. But possibly in a very different way from what she had first expected. Why they might decide to open up the house to the public, as did increasing numbers of *palazzo* owners.

Her work was compete. Checking final corrections was all that remained. It had been a stroke of brilliance, Riccardo's suggesting that the painting of the two girls bleaching their hair should be on the cover. The result was nearly as exciting to Emma as finding the painting. Carpaccio, you would approve. I know you would!

Thought was interrupted by the ringing of the bell at the water gate at the front of the house. She could hear voices outside. Someone was arriving by motor launch, someone of importance judging from the quiet purr of a powerful motor. Sam? She remembered the past year's trip to Tuscany with the Celia Drummond girls. Sam had made a surprise early appearance on that trip. It might be Sam! She hurried toward the front of the house.

The door was open wide; she could see Filiberto hurrying out, motioning to the boatman tying up a sleek motor launch. Surely Sam hadn't come by private water taxi! Emma felt certain his prudent, thrifty nature would rebel at such extravagance, sending him straight as an arrow, carrying his suitcase, to the nearest *vaporetto* stop at the train station. She heard the voice of the boatman who swiftly leapt out onto the *molo* to tie up.

"I can see Filiberto coming, Milord." Emma picked up the Venetian dialect.

"*Va Bene.* This will do fine. Let me give you some help with my things." The speaker vaulted gracefully out of the boat with the ease of a man accustomed to life outdoors in the open, at home with all weathers and seasons, Emma thought admiringly. Lord Elmley!

"Ah Filiberto," she heard his pleasing, modulated voice greeting Filiberto as he unlocked the gate.

"Looking chipper and fit as always." He embraced the old servant and stood back to look at him for moment.

"Your grace," Filiberto mumbled, almost overcome with emotion. "What a surprise. But how good it is to see you. I did not realize . . ."

"Nor did I, Filiberto. Riccardo and *Signorina* Dandolo brought me up to date with a telephone call. I thought I might come just a bit early in view of all that's been happening. And I believe I see *Signorina* Darling behind you?"

Emma stepped forward, holding out her hand.

"Good morning, Lord Elmley. We hadn't been expecting you quite yet, but just this morning I received the final proof copy of the revised catalogue."

"Splendid. I shall want to see your progress as soon as possible. And has Dr. McGregor put in an appearance?" Emma felt her face turn crimson.

"It is still a few days early. I did think the launch I heard when you arrived might have been Sam. But that was obviously a mistake." She stood waiting, feeling the childlike flush to her cheeks spreading.

"Riccardo is not here at present, Lord Elmley. He and *Signorina* Dandolo had business to take care of this morning. They should be back soon. I hope your trip was pleasant?" Emma looked up at the earl.

"Completely predictable and uneventful. The way I prefer it," the earl laughed, walking swiftly toward the entrance.

"And is that old Tintoretto?" He rubbed the dog's head as he stood like a sentinel at the entrance, tail swinging. Tintoretto's nose quivered and sniffed at the stranger.

Emma and the earl stepped inside followed by Filiberto and the boatman Carlo carrying the two cases. Emma noticed both Filiberto and the earl seemed on friendly terms with him. He must be the caretaker of the Elmley motor launch. Riccardo had mentioned there was a *Ca' Sospira* launch moored at a slip on the Zattere and brought to *Ca' Sospira* when needed, but she had never seen it. Lord Elmley turned to Emma.

"I suppose since Riccardo is not available, I might come straight away to the library for a quick look at the catalogue? That is where you are working, right?"

"Yes, *certamente* Lord Elmley," Emma replied, wondering what on earth she would say about recent developments if he questioned her. She had thought Vittoria and Riccardo should be the first to speak of events which had unfolded since she had found the letter. As he settled at her desk to look over the proof copy, Emma fidgeted in the wing chair facing him.

He glanced around the room, his eyes falling on the Carpaccio propped on an upper shelf.

"So this is the mysterious Carpaccio! Beautiful. Perfect for the cover. But tell me, what do you think of it, Emma?"

Emma felt herself relax; he spoke in such a friendly manner. She recalled her interview with him in England. How kind and considerate he had been. He seemed the same now, approachable, skillfully putting her at ease.

"Since arriving, I've been looking at what Venice has to offer by Carpaccio, which is quite a lot. The Saint Ursula frescoes in the Accademia are the most famous, of course, but there is another set of frescoes in the *Scuola* of Saint George in the Riva degli Schiavoni recording the life of the saint. The Correr Museum also has a single Carpaccio of two women sitting on an *altana*, similar to this one.

"But how much lovelier is yours, the Elmley Carpaccio! The women in the Correr painting are old, used up courtesans. The colors are dark. This one is a hundred times better, Lord Elmley. Not only is it a watercolor, a very early one, but the freshness and verve is so compelling it begs the question, were the two girls special in some way to the artist, perhaps members of his family? And look at the delicious still life of the basket of lemons, the little dog! Then there is the question: how did he know about the watercolor technique? Albrecht Durer came down from Germany to Venice in 1506, met Giovanni Bellini on that visit we know for a fact. His new style of watercolor could have filtered over to Carpaccio through Bellini!" Emma's eyes shone with excitement and her face glowed.

"Interesting, very interesting" he said, looking at her carefully as she spoke, then turning back to the painting to study it again.

"Yes, I understand what you mean, now that you've helped me see it, Emma. You do have great insight in describing paintings. I caught that passion the first time I met you. Now tell me how you discovered it."

He put down the catalogue and prepared to listen. Thoughtfully she chose her words, telling him how she, Riccardo and Vittoria had searched the upper bedroom where the great Elmley Bed stood. They found it, hidden behind the backing of Lady Sybil's needlepoint tapestry. Emma scrupulously recounted how Vittoria led them to look under the tapestry backing.

"And what first gave you the idea it might be hidden in the tapestry?"

Emma described the mighty leap by Tintoretto, the broken slat, the hidden letter. The earl gave a nod in Tintoretto's direction and the dog began thumping his tail.

"I imagine you have thoughts about what has been discovered pertaining to the family, along with this missing picture, Emma. Am I right?"

His eyes locked with hers and she felt the onrush of panic. What a simpleton I must look like she thought miserably. I should not have brought up the broken slat. She recalled advice from her grandmother Matilda from long ago when she had broken a precious piece of china. Touching it had been off limits, high on a shelf in the parlor of her grandmother's house. Telling her grandmother had been so difficult. Emma recalled the panic.

"Trials are happenings in our lives which make one grow, Emma. How you meet them determines the kind of adult you will become. See that you never let yourself be less than truthful, less than fair, less than honorable." Those long ago words, buried in her subconscious, swam before her. She plunged ahead.

"You mean contents of the letter of course? Yes, I found the letter written by your father to Riccardo. It was tied to the slat that splintered under the Elmley bed.

"The slat broke when Tintoretto suddenly sprang up on the bed. I'd gone in the room to try to work out, once again, where the missing Carpaccio could have been hidden. I was seated on the bed to get the best look at Lady Sybil's tapestry that I possibly could. I thought perhaps it might reveal a clue as to the picture's whereabouts."

"I see," said the young earl. "And you did not find the picture?" Emma shook her head.

"No, not then. Only the letter, tied to the slat when Tintoretto gave his mighty leap." Emma swallowed, took a deep breath, and resumed.

"Your father knew Riccardo would be the logical person to supervise the dismantling and shipping of the Elmley bed back to Worcestershire, of course. He was sure Riccardo would find the letter. What he could not know was when his death would occur. Unfortunately, it was earlier, and quite sudden. It came at a time when Riccardo was away visiting relatives in Switzerland.

"I opened the letter, not realizing how very private it was. It was on parchment, rolled up like a scroll around the slat. Please believe me, Lord Elmley, I would never have read something so obviously a family matter had I realized . . . ." Embarrassment raised the pitch of her voice.

"Emma, please, no regrets. Had it not been discovered, why, this whole business would have dragged on. I am certain my father had no idea it would remain hidden all these years. An impossible situation for Riccardo, don't you agree? Well, it could have continued *ad infinitum*, never been put right, if you hadn't been here. That would have been a terrible injustice." She stole a glance at the earl. His face looked earnest.

"You did us a great favor Emma. Who knows when we would have found the letter if the slat hadn't given 'way? Thanks to

Tintoretto, also, who played his part," he finished, patting the dog who had approached at the mention of his name.

Lord Elmley's forthright smile bolstered Emma's courage. She could hardly believe he spoke of the recent events so calmly. He seemed actually glad to be sharing some of his wealth with a man he had believed to be an employee of his father, nothing more. Lord Elmley seemed to read her thoughts, and continued quietly in the same reasonable tone.

"Look Emma, I have had some time to accustom myself to this, this revelation of my father. I won't pretend it wasn't a real shock. Luckily there is an abundance of wealth and possessions to share. That is not a problem, a relief, really, for as you know our family at present seems disinclined to spend much time here in Venice.

"The truth is, I had never imagined my father as being on the same plane as the rest of us everyday mortals." Here the earl's eyes took on a reflective glimmer. "He seemed a paragon to me, more temperate, more intelligent certainly, more assured. Matters I struggled over when I was growing up seemed of little consequence to him, not that they were unimportant, it was more that he was teaching me not to give in to inferior feelings, always to aim high, to keep in my thoughts the larger picture.

"In a strange sort of way, his weakness, if one wishes to call it that, makes him seem closer to me, knowing that he was human, flawed, just like the rest of us. And that like everyone else at certain times in one's life, the cards are simply stacked. By that

I mean his tragedy was that he lost Esperanza, the love of his life, and he lost one of his sons, because of choices he made. He lacked the strength to acknowledge Riccardo during his lifetime. I imagine he also lost some of the love and respect my mother had for him, although of course nobody will ever know.

"I've had to do a lot of soul-searching about Riccardo," he went on, carefully folding his hands in his lap.

"His life has certainly not been easy. What my father did to help him must have seemed a mighty little to Riccardo, if he was aware of who he was, and knowing something of the tremendous wealth and power my father possessed, *our* father I should be saying, of course." Here Emma felt compelled to interrupt.

"Lord Elmley, in his heart of hearts Riccardo may have wondered, but I do not think he ever truly believed he was the late earl's son, not until he read the letter. Remember, I gave the letter I'd stumbled upon to him, saw his immediate reaction of shocked surprise. But subconsciously, through the years, Riccardo had been behaving as if he *were* such a son, in a strange sort of way. He has shown it by the love and loyalty, care and attention he has lavished on this house and its contents. It has far exceeded the requirements of any job.

"He won't tell you of his heroic behavior during an attempted robbery a few weeks ago, and again, shortly after, when he put out a fire in the kitchen and suffered bad burns on his hands during the second robbery attempt. No Elmley son could have performed better!" she finished fiercely. She stopped, aware of what she had just said.

"I'm sorry, Lord Elmley, if I overstepped," she mumbled, fingers locking in an iron-like grip on her chair arms as she realized she was perhaps expressing thoughts the present earl did not wish to hear. But to her relief he nodded his approval.

"Of course you are right, Emma. I am in complete agreement. I want it understood that I have not come here to cause trouble. I intend to make that crystal clear to Riccardo and Vittoria. I plan to implement my father's wishes in every quick, practical way that I can. I intend to do everything possible to speed the process along. There will be no conflict whatsoever over my father's letter. And whatever Riccardo decides to do with *Ca' Sospira*, it will be his decision and his alone. I would also like to say that I especially wish to become a close friend to my new brother." He sat back.

"Now, about the collection of paintings here, which brings me to another subject I must discuss with you. I plan to speak with Riccardo about the possibility of sending a traveling exhibition of the collection to England. As he has become its owner, he will have to decide if he should like it to travel. It could bring in some useful revenue for him as well as showcase the paintings to some very important museums which might pave the way for future exhibitions. But it will become a reality only if Riccardo embraces the idea."

"That is very generous of you, sir," Emma said, shifting a little in her chair as the earl began studying the catalogue. She felt a great sense of relief that the somewhat awkward moments had been got through, and that apparently the earl was here to see that his late father's wishes were carried out rapidly, and in careful detail. She paused to think about her reply before speaking.

"What an honor it would be to have my catalogue showcased in several exhibitions in England!"

"You would be the obvious person to accompany the exhibition. I had already made inquiries in a few places like Edinburgh, Glasgow, York, Oxford and Cambridge, Brighton. You could give a splendid presentation, slides, lectures and so on and meet with local curators, Emma. How would you feel about that?"

Emma's head was spinning. "It would be a dream, sir. But Riccardo and Vittoria might want to go themselves. She is affiliated with Gallery Vianello, one of the leading art galleries in Venice."

"Those details would have to be worked out by Riccardo of course," he agreed as Filiberto sailed into the room with the tray of morning *caffelatte*.

"Plenty of hot milk and very large cups, Milord, just as you like it," he said, setting the tray on the library table in the center of the room.

"Splendid, Filiberto. When are you going to end this lengthy visit to Venice and come back to Elmley House? You know we miss you and would welcome your return." His gentle smile reflected his affection for the old valet.

He knows things will be uncertain here when Riccardo takes over. He's telling Filiberto that whatever happens, there will always be a place where he will be welcome at Elmley House. Emma marveled at the young earl's ability to put himself in others' shoes so easily. No wonder this family has enjoyed a long history with devoted servants, if the Elmleys were all as considerate and as caring as this one.

Filiberto concentrated on serving the steaming cups of *caffelatte*, eyes shining with a suspicion of mist. He turned to the earl and delivered a touching little statement.

"I sincerely thank you, Lord Elmley. When my services are no longer required by Riccardo, I will be happy to accept your kind offer.

17

An Unpleasant Intrusion Disturbs the Riposo

Quiet enveloped the house. Lord Elmley disappeared into the guest room, always kept ready at *Ca' Sospira*. His intent was to freshen up and rest a bit. He wanted no food until dinnertime but asked to be informed when Vittoria and Riccardo returned.

Emma was on her way to the Correr Museum for a brief visit with Samantha Satchell. She hoped a meeting of the friends could be arranged in the short time after Sam arrived. She would like him to know all of them, but there was hardly time for another picnic at the Lido. Her thoughts turned to Lord Elmley; he must surely need a rest, after traveling from London to Venice. She pushed back her hair and pulled on her wide brimmed straw hat, walked quickly to the heavy front door and stepped outside.

Closing the massive door she turned, surprised to see Nigel Sleight and Cyril Meadowes approaching. They quickly came to a standstill on either side of her.

"Emma! What luck to catch you. I've not seen you in ages." Nigel seized her hand, pumping it in a friendly way as though there had been no cooling of feelings.

"I just received a new supply of Polo mints through the post, slow as a tortoise as always. Here's a fresh roll for you. Put it in your pocket." He held out the small cylinder.

"No, thank you," she said quickly, shaking her head. His fondness of the English peppermints had once seemed charming. Now it was distasteful to her.

"I'm afraid I was just leaving." Her voice was cool.

"We must dissuade you, mustn't we Cyril? It is *you* we came to see. Word has leaked out you will be returning to England soon and we wanted to wish you farewell and at the same time have a peek at your new-found treasure. I mean the Carpaccio."

"So thoughtful," she murmured, "but I really cannot delay. I have an appointment and I am already late." Polite words, however the tone of Emma's reply eased across the line into hostility.

Quick as a sudden sea squall, Nigel's face changed. He frowned, his voice lowered several decibels. Jovial banter faded like a fickle wind into nothingness.

"That is too bad, my dear. You are going to be even a little later than you thought. Cyril, if you please . . ."

Nigel's eyes never left Emma's face. Emma gasped as she saw the small automatic pistol in Cyril's hand.

Nigel whirled her around and whispered in her ear, "Shall we go in, my dear? Your key, please."

Numbed into silence, she fumbled in her purse for the key and unlocked the door. Nigel opened it quickly and guided her inside as the cold metal of Cyril's gun bored into her back.

"Lead us to the Carpaccio, Emma," Nigel's voice was coated with ice.

She must raise the alarm, but how? A ladylike swoon was useless. Where before he had seemed sympathetic and solicitous, Nigel had segued into a criminal who stole paintings. The genial organizer of the Lido picnic had been only stage dressing for a petty thief who nicked Piranesi etchings. Now he was determined to purloin a valuable Carpaccio. Her assessment was clear and unforgiving.

Quick as a Houdini, Emma made a decision to bypass the library where the painting was propped on a shelf and take them upstairs instead. She kept her face blank as conflicting thoughts bounced gratingly about in her head and she began climbing the stairs.

The internal imp whined danger, danger, as she considered the odds. She knew what it was like to be tied up under protest while thieves carried off their prize. She remembered the previous summer in Tuscany when, bound and gagged she witnessed the theft of a famous painting by Piero della Francesca as she traveled the legendary Piero Trail. Well, this time she wasn't giving up the Carpaccio to these creeps, Emma fumed. Not if she could help it. The trio continued up the stairs.

"Are you quite sure it is the Carpaccio you have come to see, Nigel?" She called out in ringing tones loud enough to shatter glass. "I'll gladly show it to you, but you needn't be so rude as to keep that thing in my back. Surely you can persuade your henchman to put it away. I am cooperating, leading you to the Carpaccio, am I not? It's in the late earl's bedroom."

"My dear, I understand in that harpy voice of yours you are trying to alert Filiberto and the mastiff Tintoretto, but it is no good. We waited until we saw them leaving on a little walk, probably down to San Marco to the news agent in the piazza. We've been observing the habits here." He flicked an imagined dust mote on his lapel.

"No need for loud voices, don't you see? We are all alone." His face took on a veneer of self importance.

He must have given a sign to Cyril, however. She no longer felt the gun pressing into her back. So they had been watching the house at this time of day. They must have barely missed the arrival of Lord Elmley earlier. On impulse, she decided to try a more persuasive approach.

"You make me nervous, Nigel. I thought we were once friends, and now you and this person come along threatening me. How would you expect me to react?" She kept the pitch of her voice high.

She had reached the top of the stairs. They were approaching the bedroom door where Lord William rested. Wake up! Wake up, Lord Elmley, she whispered. But no sound came from behind the closed door.

"By the way, Nigel, Cesara is no longer working in the kitchen. She cannot be of any use to you any longer, can she?" Emma asked innocently.

Cyril, not Nigel, answered. He let out a snarl that sounded like Tintoretto's growl. Delighted, Emma was all attention as he released choice expletives just as they passed the earl's door.

Cyril expanded on "disloyalty and irresponsible behavior," finishing with, "I simply cannot understand why that wretched cook dropped us flat and refused to give us any more help. Those men from Torcello were distant relatives of my wife. Cesara claimed they were related to her. Silly cow!" His eyes rolled heavenward.

"Now my Czech buyer is having second thoughts. It has taken us far too long to produce the picture. No wonder he is disenchanted!"

"Enough, Cyril!" Nigel hissed.

Surely the earl had gotten an earful from the corridor. If that didn't bring help soon, hope would trickle away, like sand in an hourglass. Emma prayed her anxiety wasn't showing.

She led them into the bedroom where the Elmley Bed and Lady Sibyl's tapestry were dimly outlined in the pale light seeping in from shutters drawn to protect wools of the needlepoint from fading. She switched on the overhead chandelier and noticed the mattress still sagged where the broken slat had fallen. In her mind it gave the room an abandoned, violated look. Would she be able to stall for enough time? In a flash of prescience she pointed to the bed.

"Well, there it is. If you want to see it you will have to pull it from its hiding place."

"What! You are a little too clever by half, Emma Darling! Do you expect us to believe the thing is hidden somewhere in that ridiculous giant of a bed? I've been far too patient with you." Nigel's eyes narrowed, he glared at Emma while Cyril scowled in a menacing way.

"Yes, that is what you will have to do," Emma spoke calmly. "That is where it was found and Riccardo and Vittoria insisted on putting it back again for safekeeping. At any rate that is where it is they *told* me they hid it. I honestly do not know for certain." Emma's smooth countenance proclaimed innocence. In her reckless bravado, she allowed no thoughts to intrude about what would happen when they realized she had told a whopping lie. But if it would delay proceedings until help came, it was worth it. If not? Well, the imp in her head would simply expire from fright, having warned her repeatedly until he collapsed.

The men removed the covers, carelessly tossing the silken hangings in a corner. Emma fussed, making a slow, ponderous job of folding them up. Nigel and Cyril looked with dismay at the heavy mattress, covered in a ticking thick as battle armor.

"We'd need a machete to get into that," Cyril fumed while Nigel looked Emma's way, glowering.

"You will regret it Emma Darling, I promise you, if you are leading us on a wild goose chase. Don't pin your hopes on the hound and that old trout Filiberto," he warned. "I wouldn't behave foolishly, if I were you." His voice was soft but the threat was implicit. The imp trumpeted caution: watch your step. It could be tricky if he does what he says.

"Oh come on, Nigel, let's get down to it and get away before the old valet and that dog return." Cyril's impatience was growing. He looked dangerous waving the gun around. His glance toward her was full of malevolence, as evil as any she'd ever encountered.

Nigel sighed, motioned him to the unwieldy mattress and together the two men managed by pulling and tugging to wrest it off the bed frame. They propped it against a wall. Before examining it for a seam which might have been opened to insert a picture, they began to examine the slats. Emma stood quiet as a church mouse while they took each one out and turned it over. Emma raised her gaze to the tapestry above the bed, looking steadily at the house in it. She waited, heart hammering in her chest as she hoped for some sound of intervention.

"You don't suppose the painting we're after could be hidden in the tapestry she keeps staring at, do you?" Cyril half-whispered as he and Nigel bent over the slats. Emma's heart gave a leap as she managed to make out their words. Anything that gave her more time to be rescued was worth pursuing.

"Better not be," Nigel answered, out of breath from his efforts. "She knows I'm at the end of my tether. If we don't find it in a few minutes, you'll have to take over."

Nervously Nigel crunched on another Polo mint. Emma breathed in deeply five times as she watched anticipation spread over Cyril's face.

So powerful was the stab of panic she felt traveling down her back that she failed to hear the click of the door or see a distinguished figure step into the room.

"Is there some way I can help you gentlemen?" the assured voice washed over Emma like a Bach chorus as she whirled around to face the Earl of Elmley framed in the doorway.

Nigel almost dropped the slat he was holding, beads of sweat erupting on his brow while Cyril stood up, rooted to the spot, motionless like a cigar store wooden Indian.

"Crikey!" he muttered.

The earl had exchanged the suit of his arrival and, dressed for an afternoon at home, wore comfortable leather slippers, dark trousers, a snowy shirt and a beautiful but subdued lounge jacket in pewter and blue patterned silk paisley. He was not smiling.

Emma marveled. He expressed the spirit of *Ca' Sospira*, she thought. In England, he had worn blue jeans and a white shirt open at the throat when she had met him at Elmley Castle.

"Are you all right, Emma?" He moved to her side. "Perhaps you would introduce me, if indeed you are acquainted."

"Nigel Sleight, employed by Gallery Vianello, Lord Elmley, and Cyril Meadowes, formerly of the British Consulate in Venice. They saw me leaving, forced me back inside and insisted I take them to the Carpaccio." Emma's voice was flat and disapproving.

"I was explaining that Riccardo and Vittoria had replaced it in the place where it was found when you came in." Emma, limp with relief, hoped he would play along with her story, having looked at the painting with her not thirty minutes earlier in the library. His smooth gaze accepted the fabrication without the slightest lift of an eyebrow. What a picture of assurance, Emma reflected.

"We were only hoping for a look at it, Milord," Nigel said, quickly, determined to put on a good face. Cyril nodded vigorously.

"Not exactly, Sir," Emma broke in. "I was forced to bring them up here." The earl's look told her that he understood the ruse perfectly, that she had been leading the two men on a wild goose chase to gain time.

"Forced? Whatever do you mean?" He transferred his gaze to Nigel who looked down at his shoes while Cyril fidgeted.

"Nothing but a little joke, Milord," Nigel smiled weakly.

"Only a joke, the gun," he stumbled on. "Good sport, Emma. We knew she wouldn't miss the chance for a tease." He added a week ha, ha, smiled at Lord Elmley who was not amused. Emma's face began to flush with angry red streaks.

"They used a firearm to force you?" Disbelief in his voice, the earl turned from Emma.

Stepping closer to the men he said in a soft voice, so low it could hardly be heard. "The gun, if you please." He could have been asking for a cup of tea, his voice was so soft.

Emma spoke up. "The gun was pressing in my back as we came upstairs."

The earl's countenance darkened.

"I won't have firearms in *Ca' Sospira!* Give it to me at once!" Thrown off guard by the earl's sudden anger, Cyril sheepishly handed over the weapon.

"I'm sure we can work this out, Lord Elmley. There has been a misunderstanding. It was truly a joke." Nigel's words trailed off, wilting before the blazing fury of Emma's flushed face and the earl's stern look of displeasure. The earl motioned toward the open door and hallway.

"Suppose we all go downstairs now. If you two will precede us, Miss Darling and I will follow."

Emma was reeling. The power of Lord Elmley's presence had turned the two meek as schoolyard bullies. No wonder England had endured through the ages. She fell into step behind the earl as he followed Nigel and Cyril, looking like two delinquents caught stealing marzipan from the corner sweet shop.

From the entryway they heard the excited barking of Tintoretto and Filiberto's efforts to quiet him. Riccardo's quick command silenced the dog and Vittoria's musical tones of affection were heard as she tried to comfort the animal. They had apparently arrived all at once. Tintoretto's keen sense of hearing and smell had detected the presence of strangers in the house.

"What could have set him off?" Emma and the others heard Vittoria exclaim below.

The little group at the bottom of the staircase looked up as a bizarre procession came into view. An extremely uncomfortable pair, Nigel and Cyril, followed by a distinguished Lord Elmley in lounge jacket and slippers, with Emma, cheeks aflame, bringing up the rear. The earl, dressed for an afternoon at home, carried a small automatic revolver. Amazement at the procession and sight of the gun transfixed the upturned faces.

Their reactions were diverted, however, as sounds of a powerful motor launch arriving at the water gate on the *rio* filled the air. The motor cut to idling. The bell at the water gate began pealing repeatedly.

Filiberto reacted quickly, moving smartly through the entrance garden out to the gate. Tintoretto began to bark. Emma saw Filiberto quickly unlock the gate as three men gracefully jumped to the dock and hurried to the front door, where they were met by Riccardo. Two men wearing police uniforms; their superior, a tall, slender officer of about forty in a skillfully tailored silk suit, stepped inside.

The man in the suit spoke in accented English, straight brown hair falling over a high forehead under which piercing brown eyes scrutinized them. His tie of a soft reseda stirred in the breeze. What a handsome man, Emma thought, and how beautifully dressed, more so than any policeman she had ever seen. Even Charlie St. Cyr, the debonair Scotland Yard detective married to her friend Jane, seldom rose to such *brio*. It was the middle of the *riposo,* uncomfortable to be wearing a suit in the summer heat of Venice, but his appearance belied the fact. She felt instantly drawn to the man, whose eyes roaming over the group, quickly sized them up. A nice espresso tone those eyes, with laughter lines at the corners.

"Who rang the *questura?*" were his first words.

"Why, I rang," Lord Elmley, occupying the entry, answered in a somewhat surprised tone. "I am William, Earl of Elmley, and *Ca'Sospira* is my home." Emma saw him send an apologetic glance in Riccardo's direction. Clearly this was not the moment for explanations.

The earl continued in the most respectful of tones, "And you, Sir, are?"

"Inspector Dario, Luigi Dario. *Permesso?*" He gestured toward the entrance. "Could we please step inside, out of this heat?"

"*Certamente,* Inspector Dario." The earl waved the inspector and his two policemen inside, led by Filiberto.

Emma's heart skipped a beat as she stood in the shuttered coolness of the *portego* with the others. So his name was Luigi,

Luigi Dario. She recalled another Luigi, Luigi Rovere, the police inspector in Urbino whom she had met on last summer's tour to Tuscany with her students. Were rugged good looks required for every police inspector in Italy? It seemed they were, as in England, a requisite for police. Bobbies and Inspectors of Scotland Yard, all of them handsome. An age away, last summer. She had been powerfully attracted to that Luigi. Sam's arrival came at just the right moment. How immature she had been on that earlier trip!

Lord Elmley suggested Emma relate what had just happened to Inspector Dario as Cyril and Nigel, sheepish and subdued, stood, securely held, between the two policemen.

Satisfied that he had the right men, Dario gave quick orders. The policemen quickly applied handcuffs and moved toward the door with Nigel and Cyril. They would be detained at the *questura*, the inspector had heard enough. Details would be worked out later.

Sounds of the powerful motor launch filled the air. The pilot, let out the throttle and it roared off down the little *rio*, bound for the waters of the Grand Canal and the *questura*.

The Inspector turned his attention toward the others standing quietly. But before he began, Lord Elmley suggested they move to the more comfortable library. Emma breathed a sigh of relief. Nigel and Cyril were out of the house on their way to the police station before they ever saw the Carpaccio. A huge burden lifted around the region of Emma's heart.

Riccardo gave an account to Inspector Dario of previous unsuccessful attempts by the pair to steal the picture while Emma and Filiberto answered his questions carefully. Vittoria spoke up.

"I think you should also be aware Inspector of something which happened at Gallery Vianello, where Mr. Sleight and I are both employed." And she told him of Nigel's theft of five Piranesi etchings which she had discovered. Her employers were aware of the theft and were checking to be certain no other works had disappeared from the gallery.

Inspector Dario, seated at Emma's desk, listened patiently, seemingly willing to spin out the inquiry indefinitely in the cool, shuttered interior of *Ca'Sospira*.

This refusal to be ruled by the clock reminds me of Tuscany, Emma thought, but it is a feeling even stronger here in Venice. Living will not be rushed. The awareness of history, the absence of noisy, smelly motor cars, placid canals with their little foot bridges, slowed the pace of life. The very stones of Venice helped form this mind set. Heavens, I sound like John Ruskin, she mused.

Riccardo told the inspector of Cesara's involvement in the scheme to steal the Carpaccio, how her failure to report for work the morning of the fire in the kitchen confirmed her duplicity. Filiberto filled in with details. Emma told him of the meeting of Cyril, Nigel and Cesara she witnessed at the Salute church. The Inspector, comfortable in the desk chair, took careful notes in a small notebook he produced from his suit pocket. Emma watched as he jotted down an address when Cesara's house in Dorsoduro was mentioned.

Reluctant to quit the coolness of the house, the Inspector at last stood up to leave, admonishing all of them to be vigilant.

"Until we apprehend the cook, I advise you to do what is necessary to protect the watercolor," he said, peering up at the Carpaccio propped on the bookshelves. Emma could tell he admired it by the careful, unhurried way in which he examined it. Venetians naturally appreciated fine art, especially works of their own artists. It was a part of their birthright she had learned. He gave a last glance of satisfaction and turned toward the earl.

"If you are agreeable, Lord Elmley, we can offer outside surveillance for a week or so, until everything is cleared up. This is a wonderful, rare work by Carpaccio, one of Venice's most famous painters. It must be protected. I imagine that you would not wish anyone stationed inside?" He trained laser-like eyes on the earl.

The earl coughed delicately.

"Thank you, Inspector. Outside surveillance would be most helpful. Before you leave, I should like just a brief word with you and Signor Montgano if you are agreeable?"

And as his soft voice blended into the air, Emma, Vittoria, Filiberto, even Tintoretto, began edging toward the door. *Un' conversazione privata,* Emma thought. He'll be introducing Riccardo as the new owner to Inspector Dario. Lord Elmley had arrived only a few hours earlier and look what had been accomplished. Emma marveled. Benign authority, command, presence, all rolled into one.

She heard the police launch, motor idling, outside. The police had returned to collect the inspector, whenever he might be ready. Ah, Venice, even the police make life here more romantic. Unbidden, thoughts of her grandmother Matilda popped up. How much she would have enjoyed being a fly on the wall during events of the afternoon. Lord Elmley had put on quite a show in his own quiet way.

"It would have made you proud to be British, Grandmother."

Basilica and Campanile, Torcello

18

Emma Follows Cesara and Lets Down Her Guard

Summer evenings were growing shorter and a cooler breeze stirred leaves on the trees in Dorsoduro as Emma walked briskly toward the house of *Signora* Zambelli. She was on her way to the little dressmaker's cottage to collect the stoles she had ordered. Sam would be arriving very soon. Emma could barely contain her anticipation. The separation seemed more like seven years rather than seven weeks. She longed to see him.

In her euphoria she had almost forgotten to call for the chiffon stoles the seamstress had made, gifts Emma had selected for her mother and Mrs. McGregor. Time had flown and already it was too late to order a special gown by *Signora* Zambelli to wear on her honeymoon. She would be leaving in a little more than a week for London and her wedding.

It looked like their honeymoon would have to be postponed in any event because of Sam's decision to take the post in

Oxfordshire. A village near Oxford would be their immediate destination where they would begin searching for a suitable cottage. She supposed Sam had already made up his mind to take the job as recent letters from him seemed to suggest. He must be waiting so they could talk over plans face to face.

Not much use for one of *La Signora's* lovely gowns in a village in Oxfordshire, she sighed as she walked along. Something to cook dinner in and feed the chickens in was what would be needed.

What mean, spiteful thoughts, the imp hissed. The truth is, you know very little about life in rural Oxfordshire. Why, the young surgeons may have butlers and dine by candlelight, for all you know. She smiled as a picture appeared of a fiercely independent Sam, shoulders being brushed down by a faceless valet wearing a black uniform. At least I can chuckle. Laughter helps. Feeling sorry for yourself Emma? The imp whined. Yes, she admitted, but I'm trying hard to get over it.

Lost in her thoughts, she had not realized she was passing the house where Cesara lived, but as she glanced ahead she recognized with a start the familiar figure of the cook hurrying out of her front door.

"*Signorina!* What a long time it has been since I have seen you. "

Cesara's greeting was patronizing, bordering on offensive, belying the saturnine features, mouth turned down at the corners. Emma was surprised; she supposed Cesara had left

Venice. This false friendliness made a mockery of the woman's usual sour attitude.

Does she believe she can just rub out what has happened? Cesara, the turncoat? Emma marveled at the woman's boldness. Did she really believe the role she played in aiding and abetting Nigel and Cyril could be glossed over? Emma flushed with anger at the thought, remembering Riccardo's burns. How stupid she must think me, heaping on such flattery. She recalled how Cesara had rebuffed her overtures of friendliness when she first met her at *Ca' Sospira.*

"Please, *Signorina,* come inside my house for a minute. I have something important to show you."

And, as Emma gave every indication of ignoring her and hurrying along toward the dressmaker's cottage, Cesara quickly added in a low voice, "I have new information about that Carpaccio."

Did the woman not know the painting had been found? Was it possible? Emma stopped and turned to face Cesara who by this time was close by her side.

"Yes, you would like to know what I have learned, I know you would. It will make all of the pieces fit, you see. It will be a feather in your cap to have everything worked out before you leave Venice, when you present the new catalogue to Lord Elmley. He will be so pleased. Maybe a big bonus for you, eh *Signorina?*" Emma was horrified to see her wink.

As though I'm conspiring with her, Emma thought angrily. And yet, suppose, just suppose she has found out something worthwhile. It might help Inspector Dario if I could find out where Cesara was living now. Was she still at this house or had she merely returned to the neighborhood for a visit? Perhaps I can discover if she is still in contact with Nigel and Cyril. She really should be in jail for helping them. She should bear some of the blame. As her thoughts raced, she yielded to the gentle pressure on her arm and moved a few steps closer toward the tiny porch of Cesara's house.

"Just here, *Signorina*," Cesara said brightly, easing her through the small open doorway before Emma had time to decide whether she should trust this woman or was it too risky?

Suddenly she was face to face with looming and frightening shadows on the walls of the tiny room; afternoon had faded to nightfall. The open door admitted a slim shaft of light which pierced the gloom revealing a space filled with furniture.

As she crossed the threshold her eyes became accustomed to the dimness. She saw chairs, tables, a desk, misfits looking like the leavings of a furniture tag sale. Nothing matched except perhaps scratches, dents and nicks of hard usage. The house had become a storehouse for bits and pieces of the worn out, rather than the antique. It did not look habitable. Wallpaper had lapsed into exhaustion. Faded, grimy where it met handprints of the once white door frame, blue garlands furled listlessly, held together by nosegays of pale, once pink rosebuds.

In spite of feelings of unease, Emma felt twinges of sympathy for the former occupants of the house. Such squalid quarters could not have been pleasant. It was obvious, however, nobody lived there now. The house had become a depository for old, broken down junk. Her apprehensions rose.

Only the suspicion of light came in from the window; darkness had spread like a shroud. I'm a silly fool to have fallen for this, Emma thought, but before she could step back, heavy hands gripped her shoulders. In a few seconds, someone had tied a scarf over her eyes and her mouth. She heard Cesara's whispered *Va Bene!* of satisfaction before she melted away from Emma's side.

Emma's heart began hammering, she felt her throat constrict with fear. What an idiot she had been. She twisted, trying to move out of the vise like grip. She knew Nigel and Cyril were locked away at the *questura,* but Cesara was free and had not lost her duplicitous ways. Someone was helping her. Who? Whose strong hands were grasping her shoulders? Emma's nostrils filled with a sweetish, sickly odor. In the space of a few minutes, like a broken doll spilling sawdust, she slowly slumped to the floor.

~~~~

It had been two nights, forty eight hours and more. The little notes written with pencil on cheap lined paper demanding ransom money were found under the doorframe of *Ca' Sospira,* each morning by Filiberto as he opened the great door of the *palazzo*. The crude, cryptic letters held similar messages, all demanding money for the safe return of Emma Darling.

Dr. Sam McGregor had arrived from London only hours before and was feverishly working against the clock with Lord Elmley, Riccardo and Inspector Dario to find Emma. When Sam arrived at the railway station at midday, he was met by Lord Elmley and Riccardo and told of Emma's disappearance. Rosamund had rung *Ca' Sospira* at seven o'clock that morning informing Riccardo that Emma never came home from work the evening before.

"Completely unlike Emma," she had sobbed into the telephone "Something has happened to her, I'm sure of it!" But the police had found no trace of Emma. Her movements became a mystery after leaving *Ca' Sospira* around six o'clock the evening of the earl's arrival when she left for Rosamund's flat in Dorsoduro.

Nigel Sleight and Cyril Meadowes remained in jail. They had been questioned carefully by Inspector Dario, but they were bewildered as everyone else about Emma's disappearance. Cesara's unoccupied house had been searched after Vittoria recalled she, Emma and Rosamund had passed by it on their way to the dressmaker's cottage days earlier. Police learned Emma had made an earlier appointment with the dressmaker to pick up two stoles the evening she disappeared. But they found no trace of Emma, only Cesara's deserted house crammed with furniture.

"I pointed the cottage out to Emma," Vittoria told the inspector. "I'd seen Cesara going in there once before. I realized it must be where she lived. Wait, when the three of us passed by, we saw the two men whom we thought might have broken into *Ca' Sospira,* but they were never caught. I remember now. It had slipped my mind. They were approaching, gave every indication of going inside. We had to walk on so they wouldn't suspect we were snooping, you see. We also wondered if they might be the same two men who came to Gallery Vianello to see Nigel some time back. I saw them myself on that occasion as well." Her eyes narrowed at the possibility.

When Inspector Dario questioned *Signora* Zambelli, the little seamstress told them she never saw Emma again. She had failed to keep an appointment to collect the stoles. But the seamstress did recall seeing her former neighbor on the next street earlier that day. She had seen Cesara, a cook for one of the *palazzi* near the opera house, *La Fenice.* She had asked the seamstress if she would be seeing the young American girl anytime soon. *Signora* Gambelli told her Emma had an appointment to collect two stoles that very evening. However, Cesara's closest neighbors informed the Inspector they were sure Cesara had moved away. Inspector Dario threw up his hands in frustration.

"I know Emma's disappearance must have something to do with Cesara," Vittoria said, meeting with Riccardo and Inspector Dario briefly the following morning. "She lived so close to *Signora* Zambelli! I can't believe Cesara is not involved."

"But her house was locked. When we got a warrant to enter and search, we found nothing but a house full of junk and signs of a hurried departure," Inspector Dario answered, rubbing his chin thoughtfully.

"There was nothing to suggest anything unusual had gone on there. Cesara must certainly have left to stay with relatives if she is in Venice. We traced her daughter and discovered the daughter's husband has taken a job in Modena. That house is already occupied by another family."

"Yet Cesara's house is vacant? You are certain nobody's living there?" Vittoria looked inquiringly at the Inspector. He nodded.

"It's empty. Only broken down furniture. Probably belonging to the daughter, some of it. There was hardly room for anyone to sit, or sleep, for that matter. Nobody was living there, I'm sure."

Riccardo turned to Vittoria. "The two men you saw at Gallery Vianello. I remember now, we thought perhaps Nigel had hired them to break into *Ca' Sospira*. But nothing ever came of it. As I recall, someone made the comment they looked like they came from Murano or one of the other islands. They seemed like countrymen, fishermen or farmers, rather than city dwellers, those Filiberto and I encountered at the first break in at *Ca' Sospira*. I was told the two men were relatives of Meadowes wife. Maybe they are the same two related to the cook Cesara." The Inspector looked thoughtful before answering.

'We must find them! Most of all we need to find *Signorina* Darling!" Inspector Dario barked and stood up. "My men have been combing the islands of Murano and Burano. We'll continue as long as necessary." He rubbed at his eyes and muttered almost inaudibly, "So much of the work of the police is boring and repetetive. I think I could sleep standing up sometimes it is so painfully dull. Frankly," he finished, "It takes the patience of Job to take up this line of work."

~~~~

Tommaso Migliori thought of his friends Riccardo and Vittoria and the wonderful news they had received as he journeyed by *vaporetto* toward the island of Torcello. The early morning mists were lifting and it looked like a fine day to visit his grandmother whom he had not visited for a while. He knew he was her favorite.

Because Riccardo's real father turned out to be the seventh earl of Elmley, he and Vittoria would now be able to marry and live in their own house in style. Well, it could not have happened to a better fellow. Riccardo had been a friend since they were both wearing the hated short pants of their school uniform days. He smiled, remembering Riccardo's tall, lanky frame in the short trousers. Some of the boys had called him Scarecrow, and it had hurt Riccardo's feelings.

Tommaso recalled how he had stood up for his friend, given a few bloody noses on his behalf as they made their way home together from school on those days when Riccardo's mother couldn't collect both of them. She was a caring lady, and she knew Tommaso's mother could never leave work to pick them up. Her job at the Mocenigo palace on the Grand Canal kept her in the kitchen most days until dark. It had been a kindness of *Signora* Montgano to see Tommaso safely home when she called for Riccardo at the school gates. Yes, she had been a nice lady, he recalled.

School days ended, but his friendship with Riccardo endured. When Tommaso came of age, took over the family gondola and became a gondolier, he continued to meet Riccardo occasionally. When Riccardo told him about wedding plans with Vittoria Dandolo, Tommaso had treated the two of them for a moonlight ride in his gondola.

Something Riccardo told him earlier had been troubling Tommaso. The American girl, Emma Darling, working at *Ca' Sospira*, had gone missing. Vanished without a trace on the journey from *Ca' Sospira* to Dorsoduro. Police as yet had no idea of her whereabouts.

Riccardo also told him it was largely through Emma's efforts that the missing painting by Carpaccio belonging to *Ca' Sospira*, had been found, as well as the letter which brought Riccardo such good news about his real father. He frowned. *Signorina* Emma had been the one to bring Riccardo such good fortune. Quick to understand, a tireless worker, loyal, passionate about her job was how Riccardo described her. Tommaso wondered how he could help his friend find *Signorina* Darling.

Arriving at Torcello, he walked from the dock down the old road that divided the center of the island roughly in half. Soon *Santa Maria della Assunta,* the basilica dating from the Byzantine period, lay behind him as he walked deeper into the deserted woods with patches of swamp that made up most of Torcello, a once prosperous island decimated by plague in centuries past and now unable to keep up commercially with the rest of Venice. It was a tourist destination mainly, with sightseers stopping at the water's edge, to visit *Santa Assunta* or to have a meal at a well known restaurant nearby, the Devil's Bridge. Aside from the expected souvenir shops near the *vaporetto* dock, that was it. A few inhabitants lived in modest frame houses hidden by trees and brushy undergrowth deep in the island's center where they farmed a little or fished in the lagoon during the day.

His grandmother Chiara, in her eighties, lived alone. She was fiercely independent and a trial to her large family of sons, a daughter, nieces and nephews who could not understand why she would not close up the remote little house and move in with one of them. His mother had shed many tears over this Tommaso knew. There were grandchildren; Tommaso was one of ten. He turned off the well worn road to follow a faint path deeper into the woods to his grandmother's cottage. His thoughts wandered and he paid scant attention to his surroundings, so familiar was his journey. He could probably find his way in the dark, if he had to. He knew his beloved *nonna* would seldom call on her family, even if she needed help. She was too independent, not that kind of person.

They'd all insisted on installing a telephone for her in her advancing years, but she seldom used it and let it be known in no uncertain terms *she* would call *them*. They were not to waste her time with frivolous calls on the *telefono* when she was busy and had her work to do! Tommaso smiled. He admired *nonna* Chiara and liked to visit.

So deep in thought as he followed along the familiar little track becoming fainter and fainter, he almost failed to hear the sound of music floating softly on the air. He paused to pick up the sound. The noise of his shoes striking pebbles on the trail halted. He listened but heard nothing. He hesitated a moment longer and was rewarded by the strains of an unknown melody. It was a nice tune, sad sounding. A woman was singing in a sweet, pure soprano. Try as he might, he could not make out the words. He crept nearer the direction of the sound.

He was sure he had never heard the melody or the words before. It puzzled him as he tried to make out the meaning.

> *Carry me back to old Virginy,*
> *'Dare's where de cotton, corn and sweet pertatos grow.*
> *'Dare's where de birds sing so sweet in de springtime,*
> *'Dare's where 'dis old soldier's heart am long to go.*

Each day in his gondola, Tommaso met many foreign tourists whose language he did not speak with any degree of fluency. But he could understand, and give directions in French, German or English: turn right, turn left, straight ahead and so on when passengers disembarked. And he could tell them about the buildings along the Grand Canal if they wanted to know a bit of Venetian history.

But most of the words of the song floating so plaintively to his ears were strange. He was reasonably sure it was English, but most of the words did not sound like the English he had heard. Nor did it mirror the American accents he had come to recognize. People from New York sounded different from the Texans. Of course he watched "Dallas" each week on the television like everybody else in Venice. Puzzled, he walked closer to the sound and presently, through thickets of trees and undergrowth forming a dense barrier, he made out the outlines of a small house, similar to his Grandmother's, one he'd never seen before.

A new sound floated on the air.

> *Take my hand.*
> *Take my whole life through,*
> *For I can't help,*
> *Falling in love with you.*

That song and melody Tommaso *had* heard before. It was an Elvis Presley tune. Young people all over the world could identify that melody Tommaso was certain. Elvis was well known in Italy. He grinned, sure about that.

He crept closer to the house. There was a yet a different tune being sung now. It was one he recognized at once. When taking

Americans around Venice; they would sometimes break into snatches of it to express their delight at being in his beautiful city.

> *Yankee Doodle went to Venice*
> *Riding on a pony.*
> *Stuck a feather in his cap*
> *And called it Macaroni!*

That clinches it, Tommaso thought. She is an American for sure. I'm ringing Riccardo.

Retracing his steps, he resumed his journey toward his grandmother's cottage. When he saw the outlines of her house against the sky he began loping as fast as his feet would carry him. He must use her *telefono* at once to ring Riccardo. It might be *molto importante*, that call. The American might be held prisoner on Torcello!

But when he opened the tiny door of his grandmother's cottage and looked in, all thoughts of what he had just seen and heard flew out of his brain.

His grandmother was lying on the floor, one leg twisted beneath her. Her eyes were shut and she lay perfectly still, except for a slight movement of her lips. Bending over and placing his ear close to her mouth he could barely hear her words. She was praying. Fear for his grandmother's life drove everything from Tommaso mind. He hurried to the telephone on a small table in the passageway and dialed the Venice emergency number to order an ambulance boat from the mainland.

~~~~~

"I cannot hold out any longer." Sam McGregor announced to the breeze as he stood alone in the freshness of early morning on the *altana* of *Ca' Sospira* with only Tintoretto for company. It was his first morning in Venice following the nightmare he had discovered on his arrival. He'd spent the first afternoon and most of the night in a controlled panic, the horror of Emma's disappearance slowly taking hold of his brain.

"If I can't find Emma, I think I'll lose my mind."

Tintoretto gave a comforting whine of sympathy.

Every lead had fizzled in the combined efforts of police and Emma's friends. Yesterday with his help, things had not gone better. Now he knew he must try to find her on his own. He'd hardly had any sleep since he learned the news, but this was not unusual. Doctors were accustomed to long hours on call with little or no sleep at the hospital.

Sam looked out at the world that was Venice with a furrowed brow, indifferent to the beauty and freshness of a sky tinged with pink from a steadily rising sun. Straight blond hair fell over a worried brow above kindly blue eyes. Tenacity and resolve stood out in the strong chin.

"Come on, 'Tinto." He pulled his thoughts together, preparing to leave the rooftop garden. Hurrying downstairs, he turned into the hallway and glanced in a mirror, failing to register his slightly rumpled jacket over a clean shirt and tie. His freshly shaved face proclaimed respectability, but deep hollows beneath his eyes told of anxiety and a wakeful night.

His final mission with Riccardo and Lord Elmley before ending yesterday's fruitless search had been a visit to Nigel Sleight in his jail cell. He had decided Nigel was the more approachable of the two men when he sat in on the meeting with Inspector Dario and the two suspects. He'd noticed Nigel's look of surprise and a glimmer of concern when he was informed of Emma's disappearance. That look seemed genuine. It was sincere, the look of someone hearing bad news about a friend.

That decided him and now he was going back alone, hoping to visit Nigel to see if he could wring a drop more information from him, anything which might help them find Emma. A long shot, but at the moment, it was all he had. Once again the pain of losing her engulfed him and it was all he could do to keep from giving in to it.

He squared his shoulders, willed his eyes to stop welling, and patted Tintoretto. He penned a brief note to Lord Elmley and Riccardo, telling him where he was going and left it on the *cassone,* the old wedding chest in the entry. Quietly, he let himself out.

It was an hour before breakfast. Filiberto would discover the note, see that Lord Elmley received it. Riccardo would assume he was sleeping a little later or suppose he'd gone for a walk along the Grand Canal, behind the palaces, when the day was still in the freshness of morning, like some rare and precious watercolor slowly coming to life. That was how she might describe it he thought. Hope took another nose dive. Thrusting despair aside, he kept walking.

He'd be back soon. He'd either find out something useful or he wouldn't. It was that simple. His face looked undisturbed as he marched toward the Rialto, but his innermost feelings were about to implode. *Where could Emma be?*

He found the *questura*. His resolve faltered as he stepped inside the security area of locked doors with the guard. The smell of jails had been imprinted in memory ever since the dour faced Miss Isobel MacPherson took the lower form to visit the badly overcrowded two room jail at Loch Aden, the village in Scotland where he grew up, where his family still lived.

It was the stench that nauseated him, not just the faint latrine odor, but a mingling of overcooked food, body sweat and the perspiration of fear. No, decidedly not where he wanted to be. He'd choose the acrid, antiseptic smell of the surgical ward over it any day.

The sleepy guard indicated a small table with two chairs under a bright overhead light, motioned to him to sit there and wait. Presently he returned, bringing along a confused Nigel Sleight rubbing his eyes and running stubby fingers through his hair. Clearly he had been catching forty winks, Sam realized, feeling a bit sorry for him in spite of his crimes. If everyone had a foretaste of what life was like in the lockup, he would wager there'd be far fewer crimes committed. The trouble was, no criminal ever thought he'd be caught. He focused his attention on Nigel.

He decided to begin by asking him a few questions about himself to show he had not come as an enemy. Was he receiving representation? Had the British Consul been in touch? He told Nigel that he and Emma had planned their wedding before she came to Venice. It was only a few weeks away. He looked into Nigel's eyes and admitted how fearful he was for her safety.

"Surely you don't think I had anything to do with her disappearance?" Nigel asked quietly. "I have always liked and admired Emma. We were great friends before, well before all of this happened. You do realize how ghastly it is for me here, being under lock and key?"

"I'd guess it might make Wormwood Scrubs seem like a Country Club," Sam answered and the two men smiled at each other. Not that there was anything funny about the London prison, any prison for that matter. The knot in Sam's stomach eased a little. Nigel's understanding was a good sign. He hoped it meant Nigel did not think he was trying to trick him. Sam prepared to listen patiently.

"No frills, no communication with the outside," Nigel reflected, nervously drumming fingers on the table. "No visitors, telephone calls. Not that I thought I'd be having any visitors," he finished, sounding sorry for himself. "The British community, my countrymen, consider me one rung below a leper now that I'm tied to Cyril and we're in jail."

"The guard says I only can speak to you a few minutes," Sam said softly, hoping to return to the purpose of his visit. Nigel nodded.

"I've thought about Emma since last night when I learned she was missing. I keep coming back to the two men who carried out the first break in at *Ca' Sospira*. Cyril lined them up for the job. Alberto and Franco. Brothers. Surname is Pezzelli. They live on Torcello. There are lots of Pezzellis. Cesara is related to them also."

Sam wondered if Cyril was his only accomplice but did want to question him too much. He wanted Nigel to tell everything on his own, without prompting. He wanted to build on his trust. He gave a nod of encouragement. Nigel studied his fingernails before speaking.

"Then, there is Cesara."

"You haven't heard of any links to Cesara, have you? I mean, related to Emma's disappearance," Sam asked.

"No," Nigel paused, "But that doesn't mean links don't exist. These island families intermarry a lot. Relatives help each other. It is certainly possible. I had not considered that Cesara might try to act on her own, try to collect ransom money. Silly woman! So much more risky, abduction, rather than nicking a painting." He rubbed at his eyes.

"You should find those men on Torcello. Quickly. They may lead you to Cesara, then to Emma. I hope you do find her soon."

Sam was out of his chair by the time Nigel finished talking, sensing he had told everything he knew or was planning to reveal. Thanking him he left, determined to go to Torcello at once. In seconds he was striding toward the *vaporetto*, on his way to the remote island of Torcello.

~~~~

Tommaso hardly breathed as he rode in the ambulance launch with his grandmother. It had taken such a very long time for them to arrive. He had been almost physically sick with fear. The night had seemed endless as he waited for the stretcher and the ambulance men to arrive at the cottage. But the people at the emergency center had been very good, reporting back to check on him through the night. They explained there had been a boat accident on the water near Santa Lucia, the train station, and every launch had been pressed into service. They told him to cover his grandmother with a blanket, not to move her, and to keep talking to her. To give her water if she asked for it. He waited and prayed. Tommaso had never prayed so hard in his life. At some point near daybreak he heard the sound of voices coming up the path.

He did not even glance at his watch, but he could see the lightness of dawn in the sky. It took a while for the attendants to examine his grandmother and prepare her for the journey to the *ospedale*. Gently they eased her onto the stretcher and moved out. Tommaso carefully locked the door of the little house then hurried with them toward the dock.

Finally they were settled in the cabin of the ambulance launch waiting at the Torcello dock. He held his grandmother's frail hand as she lay on the stretcher. He suddenly thought of the woman's voice he had heard at the tumble down house in the woods. So much had happened, he'd almost forgotten her. Although he hadn't seen her, the strong voice told him it was someone young, and the accent sounded American, rather than English. Her choice of songs seemed to confirm her nationality.

He must reach Riccardo by telephone as soon as he had tended to his grandmother. Something Riccardo had told him recently about the disappearance of the young American lodged in his mind. Could this be the missing girl? What was it Riccardo had said? He tried desperately to remember. But the pallor of his grandmother's face turned his thoughts back to fears for his grandmother's life. Would she be all right?

At last the launch pulled into sight of the *Ospedale Civile* in the Castello *sestieri* of Venice. Tommaso gently removed his hand and wiped away sweat droplets from his forehead. In his relief they had finally arrived, he had hardly noticed he was perspiring profusely. The doctors would know what to do to make his grandmother well again.

Once inside, he felt drained as he waited for her examination, then watched them gently place her on a gurney and roll her toward the surgical ward. There was a badly twisted knee and a broken bone in her leg. He could accompany her no further. He would have to entrust her to the surgeons now. He watched her disappear through the swinging doors. There was nothing more he could do save wait and pray. He went to the waiting room, found the telephone outside in the hallway and dialed Riccardo Montgano.

~~~

As Sam's *vaporetto* docked at Torcello he watched an ambulance launch pull away, gathering speed into wide waters, bound for the mainland. Sam's heart skipped a beat as he glimpsed a figure on a stretcher inside the cabin. The pilot and two attendants stood outside, on deck. Inside the lighted cabin Sam could make out a young man sitting beside the stretcher. The prone figure was covered in blankets, except for her head which had heavy, thick hair. Both despair and relief flooded over him when he saw white hair and the face of an old woman. No possible way could this be Emma, but where could she be?

~~~

At *Ca' Sospira*, Riccardo heard the insistent ringing of the *telefono* as he tried to rouse himself from a wonderful dream.

He was standing at the front of the Miracoli church and Vittoria was floating toward him, dressed in white and on the arm of her father. From the church swelling chords from the organ filled the air.

The *telefono* continued to peal. He could imagine it on the desk of his tiny office, intruding on his dream. He groped for his robe and slid feet into his slippers. He'd have to answer it.

"Riccardo Montgano speaking. Who is calling?"

It was Tommaso Migliori. He was at the *ospedale* with his grandmother who had apparently broken her leg in a fall at her remote cottage on Torcello. Tommaso told Riccardo what he had seen and heard at the tumble down cottage hidden in the woods on Torcello, near his grandmother's house. He might have heard the missing Emma Darling's voice. He had heard a woman singing snatches of American songs from inside that house. A woman with an American accent. He told Riccardo the precise, location, only about fifty yards due east from his grandmother's cottage and well hidden by undergrowth.

19

Renaming the Devil's Bridge the Angel's Bridge

Emma lifted her eyes to the ceiling and willed herself to quit thinking about food.

"Ah'm fixin' to make yo' a big pot of greens and yo' favorite, mah skillet cornbread."

It was the voice of Rose, the cook and house keeper at Emma's childhood home in Virginia. Emma immediately felt warmed and comforted. In spite of her resolve to disregard it, the image of a Virginia platter of greens and a steaming black iron skillet of Rose's fabled cornbread affixed itself to the ceiling of the tiny room, her prison—how many days now? She sighed, struggling to remember as she tried to ignore the hunger pangs. It had been two nights and one day since she was seized in Dorsoduro. Where was she now?

She'd stopped eating anything brought to her after she smelled and tasted the drug mixed in the rubbery pasta and watery tomato sauce on her plate. It was faint but the same smell she'd gagged on when the cloth was pressed over her nose in Cesara's house in Dorsoduro. She had recognized the pungent odor. They were keeping her doped so she wouldn't try to get away. She must stop eating everything brought to her, keep her mind clear.

But Emma could think of nothing but food, she was so hungry. Images from her Virginia childhood, members of her family, bounced in and out of her thoughts. No! She should try to focus on plotting a way to escape! Luckily she was not bound and gagged. However she felt so weak she could hardly do anything but sit on the mattress on the floor. It had to be hunger making her feel fuzzy and confused. Each time they brought food, she emptied the plate down a large crack in the floor near the worn mattress after the door slammed shut. She knew she must not eat.

Where was she? Only the regularity of pealing bells assured her she was still somewhere near Venice. But the lack of city sounds, the babble of loquacious Venetians on the streets, puzzled her. Certainly the bells she'd heard were not those of *San Marco,* or *Santo Stefano* near the Accademia or *Santa Maria della Salute* on Dorsoduro's tip. No, these church bells sounded melodious, but strange to her.

There were none of the noisy motor sounds of *vaporetti,* of sleek motor launches, or heavily laden freight boats. No footsteps or the hum of activity as people moved around the city. Only the bells. She had to be on one of the outer islands. But which one? She knew many of these islands had large areas of land virtually unoccupied, even Burano the island where once lace makers had produced beautiful lace cloths, veils, collars. Now the market for lace hiccupped and dwindled, but a few lace makers carried on. She knew there were large undeveloped areas of unoccupied land near Marghera, the shipping port at the mainland end of the bridge, which was a part of the municipality of Venice. Emma faced the reality: there were hiding places on countless outer islands scattered around Venice.

She'd not seen Cesara since that disastrous encounter inside her small house on Dorsoduro. Where had the kidnappers moved her? How had they transported her? Perhaps by a small fishing boat? It was possible, under cover of darkness, with strong men supporting her, Emma reasoned.

Three different people brought food morning and evening, but she only saw their hands. Each meal followed the same pattern. The person unlocked the door and pushed the plate and jug of water onto the floor of the room. They did not step inside. She had only a quick glimpse of hands. Two sets of hands were male, showing signs of hard labor, dirt imbedded in fingertips, rough calluses on their palms. The third pair was thin, frail, trembling slightly. Spotted hands, an old woman's hands. They were the hands bringing her food most often. If ever she could force her way out, it would have to be when those hands unlocked the door. A frail older woman would give her a better chance of escape. She tried to work out a plan, but her growling stomach forced thoughts back to her hunger. Energy depleted, she only wanted to dream of food.

Light in her little room came from a clerestory window, a rectangle of glass opening high above, letting in badly needed fresh air. She could see sky through the dirty glass. If she had anything to stand on, could she escape? But no, that seemed foolhardy. The glass would have to be broken and how could she raise herself up? Impossible. Her eye fell on the disgusting hole in the corner of the room, an inside privy, a primitive gesture to sanitation. She battled feelings of frustration, anger, fear. Would anybody ever find her?

She had no view of her surroundings, only sky and occasional clouds floating by; the window was too high. There were birds outside, Emma could hear them chirping, busily at work, foraging for food. That meant trees and underbrush, she reasoned. But hunger enabled her to think of little else most of the time. To keep her mind clear, she sang at various intervals when hopeless feelings began closing in.

Like her dreams of food, they were often songs related to childhood. Why am I doing this she wondered? Because it helps you escape yourself a few minutes, the annoying imp piped up. Yes, and there was always the faint hope someone might hear.

> *Yankee Doodle went to London.*
> *Riding on a pony . . . .*

~~~~

Sam stepped off the *molo* at Torcello as the bells began pealing in the bell tower of *Santa Maria della Assunta*. He saw a monk sweeping the porch at the entrance to the church and decided to speak to him. He walked up the path to the church. The old sexton wore brown robes. Perhaps a Benedictine? As Sam came closer, the man smiled.

A good sign, he thought noting the man's kindly wrinkled face and watery eyes.

"Brother, I am looking for a remote part of the island where there are houses. I am looking for a house belonging to the Pezzelli family." The smile enveloped the man's face.

"Easier finding a needle in a haystack. Too many Pezzelli! Almost as many as the Gabanno family, my family, on Torcello. Their houses are all over." He gave a broad sweep of his arm. "Those two families were so tough they survived the plague."

"Plague?" Sam echoed with alarm.

"In the thirteen hundreds." The sexton was enjoying his visit with the British tourist.

"But why look at tumble down houses dotting the lonely outreaches of Torcello? There is much more to be seen inside the beautiful church of *Santa Maria della Asunta*. The best example of the Byzantine period in the whole world." He urged Sam to come inside.

"No, I must press on," Sam told him. "I am searching for a missing woman who may be somewhere in one of the old cottages. Perhaps another time."

"Then in that case you should keep to this road until it forks. Take the left fork. You'll have to explore the area. There will be trails, mostly overgrown, leading to the houses, most some distance from each other. Don't become discouraged. Good luck finding who you are looking for."

Sam thanked him and hurried down the path. The surrounding landscape took on a wilder aspect beyond the well kept grounds of the church. He duly arrived at the fork. A small sign to the right advertised *Osteria al Ponte del Diavolo*, the restaurant of the Devil's Bridge. Strange name for a restaurant he thought as he turned left. In ten minutes walking, the pathway had narrowed and grown more obscure.

He glimpsed a frame building through the trees and brush. He heard a radio playing violin music. Two small boys were tossing a ball in the clearing in front of the house. A woman watched him from behind a screen door as he approached.

"I am looking for a missing person, a woman," Sam began. "Is this the Pezzelli house?"

"No," The woman answered briefly, before turning away. "Gabbano, not Pezzelli." She disappeared inside before Sam could tell her he had met one of her relatives at the church, hoping she might be more helpful.

He returned to the main path, wondering how many false approaches he would be forced to make before he found the right house, and what would await him when he found it.

He was now following an offshoot of the path leading into thicker brush. It seemed unlikely there would be a house at the end. Presently the trail stopped. A footpath curved, and as he rounded it, a tumbledown house, looking more like a shed, came into view. If it had been painted long ago, every vestige of color had by now disappeared. Clapboards were leaning, whole sections missing, revealing interior walls. It was marginally habitable, that house.

He heard the baying of hounds near by. Were they running free? Would they attack? He glanced about for shelter as a figure came into view from the back of the house, moving slowly, shuffling as quickly as strength permitted. She crept listlessly along, pausing, looking back over her shoulder as though she feared someone might be following. It seemed to require great effort for her to move at all.

Sam took a few steps closer to ask directions. He opened his mouth to frame the words but the shock of what he saw silenced him.

The slow-moving creature was Emma!

Sam hurried to embrace her as she took a step forward and fell fainting into his arms.

"Emma, Emma, my darling, what has happened? What on earth have they done to you?"

There was no answer. Emma had lost consciousness.

~~~~

Lord Elmley and Riccardo stood at the wheel of the powerful Elmley launch with the pilot Carlo standing between them. They were rapidly approaching Torcello.

"Dr. McGregor may not realize how remote and solitary this island really is," Riccardo was saying, his voice tense. "I should have come here sooner looking for Emma. Torcello is isolated enough to make a perfect hiding place and we knew, Vittoria and I, of the connection Cesara had with the two brothers who had worked for Nigel. They were distant relatives of Cesara, I remember, and they live somewhere on this island. Yes, we should have searched here sooner. I blame myself for this. This is where we'll have the best chance of finding Emma and it took a stranger to Venice, Dr. McGregor, to lead us here!"

He had been feeling terrible ever since he'd received the call from Tommaso Migliori earlier that morning. Tommaso told him about an incident on the way to visit his grandmother's on Torcello the afternoon before. He had heard a voice singing in the forest and had followed the sound to a tumble down house near his grandmother's cottage. Tommaso remembered what Riccardo had told him of the missing American girl, Emma Darling. But when he reached *nonna* Chiara's cottage, he'd found his grandmother unconscious from a fall and had spent most of the night holding her limp hand, waiting on the ambulance launch. As soon as his grandmother was settled at the hospital, he had rung Riccardo. Then Riccardo read Sam's note, brought to him by Filiberto who had found it on the large *cassone* in the hallway. He and Lord Elmley had quickly drunk some coffee and boarded the launch idling outside *Ca' Sospira*, bound for Torcello.

Lord Elmley reached over and touched Riccardo's hand. "Don't look back, Riccardo. We are here now, that is what matters, and with luck we shall find Emma." The earl spoke softly with great confidence.

The two men made their way quickly past the church and hurried toward the deserted, fallow land on the island, taking the left fork and moving quickly into the deeper forest. Carlo remained with the boat, keeping it ready for a quick departure if necessary.

Riccardo remembered a childhood visit with Tommaso many years earlier when Tommaso's mother took the two boys with her for a picnic and a visit with the old lady. He thought he could find her house.

Lord Elmley had taken the precaution of alerting Inspector Dario, telephoning him at the *questura* of their plans before they left for Torcello. The inspector had not yet arrived and so a message was left for him. Lord Elmley knew time was of the greatest importance. The officer he spoke with urged caution and promised the inspector or someone from the *questura* would join them on Torcello within the hour.

~~~~

Sam lifted Emma in his arms and began striding toward the basilica. He knew they would find safety at the church. The sexton would help him get Emma to a hospital. He tried speaking to Emma, but she remained silent, eyes closed. His anxiety grew as his legs tired and he began to slow the pace. Would the kidnappers find Emma missing and try to overtake them? He thought of the barking dogs. He would be powerless to fend them off if Emma was still unconscious. Thankfully, he hadn't heard them again. There was no sound of barking. He hoped they had been fed and penned up.

He spotted a fallen tree near the edge of underbrush along the path, its large trunk probably uprooted in a storm some winters past. Quickly he carried Emma to it, sat down, and, supporting her on his lap, checked her pulse at the wrist with his free hand. It seemed just a bit below normal. He began fanning her briskly with the summer Leghorn he'd worn to ward off sunburn.

It took only a few minutes for the rush of air to revive Emma. She opened her eyes and looked up into his face.

"Goodness! Sam? This is not the welcome I planned for you. Where are we?"

Sam's look confirmed a great weight had lifted from the region of his heart.

"I'd hoped you might be able to tell me."

"I was in a tiny house on Dorsoduro the last moment I knew where I was," she sighed.

"Now, after being drugged for two nights and a day, everything seems fuzzy. I have not a clue."

"I can tell you we are on the island of Torcello, quite a way from Dorsoduro, and *Ca' Sospira.*" Warning flags waved before his eyes at her mention of drugs. What was that about? Emma told him that they had tried to immobilize her by putting a drug in her food, but she simply stopped eating anything brought to her.

"Oh Sam, darling Sam. Thank you for finding me, wherever we are. I want to tell you everything. Maybe we can piece together who brought me here and then we can send word to Inspector Dario, but first Sam, at this very moment I am simply perishing from hunger. I haven't had anything but water for so long, you see. I'm weak and fuzzy feeling but most of all hungry. Sam, could you possibly find something to eat?"

"My bonny lass. Havers! Of course, you must be starving! There's a place ahead, just past a fork in the pathway. We'll go there, they will give us a wee bite to get you going again. The sign called it The Devil's Bridge, but I'm calling it The Angel's Bridge, in your honor."

Emma smiled up at him. Dearest Sam. She loved this sentimental turn of mind and the way he lapsed into the vernacular of his native Scottish Highlands when he became anxious or upset. He gathered her in his arms and started off again, energized by the good luck of finding her safe with apparently only hunger making her so weak.

"Do you think they know you got away? Will they follow us?"

Emma was silent for a minute, struggling to put her thoughts in order.

"No, I mean no, they won't follow us, at least not for a bit. But yes, someone knows I got away. This morning, the old woman opened the door, set down the food as usual; then, surprisingly, she stepped in and looked at me for the first time and her eyes began to overflow. Always before she had not shown herself, nor had she peeked in at me. I had no idea what she looked like; I'd guessed she was old because her hands had brown spots on them and trembled when she set down the jug of water and the plate. This morning it was the sight of me, such a mess, that touched her when she brought my food. I suppose the two men in the house had left to go to work somewhere in Venice, or perhaps they are fishermen. Only she and I were in the house, I think.

Salome Dancing, Mosaic, San Marco 14th century

"'*Povera ragazza, povera Signorina,*' poor girl, poor miss, she kept repeating as she looked at me. Suddenly she pointed toward the open door and said '*Mi lasci in pace,*' which I took to mean 'leave me alone, go! Leave me in peace!' And I bolted. You see, Sam, she knew it was wrong to keep me prisoner and drug my food. I'd been held two nights and one day. It worried her, doing something evil like that. And she couldn't stand it any longer. But Sam, when Cesara or those men return, well, I fear for her safety, poor thing."

He kissed the top of her head and burrowed his nose in the wonderful sandy strands of hair.

"Courage, lass. Courage. Of course we'll see she gets help, just as soon as we can notify Inspector Dario that you are safe. The unexpected places you land in! Sometimes I long for a lass a bit more restful."

~~~~

They found Sam and Emma at the *Osteria al Ponte del Diavolo.* Riccardo and Lord Elmley had retraced their steps to the fork in the road after Riccardo had been forced to admit he did not remember the way to Tommaso's grandmother's cottage after all. Hopefully someone at the restaurant could direct them.

They noticed immediately upon entering that the *osteria* had only two customers, a couple. Most of their trade would arrive later, for the noon meal. A young man and woman sat at a table near the window, heads close together, drinking tea and eating buttered toast. A teacup and saucer and a pot of tea stood beside the toast rack. The young man was Dr. McGregor.

"*Dio Mio!* It's Emma!" Riccardo cried out and hurried to the table where she and Sam looked up in amazement. Rapturous greetings were exchanged as an alert waiter quickly drew up chairs and returned bearing coffee and pastries, almost before Riccardo and Lord Elmley had time to greet Sam and wring Emma's hand. Color returning to Emma's cheeks would have done credit to a painting by Titian, perhaps even Giorgione, Sam whispered in her ear and Emma glowed with pleasure. A contented euphoria enveloped her once again she gave the facts about her ordeal and escape.

Lord Elmley dispatched one of the waiters, absorbed in the unexpected drama, to bring a telephone. He wanted to ring Inspector Dario.

The Inspector's words were brief.

"I'll be out with five men before the hour is out, even if I have to swim across. Stay at *Il Ponte del Diavolo;* we'll meet you there. We cannot be sure what we'll find at the house."

20

Tommaso's Gondola Joins a Wedding Regatta

Emma heard chatter in the parlor of Rosamund's flat as she lay half asleep in her little room with the roundel overlooking the Grand Canal and the Accademia. Slowly she battled her way into consciousness. It must be late morning. Sunlight painted cheer on the walls. She sorted out various voices coming from the front of the flat: Rosamund, Sam, was it Samantha Satchell? Vittoria? With a start she remembered. She was taking Sam to the Accademia today, but wasn't the visit planned for afternoon? Why was she hearing voices? Was she dreaming? She had been enjoying nights of long, uninterrupted sleep following her ordeal. What a godsend to be free, away from the horror of Torcello and in the cozy comfort of her little room.

Sleeping peacefully, thinking of little else but safety, the relief of knowing, after Inspector Dario's brief visit to Rosamund's flat, that the brothers Pezzelli had been apprehended and were being held at the *questura*. The old lady, Rosella, had been found unharmed and taken to the Sisters at the convent of the Church of the Frari, *Santa Maria Glorioso dei Frari*, and was being looked after.

Sam and Rosamund had agreed, Emma must have plenty of sleep to recuperate. She had raised no objections. Now, energy replenished, she roused herself and hurried to the tiny bathroom, dashed cold water on her face and returned to fling on a fresh skirt and blouse. She brushed her hair a few strokes until it gleamed, applied a little lipstick and stepped into penny loafers. She could not bear the thought of missing anything. Catching her reflection in the window, she gave a quick nod of approval and hurried down the hall into the parlor.

"Surprise!" Friendly voices greeted her. Along with Rosamund, she saw Peter Law from the Consulate, Samantha and Vittoria, Sam; the young Italians from the Lido picnic were present. Massimo, Luciano and Guido sprang to their feet like lightening bolts as she appeared, offered deep bows and warm congratulations. Only Riccardo was missing, he was with Lord Elmley of course. She had hardly expected to see either of them. There must be many necessary conferences with the lawyers to smooth the turnover of *Ca' Sospira* and its contents from the Elmleys to Riccardo.

Rosamund hurried to embrace her. Sam motioned her to his side and gave her a quick kiss on the cheek.

"It's only a coffee morning, Emma," Rosamund whispered. "That was the only thing we could manage, what with your departure coming so soon. And even Riccardo couldn't get here, they're so busy over there." Rosamund fussed about Emma, placing coffee beside her on the little table crowded with a collection of tiny Murano animals.

The days in Venice were slipping away. The Lido picnic Emma had hoped for would not take place. This morning would be the final gathering of the group, and it was not the same, really. Nigel Sleight was absent, behind bars she reflected, recalling her lucky escape and feeling a lingering frisson of fear mixed with relief. She still felt nervous and a bit jumpy. Her thoughts segued to the present. Most of these friends she would not see for a long time, perhaps never again. Sadness overtook her.

"All the more reason to make the most of it," she thought. Setting down her coffee cup she began a circuit of the room, greeting each guest warmly.

"Now, Emma, is this a demonstration of Virginia hospitality? If it is, it will take up most of the morning." Sam's tone was good natured. His joy in finding her seemed almost tangible, wrapping around him like a cloak. He couldn't, nor did he attempt to conceal his adoration.

Emma smiled at him. "I am afraid so, Sam. It is the only way I know." He took a step closer and hugged her.

"Always stay close to me, bonny lass," he whispered.

"*Brava, Signorina* Emma! *Bravo, Dottore*! Perhaps that is why we think you are so *sympatico*. You are true Venetians at heart!" Massimo spoke up, voicing his approval of the affectionate moment shared by the couple.

"*Auguri! Auguri"* The others took up the cry of best wishes. Emma felt a tingle of pleasure as guests joined in with shouts of "*Brava! Bellesima!"* When the room became calm, Rosamund gestured toward Vittoria. She nodded from her seat on the sofa.

"I have been asked to be the messenger of good news. Riccardo asks me to tell you the facts straight from Inspector Dario.

"Nigel Sleight has been turned over to British authorities and is, as I speak, on his way back to England where he will answer for his crimes. It seems there are also, ah, indiscretions there he must account for." Brief silence was followed by a low hum of voices steadily rising in volume. Vittoria continued.

"The fate of his partner, Cyril Meadowes, is not so clear-cut. He was living in Prague at the time he was taken into custody, and Venice seems reluctant to hand him back He is also married to a Venetian as you know. Although he carries a British passport, he remains in jail in Venice."

"With Cassandra as his wife, Meadowes may prefer jail," Guido, one of the Italians observed dryly in his slow and thoughtful English. A burst of laughter erupted. Cyril's wife

Cassandra possessed a legendary temper, its intensity to be avoided at all costs.

Emma stole a look at Rosamund who was carefully refilling Peter Law's cup. Her embarrassment dwindled in direct proportion to Peter Law's thoughtful attentions Emma noticed, not for the first time. Vittoria resumed.

"As for the house on Torcello, Rosella has been settled in one of Venice's homes for the elderly. The two nephews, Alberto and Franco Pezzelli, brothers who lived with her, are being held for questioning by Inspector Dario. Cesara, the cook who apparently planned Emma's abduction, is still missing. The search has moved to Modena where the daughter and her family have relocated. Cesara will have her day in court, Inspector Dario promises that."

Emma hoped he was right; she had been told earlier by Vittoria that Venetians considered Inspector Dario one of the most dedicated men on the police force. Like a dog with a juicy bone, he was patient, unwilling to give up the tiniest morsel of information that might lead him to a criminal. He would pursue Cesara to the ends of the earth, if necessary, to see justice done.

~~~~

It was later that afternoon when Sam and Emma slipped away from the impromptu, noisy luncheon party hastily organized by Peter Law and the three Italians at Quadri on San Marco.

The coffee morning to honor *Signorina Emma* had not lasted nearly long enough to complete their farewell tribute to such a *bravissima signorina*, Massimo complained. Why they all were just beginning to become great friends! And since they would not be present for the wedding in London, surely *Signorina* Emma and *Dottore* Sam would give them a few hours more to celebrate their approaching nuptials! Samantha Satchell and the other girls took up the entreaties of Massimo, Guido and Luciano.

The party traveled by *vaporetto* to the restaurant on San Marco for a spontaneous, happy luncheon. Emma took a moment to reflect. *Molti anni fa'*, many years ago, her fellow countryman, the writer Henry James, had taken breakfast at Quadri every morning when he lived in Venice at the sumptuous Barbaro palace on the Grand Canal. There, at the Barbaro, he finished his novel of the doomed Milly Theale. It became his tribute to Venice, *The Wings of the Dove*. Perhaps someday she might write a novel about *La Serenessima*. Could it be possible? Venice forever would be an inspiration.

"I happen to know Peter Law has been working on the most wonderful toast for the picnic at the Lido we couldn't fit in," Samantha whispered to her as the meal ended and time for toasts arrived. "It's the moment for him to deliver it now."

Peter gave a lengthy and admirable toast. While Emma listened, she glanced over at Rosamund, whose eyes glowed with pride. Certainly a growing attachment there she thought with delight. Peter and Rosamund complemented each other.

When the final glass of *prosecco* had been drunk and Emma was beginning to feel bubbles dancing in her head, she and Sam left Quadri, walking in the general direction of the Accademia Bridge. Sam proposed a ride on the gondola ferry, the *traghetto*, on the San Marco side of the Grand Canal, which would quickly take them across to the Accademia. Several times earlier, Emma had planned to take him to see the Carpaccio frescoes of Saint Ursula; now only this afternoon remained free. They had barely more than an hour before closing time. At Sam's suggestion, they pressed on; planning to go straight through to the Carpaccio rooms when they arrived. They hurried toward the ferry.

They approached the back of the Gritti Palace hotel. They could see the ferry dock to the side. Following a twisting winding street only wide enough for two to pass, they hurried past the rear of the hotel toward the dock. The gondola, ferrying its single row of standing passengers, had just moved off, bound for Dorsoduro. Tethered to a post at the *molo,* dock, was a two passenger gondola with comfortable padded cushions. The gondolier waved to them. To Emma's amazement, Sam grasped her arm firmly and hurried toward the dock.

"Is that you Tommaso? I'm here, with *Signorina* Emma!"

"*Perfetto!* All is ready, *Dottore!*" What had Sam been plotting? Emma looked up at him, but he gave nothing away.

They stepped up and Sam performed introductions. "This is Riccardo's good friend Tommaso Migliori, ready to take us on a gondola ride, Emma."

Both surprised and pleased, Emma shook his hand. "I am so happy Tommaso, to be meeting you at last. Now I can thank you properly for helping find me. Your information made the search so much easier. How is your Grandmother?"

"*Molto bene, grazie,* because of the excellent care she has received. She is at present with one of my aunts. But soon she will return to Torcello. I am so happy to see you also have recovered, *Signorina* Emma." He searched carefully for words. "Because I was so worried about my grandmother, I was late in giving Riccardo information of your whereabouts, but *Dottore* Sam did not waste a second in hurrying to find you. Come now, for a ride in my gondola."

So Sam has been busy plotting, Emma thought, smiling at Tommaso, then looking up at Sam as he helped her into the graceful boat, all visible surfaces polished and shining. Sam, with Tommaso's help, she amended. They must have met through Riccardo, while she was held prisoner on Torcello. Except for the impromptu lunch at Quadri, which meant the visit to the Accademia would have to be fitted in some other time, everything was moving along, better than a dream. Some dreams, she amended, remembering being taken on a disturbing trip to *San Michele,* the graveyard island, in a bad dream one restless night.

How could Sam have guessed this was one pleasure unique to Venice she wanted so very much to share with him, even though Lord Elmley had put the *Ca' Sospira* motor launch and the pilot Carlo at their disposal? A ride in a gondola, with the man she was marrying. Surely every girl dreamed of this.

They glided along the San Marco side, toward Saint Marks basilica, looking at splendid views of Dorsoduro on the far bank. The distinctive, unfinished *palazzo* Venier housing the Peggy Guggenheim Collection of Modern Art, other great palaces in varying states of repair swam by them. Emma recalled Hidden Nest, cottage of the Americans Ezra Pound and the violinist Olga Rudge on one of a network of tiny canals and narrow passageways behind the great *palazzi*. That house was fast becoming a mecca for poetry and music lovers. Tucked in a side street behind those sumptuous *palazzi*, Hidden Nest was near Cesara's house. A sudden shadow enveloped Emma.

Where was Cesara? Had she escaped? But Emma refused to dwell on worrisome matters. She had triumphed in the battle of wills with Cesara. The Carpaccio was safe. She was safe and seated beside the man she loved, enjoying a gondola ride in the world's most beautiful city. Her cup was full. She relaxed and gave herself up to the afternoon, oblivious to tourists aboard passing *vaporetti* who focused their cameras on Tommaso, his gondola and the handsome young couple who were his passengers.

On the San Marco side they passed the Bauer Grunewald Hotel, the Hotel Europa e Regina. Terraces of the beautiful Hotel Monaco swam into view. They saw a wide circle of eighteen or twenty *goldole* moored around an empty, flower-bedecked wedding gondola waiting at the hotel dock. Some of the *gondolieri* wore striped shirts and straw boater hats while others wore dark trousers and white shirts and were hatless, like Tommaso. Calling to Tommaso to join them, the boatmen gestured toward an opening in the circle, waving and shouting encouragement.

"What is happening, Tommaso?" Sam asked

"It's a wedding. The wedding banquet in the hotel must be finishing soon and the couple will be going back to their parish, to the church where they took the vows. My fellow *gondolieri* are inviting us to join them."

Emma could hardly believe her ears. The chance to watch the unfolding spectacle of a real Venetian wedding!

"Sam, can we please join in?"

"*Carpe Diem!*" Sam answered. "Seize the day." His words prompted an abrupt change of course for the gondola and a wide grin spread over Tommaso's face.

They pulled up beside an ever growing circle of gondolas whose passengers thought they had arranged a ride to look at the beautiful sights along the Grand Canal. Rather, it was their good fortune to be joining in the *spectacalo* of a Venetian wedding regatta.

Applause and shouts of *Auguri!, Auguri!*, broke out as the *gondoleri* spotted the wedding party leaving the hotel and begin making their way toward them. A story book couple floated into view, the groom, tall, slender, dark wavy hair, wedding tuxedo in correct black with a white shirt tucked snugly into a dark red cummerbund; the bride, blond and petite, wore satin shoes with stiletto heels, dress gracefully billowing behind her in the gentle breeze. She had taken off the customary heavy veil and train, revealing an elfin, heart shaped face and eyes sparkling like sapphires. Her smile mingled shyness with happiness as she accepted good wishes from wedding guests, family and strangers who crowded onto the dock. *Auguri! Auguri!*

Members of the wedding party, two priests and an altar boy, parents of the couple, younger siblings, a host of relatives and friends, began climbing back into the flotilla of small boats and launches moored around the *molo,* just outside the circle of *gondole.*

Emma's eyes fastened for a minute on a trio on the dock united by identical long straight noses. An attractive grandmother wearing lilac silk, a trim, blond matron in blue on one side, and a little girl of around eight on the other. The child was long legged, with white-blond hair worn in a Dutch boy bob. A giant bow matched the lavender of her dress, a slightly deeper shade than the dress worn by her grandmother.

Three generations, Emma reflected. Here, in this beautiful city, where history and tradition counted for everything, Venetian families lived out their lives, preserving good memories of the past and facing the future united. If they rejected the determination and ambition to "get ahead" at any cost, there were many compensations. Life lived deeply, completely as it was in this city offered many rewards.

The bride and groom settled in their gondola. The priests and the altar boy stepped into another directly behind.

"Where now, Tommaso?" Emma could not bear the thought of losing them, just when the *specatalo* was beginning.

"I'm not certain which church, but they will be returning to the church where they took their vows. We'll find out in a minute. We'll follow. Okay?"

She nodded. What bliss. Beside her Sam was holding tightly to her hand. She felt this was a wonderful way to make one's wedding vows. To share the event with everyone, friends, relatives, strangers.

"Happy?" She looked up at Sam.

"What do you think? It's a preview." His eyes told her that deep within, Sam harbored romantic leanings, no matter how carefully he tried to conceal them. The encircling *gondole* stayed abreast in several rows, slightly behind the boat bearing the bride and groom. They had left the dock area and were making for the open waters of the *bacino*.

"It's *Santa Maria delle Salute*," Tommaso told them. "That is the church they are bound for, just across the basin, on Dorsoduro, at the tip." Emma nodded. She knew it well, having spent part of an extremely warm afternoon outside the entrance, secretly watching a meeting which had brought Nigel, Cyril and the cook Cesara together. It was Emma's proof that the cook was the spy inside *Ca' Sospira* working with Nigel and Cyril, determined to steal the Carpaccio. Well, it's safe now, she sighed gratefully.

A flotilla of boats of all shapes and sizes bearing relatives and friends fell in behind the wedding party. A wedding guest on one of the boats began strumming a guitar. A groomsman, clad in a snug fitting tuxedo, stood up somewhat shakily in his boat and began a chorus of *O Sole Mio* which was quickly taken up by his audience on the boats within range.

They drew closer to the famous church which shared the westernmost tip of Dorsoduro with the enormous, ship-like *Dogana,* the customs house of Venice, facing eastward toward the Adriatic. Here, Emma thought, were the two great symbols of ancient Venice, the customs house where all sailing vessels first docked, then the church.

Sam asked her about the church's name, *Santa Maria delle Salute.*

"Santa Maria, Giver of Health. That's the translation," Emma said. "It was a church built in gratitude by Venetians who survived the plague, one of several famous churches in Venice similarly dedicated in gratitude."

"Yes, I can see how plague would easily get a foothold here," Sam answered, his gaze on the church's beautiful domes. "Surrounded by water, much of it swampy, living in close quarters as people have to do in the city. And of course, it took a long time for men of science to discover the plague was highly contagious. The church often led resistance to observances of hygiene in that regard. To them, it was more logical to blame witches for plague rather than unsanitary conditions." They both sat quietly for a few moments, Emma reflecting on the city's long and troubled history.

"They're going ashore now," Tommaso called to them as they approached the dock in front of the church where wide steps led up to the entrance. "The priest will give a little introduction of the couple to the parish on the steps, then he will take them on a walk about their neighborhood. They won't go inside the church again, having already completed their vows.

"Would you like to follow a little with the rest of the crowd? They will make their way, through the neighborhood, then I imagine they will go to the house of either the groom's or the bride's parents where an all-night celebration will begin, with another banquet around midnight." Tommaso rubbed his chin thoughtfully.

"But before this second banquet, I am sure the bride and groom will manage to slip away to Santa Lucia, the train station, hopefully shaking off priests, parents, siblings and well wishers, as they begin their honeymoon, traveling to some secret destination."

"This is truly the Venice I have heard about, but I didn't dream I'd really see it, let alone be a part of it." Emma stood up, taking Tommaso's hand, and prepared to step ashore.

"Just a minute," Sam chimed in. "I just had the thought! You aren't planning to settle here, are you Emma? You'd best think twice about that. My Italian is so poor, horrible mistakes would surely occur if I tried to practice my surgical skills at some hospital in Venice." Tommaso grinned.

"I am certain nothing could hamper your expertise, *Dottore!* We would be lucky to have you here in *Venezia*," the gondolier declared gallantly.

"When your walk through the neighborhood is over, come back here and I'll take you along some of the smaller canals on Dorsoduro, bound by the Grand Canal on the north and the Giudecca the finger like island on the south. While you are in the procession, I'll try to learn more about the couple from some of my friends here," he said, making a wide sweep of his arm toward the flotilla of gondolas.

As Tommaso predicted, the two priests, carefully minding clerical skirts and birettas, stepped ashore after the bride and groom. The older of the two priests took their hands and led them to the top of the wide steps of the church. He gave a brief blessing, still holding their hands. then introduced them to the swelling crowd of well wishers on the steps below. The flotilla had docked, and everyone was scurrying to get closer.

"Auguri! Auguri!" Best wishes, best wishes. The crowd rained good wishes on the bride and groom as they slowly walked with the priest, moving away from the church into the neighborhood.

Emma and Sam walked well behind the wedding party mixing with relatives, friends and strangers, a happy, friendly crowd filled with good will. Emma yearned for her own wedding. They followed as far as the house of the bride's parents, where they could see many tables set up for the banquet in a small courtyard glimpsed through the open gate. Sam and Emma joined other well wishers as they retraced their steps back to the dock.

Tommaso had gathered scraps of news about the newlyweds from the gondoliers as he awaited their return. The groom was a student at Padua, studying law at the university. The bride designed jewelry made from Murano glass. Her small studio on Dorsoduro near the *Salute* church, was also near the home of her parents. The couple would live in a house nearby, not far from Hidden Nest, Tommaso discovered.

Emma listened as she dreamed of her own wedding soon to take place at St. Margaret's, Westminster, in London. Then she and Sam would create their own memories to relate to their children and grandchildren sometime far into the future. Returning her attention to Tommaso's revelations about the bride and groom, Emma let her thoughts run free. Venice, *La Serenessima,* the old sorceress, was unsurpassed in the business of creating dreams. She had learned it only too well.

21

Moments on the Roof Garden During the Party

Before the farewell evening for Emma at *Ca' Sospira* got underway, a very private meeting took place on the *altana* of *Ca' Sospira* between Riccardo Montgano and William Elmley at the latter's suggestion. Lord Elmley would be returning to England soon after the departure of Emma and Sam. Onerous duties in the running of the Elmley estates as well as the needs of his wife and three children awaited him. He also yearned for long walks over his fields and forests which he realized would be tinged with the gold of autumn now, as summer waned.

The two men sat a for a few minutes in companionable silence, sipping flutes of *prosecco* mixed with the juice of white peaches, a Venetian favorite for many years before the tourist mecca Harry's Bar, launched the Bellini, now the watering hole's specialty by all accounts.

The earl looked over at a man who had changed considerably in a few short weeks. Riccardo seemed strangely younger yet more mature, less temperamental and moody, yet his face showing a lingering anxiety as to the permanence of his good fortune. I must try to do something to ease that worry, the earl thought, beginning his little speech.

"Riccardo you cannot know how much these past days have meant to me, the beginning of our friendship. I never had the closeness of a brother growing up. Only James, very much younger as you know, whose birth occurred after I had gone away to boarding school. Working with you side by side these past days has awakened feelings of great strength and contentment I never knew I possessed. I believe I am right in judging this new feeling is good for you as well?" Riccardo nodded, smiling.

"I am greatly pleased with the plans for this house you and Vittoria have shared with me, ideas which I believe will greatly benefit *Ca' Sospira*. Your hopes for the future, what you wish to do with *Ca' Sospira* sound inspired and solid to me. As to you and I, I believe we have laid the foundation for friendship of a mutual benefit, one which I earnestly hope will grow stronger each year. Trust me with your concerns, give me your inner thoughts, your ideas; in short, keep me in your confidence. I promise to share in the same way with you. If I make a misstep, tell me. Only with this sharing, as we've experienced recently, can we make our kinship meaningful to both of us. I hope we shall see each other every year. I want you and Vittoria to visit Elmley Castle as soon after your wedding as is possible."

The silence grew for a few minutes. In the semi-darkness the earl did not realize a struggle for composure was taking place within Riccardo. He peered at him more closely in the early darkness of evening.

"How could you hope to understand the loneliness and fear I've felt, when you grew up surrounded by such a large family?" Riccardo spoke at last, trying to regain his voice.

"How could you have known my pain, feeling so very much alone in the world? Vittoria understood, of course. Emma Darling sensed it when she first arrived. She had begun to help me crawl out, by her fairness, her warmth, the simple fact that she seemed to care what happened to me. Then you came, and you also knew my feelings! You have strengthened me beyond measure, not just with the money although certainly that is welcome. I mean your acceptance of me, your welcoming my joy at being part of a family I had admired for so many years. I no longer feel left out and alone in my thoughts.

"I intend to keep the trust you have placed in me. Keep me close in your sights. Come back when you can to *Ca' Sospira.* You and your family will be forever welcome." The men stood up, embraced, and quickly made their way downstairs.

~~~~

Lights in *Ca' Sospira* twinkled. Doors and casements were thrown open to the glorious approach of nightfall in Venice. Days were becoming shorter, yet the warmth of the old stones caressed by cooler evening breezes still held. A perfect night for their farewell, Emma thought, feeling misty-eyed in spite of her best intentions.

She went up to the *altana,* with Sam and Tintoretto, seeking respite from the babble of musical Venetian voices below, the hum of strings as a trio of violins played. This last evening shared with Sam before returning to London and their wedding seemed somehow incomplete to Emma, and she knew exactly why.

Emma and Sam had not yet spoken of plans for after their wedding. He had not mentioned Oxfordshire once, and she had skirted around it, afraid their feelings might blaze up in an unseemly quarrel, marring the perfection of their Venetian idyll moving so swiftly to its conclusion.

It has been almost like a honeymoon Emma realized, looking at Sam's profile as he stroked Tintoretto's noble head. Always perceptive, the dog seemed to understand when suitcases were being taken down and repacked, traveling itineraries examined. Someone was leaving. Emma's belongings of course remained in Dorsoduro at Rosamund's flat. But Tintoretto, in some inexplicable state of prescience, sensed that Emma and Sam, and possibly Lord William as well, were going away.

Emma sighed, knowing what she must do. She had been far too slow in casting off doubts and welcoming the move to Oxfordshire. She owed Sam her support. Of course their time had been shortened when he first arrived because of her interlude, if one wished to call it that, on the island of Torcello.

But that's finished, and everything worked out beautifully the mischievous imp in her head reminded her. You survived with nothing worse than hunger pangs, and my dear, you had been indulging too often in those little meringue swans filled with whipped cream from *Romolo,* that *pasticceria* so very close to you and Rosamund on Dorsoduro. Your skirts were a bit too snug. So you can afford to be magnanimous, now that you are safely off Torcello and slim once more.

Emma brushed away the irritating criticisms of the imp, like a worrisome bee's drone, and returned her focus to Sam. "I'm ready for Oxfordshire."

"You're what?"

"Ready to make our start in a village somewhere in Oxfordshire," she repeated, fingers absently tracing a design of mottled flowers on the watered silk of her long skirt.

"But, I thought," Sam began.

"Shhh! Hush! Of course I'm ready. This is what we both want. We'll be in some of the loveliest country in England. I'll learn to ride horseback, chase hounds, exchange recipes for quince jelly, join the Women's Institute. Maybe I'll arrange flowers at the village church, sing in the choir, perhaps . . ."

Gently he put a finger to her lips. "I say! Could I possibly have a word?"

She subsided.

"I have been waiting for the right moment to tell you," he began.

"Tell me what? You have my absolute and undivided attention. And my silence," she added as an afterthought.

"It seems there is a house we *can* afford in the city of Oxford after all, rather than off in a village somewhere," he said, studying her face.

Oxford. The Ashmolean museum, The Bodlian library, the Oxford Press, the colleges and their collections of paintings, punting on the Isis, Shakespeare on the lawns in summer. Emma's face softened, taking on a dreamy look as all her memories of Oxford juggled for position.

"We might live in Oxford? What bliss! Why haven't you told me?"

"I, I don't know, really," he said, his tone uncertain. "That is not quite true. I suppose I wanted first to hear something from you about how you felt about moving there. Oxfordshire won't be like staying in London, I know. I needed some indication from you before I gave a final answer. I don't propose to order you around, Emma, before or after we are married."

"I didn't expect that you would," she murmured "I didn't speak about it for a long time simply because I did not believe

I'd be happy in a village where so many people ride and hunt. Period. And the domestic duties in a village seemed onerous. Perhaps I've been reading too many period novels about vast unheated old houses, cold water taps, snow blocked roads and mud tracked into the parlor." She laughed, taking his hand.

"Tell me about the house in Oxford."

"Actually, it is not in Oxford proper, a bit out, a suburb. It is in Summertown, full of artistic and literary associations yet far enough away that Oxford's clanging bells don't give you headache every hour!" Sam waited. Emma's eyes shone with her dreams.

"Summertown? Blissful! What literary associations?"

"Well, there is a discreet plaque on the house next door to us, that is, if we take the place where I've put down a wee refundable deposit. A distinguished author lived there, raised a large family and wrote famous novels in the garden, just next to what will be *our garden,* if it pleases you." He brushed an imaginary speck of dust from his trouser leg and remarked as an afterthought.

"Funny thing, there is a round window like you have in your little cubbyhole at Rosamund's. Strange feeling I had when you showed me that room the other day."

Emma sat silently a few minutes observing a cryptic smile on Sam's face reminding her of Edward Lear's Cheshire cat. It would mean I could always be reminded of Venice when I looked out. No matter what the view there, I could change it into the Accademia and the bridge, if I wanted, she thought.

"Oh Sam, you always go right to the heart of every problem. You knew I would be missing Venice terribly. Having such a powerful reminder would be a comfort! Are you going to tell me more about the famous person who lived next door?"

"I won't give you the name on the plaque until I take you to see the house and you read it for yourself. Let me see, a clue? Ever heard of the Inklings?"

"Sam! Not the Inklings! The writers who met at the pub each week to read their works together? At the Eagle and the Child pub at the end of The Broad? Everyone in Oxford calls it 'The Bird and Baby' I remember. The Inklings! C. S. Lewis, J. R.R. Tolkien and the others? Oh Sam, you cannot be serious!"

He nodded solemnly. "I wouldn't trick you Emma. You know that. I'll show you." They sat side by side for a time, holding hands and watching the stars become brighter, allowing a contentment to envelop them.

"Sam, are you sad we are leaving?" Emma looked out on the city beneath them. Venice had made her so happy. Sixty two days of happiness, even the days on Torcello seemed bearable, viewed through the prism of freedom and a few tweaks of her memories. She felt she could hardly bear to give Venice up.

"Of course not, Emma," he answered softly. "We have so much to look forward to," he reminded her. "I have no doubt we'll see Lord William again in England. Remember, the *Ca' Sospira* collection can travel, because of all of your hard work. I know Riccardo and Vittoria will want you to have a part in their wedding plans. We could not let them tie the knot without us! We might even entice them to Oxford sometime after we are settled.

"Then there is the emerging romance between Rosamund and Peter Law. Why we might even have to return here for their wedding! It's not impossible, you know. And you will not want to forget Filiberto and Tintoretto. You must return to keep up with all of your friends, *Signora* Puglio. The flower seller on San Marco, Guido, Massimo and Luciano and . . ." She put a finger to his lips. He took her hand.

"I just hope I shall be able to supply the kite strings of travel tickets we shall be needing. I'm not running the Bank of England, you know!"

"I say, we might come back again, after we've settled in at Oxford? That must come first, of course!"

"Of course. That is exactly what I told them when I made inquiries at the travel agent Thomas Cook on San Marco yesterday. After we make the move, and before I start working at the hospital. There should be time for a proper trip."

"Sam, you didn't!" She hugged him rapturously.

"*Carpe Diem!*" Sam sighed, looking down at her.

Emma put her faith in Sam. She *would* return to take that breathtaking ride of her first hour down the magic waterway of ancient palaces, the stones of Venice. Life was an exciting, uncharted journey, whatever it might bring, provided Sam went along, of course.

"*Carpe Diem!*" she echoed softly, looking up fondly at him. "Seize the day."

ACKNOWLEDGMENTS

Thomas Moran, the American artist (born in England) whose *View of Venice* embellishes the cover of this book with the romance, color and drama defining the city, was, like many of us, powerfully drawn to *La Serenissima*. It is a matter of record that he bought a gondola in Venice, had it shipped home where it floated on a nearby pond, a daily reminder of the place he loved so much and useful in subsequent Venetian paintings. It was fortuitous that I saw his marvelous painting for the first time in the Maier Museum of Randolph College in Virginia one spring afternoon when I had been working hard to complete this third and final book about American Emma Darling's adventures in Europe, and had sought respite looking at pictures. I was working hard, and the book needed a cover image. Thomas Moran's masterpiece jolted me like a thunderbolt. Here was the perfect fit. I am so very grateful to Interim Director Martha Kjeseth Johnson and the Maier Museum for permitting Thomas Moran's painting to appear on the cover.

So many others, both aware and unaware, had an influence in the creating of this book. To the people of Venice whose charm, courtesy and patience through the many times I have visited has never flagged. To the Correr Museum when as a student, I received help when I was searching out information about an obscure artist of the Veneto, even more elusive than Vicenzo Dalle Deste, mentioned in this book. Our university group stayed that year in an hotel on San Marco now much changed and "tarted up" as my fellow students would have expressed it, and shockingly expensive. We were students drinking in the wonder of Venice then; we hardly noticed our living quarters.

Thanks to Reed and Lucretia Findlay, who brought us in great depth the flavor of Venice in a faded palazzo-cum-hotel called *Bon Vecchiata* on San Marco during an eventful February opera visit. Thanks also to Massimo, Guido and Luciano who enriched my knowledge of Dorsoduro on a September visit when my husband and I stayed at the *Pensione Accademia,* located among verdant gardens within the shadow of the fabled Accademia Museum and the Accademia Bridge. Finally, to the Lygon Family and Kinsman Association whose volumes of information about my English forebears provided insight into the fictional Elmley Family history.

Grateful thanks to Molly Jenkins for her careful checking of the manuscript and to my husband Jim and my daughters Holly Williams and Daisy Warnalis, who, as always, were unstinting in their efforts to help me turn this manuscript into a book. Finally, several books which were helpful for my research: *Paradise of Cities* by Vicount John Julius Norwich; *Lucia, a Venetian Life* by Andrea di Robilant; *City of Falling Angels* by John Berendt and *A Thousand Days in Venice* by Marlena di Blasi.

Venezia La Serenissima